ORR: THE NOBEL PRIZE MURDER

By Lynn Marron

A Grace Farrington Mystery

Enjoy!

Lynn

D1562123

This mystery is a work of fiction with all names, characters, places and events created in the mind of the author or used in a fictional manner. I hope you enjoy it.
 My best, Lynn

ISBN Paperback NUMBER: 978-1-942888-03-1
ISBN Ebook NUMBER: 978-1-942888-04-8
LIBRARY OF CONGRESS NUMBER: 2015937416

This book is dedicated to
Leonard J. Bloom, Jr.
My greatest fan
as I am his.

Prologue

Her fingertips prickled. Now she could feel them drawing closer.

Mid-day, yet the rooms seemed to be darkening. It was coming. She must light a kerosene lamp to go down to the Elder ones. With trembling fingers, she scratched the wooden match stick along the fireplace's stone mantle. It flared brightly, but her hand was shaking so. She must steady herself. They were returning--the cursed three brothers! Coming back by her command.

Their ship could not have full oil barrels, not in the mere five months they were allowed to hunt, she was sure of that. They were returning because she had lit the candles, made the required sacrifices to the Elder ones. Her invocations summoned all of them--Benjamin, Wardell, and Lemuel. Summoning the cursed brothers to their righteous rewards! Summoned the crew of the *Siren* to their deaths!

As she hefted the smoking glass lamp, its burden of smelly kerosene sloshed. Outside she could hear the rising winds as branches scraped the windows. It was June yet the fingers of a winter's nor'easterner clawed up the harbor's waves. Those proud sailors would return and be met by the full fury of her storm!

This she had been promised. Her vengeance on they who had wronged her.

When the *Siren* sailed into Oyster River, she would be waiting, watching. It was only through her strength and vigilance that they would be punished. She must not weaken with thoughts of gentle Lemuel! Not now! Not with vindication so close!

Soon, she would don her storm cape and go stand by

the shore, watching the harbor entrance. She must see them die–but first she would have to make her last obeisance. She kicked off her slippers, then hurrying to the Chinese vase she picked out a bouquet of white snowballs, cut fresh this morning, as the thin mares tails whipped across the wide blue sky.

On a silver serving tray she placed the lamp, the flowers, sugar and salt, shredded brown leaves and a jug of slaver's rum. It was difficult carrying that heavy tray and opening the door that led down to the damp cellar. Awkward maneuvering with her confining skirts, usually she worshiped in only a thin, cotton petticoat. Now she must tread so carefully on the steep steps.

She must not fall. Must not die, not until she had her vengeance against them–all those proud, honorable men who shamed her in the dark. Captain Benjamin must see his brothers die! Until he, Lemuel and sweet Wardell were under the water, she must maintain her prayers. Must grow her hatred or her vengeance would be lost! Her naked feet trod on damp packed soil, across the basement, then she set the tray on the mothering earth as she unlocked her special place with its deep cabinet. Not that anyone else came here.

Inside tall, smokey candles were already lit. She kept them burning day and night. Blue for St. Ulrich, Agwe Tawoyo, who owns the sea; the white snake, St. Patrick, Dambala Wedo; and the green for Gran Bwa lie, spirit of the wilderness. She lit smaller tallow candles about the altar, sprinkled the sugar and rum and set out the bowls of salt and the tobacco. Let the Snake feast. Head bowed, eyes averted, she laid the white flowers in sacrifice to Ogou Feray.

Then she lowered and bent to the earth, her knees and head touching dampness as her arms rigidly extended. "Avenge me. Avenge me, my spirits! We have been most grievously wronged. Bring forth the *Siren*. Pull her to me! Drown her cursed crew before me!

Soon her knees ached, her arms stiffened with pain, but she prayed long before the tall blue candle. Then before her, its flame drown in its own wax. Finally she rose, knowing that her months of torment were almost at an end.

Rushing upstairs, she fetched her cape, setting the hood on her long hair. At the door she hesitated. Should she bind up her hair? He liked it that way. It was most proper. No. She went out, hair unbound, feet still naked.

The grass underfoot was dry, yet the wind rushed like a river. Although directly above her the sky was pale blue, the harbor now whitened with foaming waves. The heavy, clotted cream clouds swirled about the edges of the sky, as if she were standing in the eye of a storm. She smiled as the clouds began to close in, darkening and cutting off all blue sky like the deadly garrote of the Indios.

As she had felt, as the thrown bones had revealed to her, there were gray sails at the horizon. A whaler was headed for Oyster River Harbor under full canvas to beat the storm to safe anchorage. But they would not beat it, not those beasts! Not while she chanted to the spirits who loved her.

The clouds overhead blackened as they joined and blotted out the midday sun. Desperately the *Siren* tacked, entering the Harbor where the fools expected safety. There would be none for the cursed three, not if she could prevail! She chanted louder, as the wind and waves rose to do her bidding.

A wet splash on her cheek. Another. The skies openly weeping, pelting, pouring rain, blotted out her vision. Could she hear the three brothers scream and cry? Hear the sails rip asunder? Past the point, there were rocks in the water. Rocks her will would force the *Siren* on to! Rocks that would rip out the ship's hull. Rocks that would feed Dumbala!

She prayed to the powerful ones, all who would listen. The *Siren* must sink! None of her crew must reach the shore! With eyes blinded by her storm, the dark witch prayed her tormenters to perdition.

Chapter 1

Present Time October,
Oyster River Harbor, Connecticut

When she opened her condo door, Bobby Jamison was there holding a single red rose in consolation; as she took it, Grace smiled wryly. "The Nobel Prize list is out, and I'm not a winner...again."

"Well, you're awfully young at forty-two."

"I was twenty-eight when I first published my Popcorn Gene Switch Theory."

Bobby shrugged. "Because Einstein's Theory of Relativity was highly controversial, they awarded him his Nobel for discovering the Law of Photoelectric Effect. Maybe you'll get it for your early gene switch negation work? Or your theories of genetic evolution? Or any of your Farrington Fusions?"

"Or I might not get it at all." she spoke with resignation.

"Naw." He smiled confidently. "You'll get it. Einstein's projected Nobel winnings were part of his divorce settlement–two years before he actually won it."

Her lips twisted with distaste. "And there's always next year."

"Someday I'm walking in here with two dozen, blood-red roses."

"Actually make them yellow, for the gold the award will bring in. I don't need more notoriety, I do need money to upgrade my DNA sequencing equipment." Wanting to change the topic, Grace looked past Bobby down to the first floor landing. "Is Sara coming?"

Bobby and his pregnant wife lived in the Oyster River Research condo beneath hers. He shook his head. "Couldn't get anybody to babysit for Ginjer, so Sara's gonna miss this one." Bobby was five foot eight, black haired and Irish strong. As a graduate student, he did lousy academically but was dogged in his research, and none was his superior in organizing the laboratory's Friday donut feasts. As he came in, Bobby continued. "If you had your Nobel, they would be announcing you as our new Head of Research."

"With my ridiculous hermit reputation? I doubt if the Board of Directors are that impressed with my administrative ability and Adam Greenfield knows Fritz really wants it."

Bobby shook his head again. "He wants it a lot, but Dr. Fritz Wilshusen does not have the ring of eminence. Depending on the new head he might be out of here." He looked worried. "and me."

Grace wanted to be comforting, but with Eric Larsen dead, Bobby's position hinged on the whims of the new Director. "We'll all put in a good word for you."

"But like Fritz, I don't have the credentials."

"You'll get them–if you would just stop doing everything here and complete your dissertation. How's it going?"

Bobby not so adroitly changed the subject. "Kurt's got to worry too. Larsen supported all his work, but Kurt's mostly self taught. That Internet Doctorate of his is iffy..."

"They might even kick me out," Grace said as she reached for her jacket.

"Nope. Even without your Nobel you're bringing in the biggest research grants." Bobby looked her over critically. "We are expected at the Captain's Roost now–don't you have to change?"

Grace realized he was in an unaccustomed suit and tie. She glanced at her oval mirror over the sideboard. She was tall and angularly thin, with short, black curls that had touches of gray. She had just thrown on black slacks and lilac-print polyester top, her nominal laboratory working clothes. "I have."

Bobby shook his head. "You have a formal gown?"

She looked at him, what did he want? "Formal?"

"Something to the floor in silk? Or wool–it's chilly for early October."

"No."

"You'll need one for Oslo."

At the moment any Nobel Prize ceremony seemed light years away.

Bobby maneuvered past her headed toward her bedroom. "It's a champagne reception for the announcement of the new Head of Research. All the big buck patrons and potential money backers will be there. You will definitely be on display, Grace, you've got to have something better?"

Grace found herself being faintly embarrassed following a man into her bedroom. Although she had shed almost all of her ingrained childhood training, her New England prudishness conflicted with Bobby's baby-brother-of-seven sisters. He was already rooting through her rather sparse closet. He pushed aside her well worn lab coats, pulling out a yellow silk, dragon embroidered, Chinese blouse. "You got this when you were guest of honor at the Beijing Genome conference?"

"Yes."

"Good, but get it professionally pressed and it needs a long skirt. Get... dark brown velvet to go with it." He rehung the blouse, then shook his head disapprovingly. "No formals. Don't you have any cocktail gowns?"

"This is a wine reception."

"Champagne maybe. Or a New York State clone." He muttered, staring disapprovingly into her closet.

She shook her head. "Can't I just be the eccentric scientist?"

"Dr. Kurt MacKay's got that one nailed down. Saw him headed up to the Captain's Roost wearing an Irish Fishman's cable-knit sweater and black blue-jeans."

`   "Oh, god, Adam's going to love that."

"Yhep. And Kurt's employment is almost as wobbly as mine." Bobby was trying to push open the tops of boxes on the upper shelves. "What do you do for funerals?"

To get this embarrassment over with, Grace reached for a hanger pushed back against the wall. She pulled out a plain, three quartered sleeved shift of smooth cotton.

Bobby stared at it disdainfully. "It's black."

"It's for funerals."

"That dress will depress the departed." He gave another despairing look over her meager closet. "My wife's got more dresses in the laundry hamper. You should be in something Chanelly, with trim lines, classical styling. You're too tall and thin to wear Sara's stuff."

"Lords & Toms is closed by now."

"And there is no time to borrow anything." He shoved the black dress at her. "Put that on. Do you have any pearls?" He said before headed back to the living room.

Grace decided to put on the dress and even a little make-up. She normally wore nothing but a little hastily smeared on lipstick. Now she rooted in the back of the bathroom drawer and found an old rouge. It was pinkish. Her lipstick was beige. Wasn't that a wrong match? Who cared? With the Nobel Committee passing her by again the night couldn't get worse.

But it could.

Chapter 2

As Bobby escorted Grace up the small hill to the back steps of the Captain's Roost, that twentyish newspaper reporter was getting out of her car. Grace noted it was that nasty red head-- was it Sonya something or other? The one Grace always avoided, so the red-head wrote a nationally bylined story trumpeting that the renowned Dr. Grace Farrington was a recluse. A hermit barricaded in her lab. Getting interviewed by that bitch would make tonight even more special.

They climbed up the back step entrance of the towering, gingerbread trimmed building. The Italian Renaissance Revival Mansion had been the home of Captain Benjamin Smith when whaling ships regularly sailed out of Oyster River Harbor. In the 1890's the Captain's Roost was converted to the heart of the Oyster River Harbor Research Institute, which today owned the whole peninsula with its eclectic, period jumble of scientific buildings.

Her friend Freya's local 'haunt tour' claimed that 'sensitive' people had seen the spirit of Jersillda Smith, the Captain's wife standing on the widow's walk, vainly looking out over the Harbor for her beloved husband's return. Freya got twenty dollars a person for her walking tour and twenty-five for her self printed '*Harbor Hauntings*' book, which she sold in her new age shop in Oyster River.

God, losing the Nobel again. Tonight, Grace just wished she could just go over to Freya's and have some wine and silent sympathy. Instead she was climbing wide wooden steps to be chief freak in a marketing circus.

With the exception of an oversized kitchen area in the back addition, the lower floor had been converted into a twelve foot high meeting hall. At the back entrance Grace gave up her jacket, but wished she had a sweater. Surprisingly cold for a room crammed full of chattering people.

Bobby was standing protectively by. "I'll get some

drinks. What do you want?"

"To go home."

He shook his head. She thought again. "Plum brandy?"

"Think we've got a free wine bar. Probably the best you can hope for is white or red."

"A sweet red, but ask if they've got scotch, something strong," He was gone and she missed him already. It was going to be a long night. No matter how many classes she taught, how many symposiums she chaired or how many grant proposals she pitched, Grace never got comfortable being showcased before large groups of strangers.

"Dr. Farrington?"

Grace turned to see two women bearing down on her. She tried to smile, fawning strangers made it worse. She vaguely recognized Adam Greenfield's wife, Rachel, introducing her to someone layered in diamonds.

"Ellen, this is the renowned Dr. Grace Farrington. You know, the 'Popcorn Gene Switch Behavioral' theory. She didn't get the Nobel this time, but we know it's coming."

Grace smiled and tried to look modest. Soon they were all talking about the cooling weather and the reddening of New England's trees.

Fortunately Bobby was back, forcing a cold, wet glass into her hand. When the ladies moved on to their next prize catch, Grace desperately sipped, finding the sweetness of a whiskey sour! Bless Bobby.

Raucous laughter from over by the massive carved limestone fireplace with Kurt MacKay holding court in the center of a knot of men. She could go over there, but it looked like a stag party. Standing by the foyer entrance was eighty year old Steward Brewster and his wife Joyce. That was nice–she was sure some on Oyster River's Board would have rather kept their skeletons across the harbor, but Adam Greenfield was principled man. Dr. Brewster could claim responsibility for much of the Institute's success as well as its disgraces. He should have been invited. Grace started walking towards Steward, then she saw the Wilshusens.

Fritz and Margery, both there. Shouldn't they be walking in with Adam for the great announcement? When was Adam going to announce the new head? Where was he? When could she go home? If Dr. Fritz Louis Wilshusen was in the audience, he probably didn't get the promotion. Both he and his wife Margery were looking grim, better not congratulate them.

Rachel Greenfield was back, with another obviously well heeled patron in tow. Grace braced herself and forced yet another smile.

"Dr. Farrington, this David Gardiner."

She was being presented to him? This Mr. Gardiner must truly be a well off patron.

Rachel was still talking. "He is thinking about becoming a member of our Board."

Well heeled indeed. His trim body, straight back made him seem taller, but Grace noted he was a man about her own height, five foot eight, with sandy hair and pale blue eyes. He stood with an ironic smile on his face and unlike Bobby's suit, Mr. Gardiner's seemed to fit, and he seemed comfortable in it.

He was speaking to her. "I've been very interested in your work..."

But Grace's eyes were drawn to the front entrance as Adam Greenfield was walking in with a smiling, triumphant man. Grace nearly dropped her drink. The hair was white, not the pepper-salt she remembered, but he still had that unnerving, patronizing little smile on his lips. Oh, shit, not him!

Walking to the center of the room, Adam proudly announced, "Ladies and Gentlemen, I have the pleasure to introduce Oyster River Harbor Research Facility's new Director, the renowned, Nobel Prize winning, Dr. Charles

Theodore Marshall."

All the eyes in the room looked to him and there was splatter of applause from somewhere, that seemed to die as fast as it had started but Marshall just appeared to draw himself up prouder. Grace was furious–the smiling, renowned Dr. Marshall had his Nobel Prize, actually, he had hers, or at least what would have been her first shot at it.

Grace couldn't even manage a smile. Looking for an escape route, she found herself staring into the eyes of that red-haired reporter. Did her hatred and revulsion for Marshall show on her face? Grace struggled to calm herself. Be professional.

Others were going up to congratulate Dr. Marshall, shaking hands with him. Grimly Grace noted that none of the main researchers were on that line. The Wilshusens just stood there, the Stewards stayed at a distance and Kurt was headed to the bar. Where was Bobby?

She turned and looked. Dr. Marshall seemed to be staring directly at her, as if daring her to say something. Grace looked for a place to put her glass down and leave.

But Marshall won't let her get away. In a loud authoritative voice he called out, "Dr. Farrington? Don't you remember your old Professor?" He had a challenging, cool smile on his lips.

Grace turned and with an equally cold smile said, "How could I ever forget?"

"We'll be working together again." Satisfied he made his point, Marshall turned his back toward her.

Grace slipped outside, keenly feeling a bit of a chill from the sea grass encircled tidal basin below. This had been her harbor haven after she fled from California and Marshall, the Dr. Josef Mengele of research science. She wasn't the only one he had screwed professionally. As a graduate student he stole her research, if she remained in Oyster River, he would steal it again.

Only how long could she remain here? How long could his massive ego tolerate a star almost equal to himself? He hadn't in the past. Years ago he ran off a seventy year old laureate. Marshall regularly spiked the careers of his most promising research assistants. She'd been there when two scientists working in the university lab produced cultures that were showing a promising break through in treating encephalitis. On Spring break, Charles Marshall 'accidently' turned off all the laboratory power, destroying their experimental chain beyond recovery. If Marshall's own cultures weren't the publicity winners, then no one else's would be.

How much of her work could she finish before she had to leave? Better dust off the old curriculum vitae. Hearing steps on the pathway behind her, Grace turned to find Bobby catching up.

He grimaced. "Fritz took that pretty well? But he should've seen it coming."

"I thought Adam would give it to him, Fritz is close to retirement."

"But no Nobel, no hope. Eric Larsen is dead. Branson now hangs his Nobel at Woods Hole. And until you get yours, we're looking mighty thin here."

"I won't get a box of girl scout cookies while the renowned Dr. Marshall is in charge." She said bitterly.

Bobby looked over this shoulder. "From what I've heard neither will any of us. Hell, I don't know if I'll be working here past next week."

Oh, shit. Bobby had been working for Eric before his stroke. With him gone, Bobby's next assignment would be totally up to Marshall. "Just stay cool. You need that PhD., then you can move on. Just keep your temper!"

"Me? Like I have problem?"

Bobby had been known to smash a telephone through the wall because the phone tree was taking too long. "You do have problem—that Irish temper of yours. You've got to cool it."

When she got back to her condo, she pulled off the funeral dress—how appropriate. She sat down before her laptop and tried to pull up her old curriculum vitae. Couldn't find it, and realized it wasn't even on this computer, since for years she hadn't even thought of looking for another job and had never even bothered to update it. And if she had, where would she send it? Where else would she want to live but here? Half heartedly she pulled up web sites of universities and research centers. Finally after an hour or so, too depressed to continue, she logged off and went to bed.

In the mornings, she usually drove to the town of Oyster River, on the other side of the harbor. A tiny New England village, where the white clapboarded houses still looked as if they were waiting for their sailor owners to return from their whaling voyages. Grace parked behind the library, with its small grassy park that ending in the Harbor. She got out, did some stretching exercises, then took off on her usual run. Not much traffic, nice views. Down along the shore to the dead-end at the gas tank farm. Driving back to ORR, she stopped for a danish and newspaper, then Grace parked the car near her condo and enjoyed the walk back to her laboratory.

Reaching the door, Grace moved to unlock it, then realized it was open. Who was in there? Too early for either of her assistants—cleaning people? She walked in to see Charles Marshall sitting at her desk, reading an open file of her latest printouts, obviously having gone through them. Furious she demanded, "What are you doing?"

"Grace." Marshall gave her a wide, ingratiating smile.

"That is my desk. I do not want anyone going through my personal research."

"Well, as Director of Oyster River..."

"Here at Oyster River we each get our own grants. As individual scientists we control and are responsible for our own work."

"Adam mentioned that, but it's a very inefficient way to operate. I'll be changing that."

She just stared at him, not believing this was happening.

After a moment Charles closed her file and got up. "As the new Director of Research, I want a complete report on all the projects you are working on, theories, money sources, and work already completed. I'll expect it by next Monday."

"As I explained, that isn't the way it's done here. I work independently."

"That is the way it was done before. Now I am changing it!" He was an imposing man at 6'2". "There are going to be a number of changes around here. People, whose science is marginal, will be leaving. I do not expect you will be in that group, but I have very high expectations for what Oyster River Research is going to be–my living memorial." He studiously looked about her laboratory, walking to her Beckman Coulter Genetic Analysis System.

"You have a CEQ 8800? Nice. I could use this myself."

Grace felt her skin crawl as Marshall put a possessive hand on it. "No–you can't!"

He spoke in a fatherly, authoritative tone. "Since it is Institute property..."

"It is not!" She sounded petulant when she wanted to be professional. Grace took a deep breath, before speaking again. "Most of the equipment in this room is my own personal property, paid for by myself from my own grants. If you have any doubts speak with Adam Greenfield."

Marshall was still looking at the analyzer. "Maybe I could just borrow it. The local papers are coming to interview the renowned Nobel winner in his lair. Maintenance could just carry it over for a day."

"No." That sounded so childish. "It will disturb my on

going work. I don't want to have to re-calibrate it. How did you get into this lab?"

"It was unlocked."

"No it wasn't!"

"That's true. I forgot. I've had security's keys duplicated." He fished a jingling ring from his pocket, almost taunting her. "After all, I'm in charge now."

Her laboratory was ORR property and the condo she lived in was Institute property. She'd speak to Adam, but Marshall already had all the keys.

Marshall was giving another encompassing look around her lab. "Many of the resources at Oyster River are being underutilized. You, one of their top producers, are living in a condo in a dinky, two- story walk-up. That has been Wilshusen and his wife are living in a ten room mansion, on the end of the peninsula over looking the ocean."

"You're going to take that from them for yourself?"

"Actually my wife and I have another house in mind. Close enough to the laboratories, but off the property, allowing more privacy. But, since that old dinosaur must move on, I was thinking of the Wilshusen mansion for you?"

"I am quite satisfied with the present arrangements." Especially if meant pushing out poor Fritz and dragging Margery from her beloved gardens. "Perhaps you should settle in and understand the workings of ORR before you restructure."

"I understand this Institute of ours is being represented by a red-necked, self taught buffoon. A Curtis Macfey."

"Kurt MacKay is considered one of the leading sea life behaviourial experts on the East Coast. Maybe the world."

"A member of the Ku Klux Klan?"

"And Mensa. He gets his jollies from getting a rise out of people. He loves the shock effect."

"He's not a proper representative of Oyster River."

"Oyster River has never required a political litmus

test."

"Maybe it should."

"I'm sure Kurt has a contract but that is something you will have to take up with Adam. Right now, if you would please leave, I have work to finish."

"This Kurt. Is he your lover?"

Chapter 3

"My what?" He was a bastard!

"Your lover. You're defending him so passionately."

"He is a valuable colleague, who does not deserve to be dismissed without cause. "

Marshall smiled benevolently at her, then checked his watch. "Actually, I am late for an appointment. We can continue your pleading some other time."

Wanting him out, Grace moved to open the door for him, he walked past, giving her a patronizing smile and she immediately locked the door behind him. She found herself breathing hard, as if she was just in some sort of battle. Trying to calm herself, Grace returned to her desk, but with Marshall having just been sitting there–she couldn't. She moved over to the screen by one of her assistants' microscope set ups. Grace had that new data from Australia, anomalies to her Popcorn Gene Switch theory, which she had to study it and understand. Usually she could instantly sink into her work and the world would slide away for hours. Now she kept picturing Charles Marshall with his proprietary hands on her DNA sequencing equipment. His hands were going to be on her life.

No, there would be no submersion into figures and percentiles today. No sudden Farrington Fusions--realization that this was the way it was–after such a realization, Grace always knew it couldn't be any other way; then the only question would be why hadn't she seen it sooner? Sighing, Grace walked about her lab–she'd miss it here. Since Eric died, she had been losing day after day on her self-imposed schedule. She had to pull it together, but not today... Grace turned the lights off and locked up the lab again. Not that it mattered with Marshall having all the keys.

Outside ORR's grass was park like, with tall maples turning yellow and red, edged with beds of orange and white mums. Looking down the peninsula, she could see Oyster

River Research's mishmash of architectural styles: classrooms in an 1870's firehouse; glass walled modern labs; yellow brick cafeteria and dorms; her two story, eight apartment concrete block building was Contemporary from the 50's, while the guest lecturer's suite was over an 1920's boat house.

In the late 1800s, Oyster River Harbor Research had been started by a few wealthy summer residents who wanted to further the quest for knowledge. Early on they focused on curing cancer; from the 1920's to the 1960's some inspired scientists found a quiet, supportive place to advance their work in cell process studies. Stewart Brewster started as a lab assistant and rose to Director, always refining the scientific direction of ORR, as he advanced his own unlocking of the secrets of DNA. Under him this little toy campus produced a surprising percentage of Nobel winners and, more importantly, some of the current successful cancer treatments.

ORR had been a refuge for her when she ran from Marshall's scientific theft and chauvinist abuse. Here Grace had found a sheltered cove of incredible peace. Why hadn't she appreciated it before? Only now that she was losing it, did she realize the absolute beauty of Oyster River Harbor. Reaching her condo building, Grace opened the lobby door. No one ever bothered to lock it. They never really had needed to lock anything here, it was safe–or had been.   As she opened her mail slot in the lobby, a voice called out. "Bobby?"

"No, Grace." She moved towards the two back, downstairs condos.

The door to the Jamison's was open and Sara walked out slowly, protectively holding her growing belly. "I was hoping it was Bobby," She said miserably.

"You okay?"

"Of course–no." Sara's whitish facial skin now had the red-pimpled mask of pregnancy and she looked terrible. To save money for them, Grace had cut Sara's red hair near her ears, making it easier to wash but it came out a bit uneven. Bobby was helping Sara out with the cooking, but...

"Do you need him?"

"No, I just want to talk to him–I called Eric's lab. Some woman answered the phone. She wasn't friendly. I'm afraid to call again, but maybe I should..."

Not while he is working in Marshall's lab, the famous doctor once fired an assistant for staying home with double pneumonia. Grace murmured, "Maybe you could call his cell?"

"We cancelled it. Money's been so tight and Bobby's been worried since Eric's death."

Grace followed Sara back into her condo. The two floor building had eight apartments for ORR staff. The Jamison's first floor rooms were a duplicate of Grace's above, only the extra bedroom Grace used as an office was princess pink for little Ginjer. And where Grace's wall of sliding glass doors opened out on to a balcony overlooking the harbor, the Jamison's doors accessed a small concrete patio. Outside it Bobby had rigged up a make shift, chicken wire fence to keep Ginjer from running down the grass to the rocks lining the harbor.

"Maybe you should see your doctor?"

"I did–today."

"What did he say?"

"Rest. Put my feet up."

"Good advice."

She made a wry face. "With a three year old?"

Grace should offer to take Ginjer upstairs, not that she was that great with kids, but the mother looked beaten. Sara had worked through her first pregnancy perfectly with no problems but the next two babies were late miscarriages. Now Grace knew the Jamisons were both scared that this one wouldn't make it either. "The doctor said everything was okay?"

"Sure." Sara bit her lip. "No. It's okay–sort of."

Grace waited patiently for her to continue.

Finally Sara looked at her directly. "I've been having trouble. Months of throwing up and my hormones have been testing abnormally high. I mean with Ginjer, I never had any problems..."

"I hear each pregnancy is different."

"Well this one certainly is. It's twins."

Oh, my God. Three kids under five, in a two bedroom condo, with one parent a homemaker and the other soon to be without a job. The situation sounded hopeless, yet Sara was searching her face for some kind of comfort. Grace forced a confident smile. "That's wonderful news."

"It's like making up for the other two we lost. I shouldn't have told you. Bobby should know first."

"I won't say a thing, and he'll be relieved that there's a positive reason for your problems."

Sara's smile faded. "This Dr. Marshall–you know him?"

"Of him."

"Bobby said you worked with him?" said Sara hopefully.

"For a short time."

"Could you talk to him about us? That Bobby was Eric's assistant and because of that we have this condo..." She sounded so worried.

"I have no influence with Charles Marshall." Grace said in a dead voice.

For a moment Sara nothing. "I don't mean to beg, but before Eric hired Bobby and let us use this condo, we paid three weeks salary for damp basement, four tiny windows at the ceiling. Ginjer couldn't even see the sky."

Grace sighed. They'd be lucky to get that again. "Just in case, Bobby should update his resume. Have him take the old one to Gail in Administration. She'll spruce it up, maybe rewrite it a bit. Gail's good at that and I have friends at Yale and S.U.N.Y. he could apply to. "

"Bobby doesn't have his dissertation done yet. He's always working and he's not too good at writing..."

"Well, he's going to have to finish." Grace didn't want to dwell on that. "With your body under stress, it makes everything seem worse. Can you rest until Bobby gets home? Is Ginjer awake?"

"Watching cartoons."

"Good." Grace nodded. "Now you sit down, put your feet up. Do you need me to do anything? Laundry? Shopping? Take Ginjer upstairs?"

"No." Sara's bright smile flashed back. "It's just so great to have you living here."

She left Sara waiting for Bobby, waiting to tell him that probably soon with no job, no place to live and no doctorate, he would have two more mouths to feed. With Sara using their friendship as a lifeline, Grace didn't want to explain that she was going upstairs to start looking for another place to move to.

But even that was beyond her. She was so exhausted she just stretched out on the living room couch, must be coming down with something. Later she phoned instructions for her assistants and just went back to sleep on the couch again. At supper time Grace zapped a frozen crab cake dinner as she recalled all her happy years at Oyster River. Afterwards she slipped her jacket over her shoulders and walked out on to her balcony that overlooked the harbor and the shore across the way. Old clapboard and shingled houses, with white painted docks. Must look pretty much like it did in the days of the square riggers, with whalers returning home after years of hunting.

Watching the orange and pink clouds at the sunset was quieting and she felt comforted as the water stained from green to dark black, as one by one the stars seemed to shine on. How many genetic coding problems has she worked out on this balcony? Now it was over. Even if Marshall allowed her stay among his privileged few, she would have to leave. What about her contract with ORR? It had two more years to run, but Adam was an ethical guy, he couldn't hold her to it, could he?

Where would she go? Finding Oyster River had been a lucky fluke. When she was an undergraduate, Eric Larsen had been a guest speaker at the University of Vermont and afterwards he invited all the students for dutch treat at the local pizza parlor. She jockeyed to sit next him. Over a slice of oily pepperoni she questioned some of his research and he seemed impressed with her ideas.

Eric asked her to outline her theories and sent them to him, then he took his valuable time to sent back his insightful comments. For a few years they intermittently kept up a correspondence and--for her graduation as a present--he lent her his code allowing her to get on the Science Foundation Network. That contact with Eric had been so important to her, but over the years they both let it drop off.

She received her doctorate in Pasadena, and was on to something important, before the big blow up. When Charles Marshall had stolen Grace's research, she had tried to speak up. To fight him! An inquiry was called and he lied openly, telling the college's disciplinary committee that he and Grace were having an affair and that her claims of stolen research and sexual harassment were revenge for his dumping her. He had friends on the faculty, she didn't. She lost her position and her scientific reputation.

But Eric had heard about Marshall forcing her out, and he contacted her again. He had persuaded ORR to offer a fellowship to a young, disgraced researcher. In those days she really had no idea of ORR's facilities or personnel outside of Eric. All she knew was that because of Marshall, no other place would have her. Grace packed up and moved back across country to Connecticut.

At first she was forced to do lab assistance and routine teaching duties, but soon she was working on her own projects. After Marshall's unwanted sexual advances Grace found herself afraid that Eric would expect some sort of pay back for his recruitment, but he didn't. Under Eric's tutelage, she soon planned her own work protocols, as he introduced her to possible grantees. Her temporary living arrangement in the guest speaker's housing became this cozy condo over looking the harbor.

In the town of Oyster River she found a safety and friends. Freya, Mac, Bobby, Kurt–the others–she would miss them so much! And this time she didn't have Eric's help to relocate, but this time, she didn't need his help. Grace had a positive track record that Marshall couldn't deny. She could pick and choose what lab she wanted to go to.

And there were some good ones. A lot of her work was with sea creatures, maybe Woods Hole? Would they have an opening? She could go inland to the University of Chicago? There were lots of places that her research could flourish, but somehow she didn't think the new place would ever bring her such close supportive ties again. After an hour of just staring out at the sea, she went to bed. But it was another hour or so before her mind was quiet enough to sleep.

She woke abruptly. Hammering at her door. Grace looked at the clock. 3:12 A.M.? Sara? Miscarrying? Barefooted she ran to the door. More hammering. Why didn't Bobby use the bell?

Grace pulled the door open to see Katherine Marshall staring at her. Not the perfectly coifed wife of the eminent Charles. No, this was a crazy lady, hair disheveled, her breath stinking of whiskey.

"Where is he?"

"What?"

"My husband!" With anger and booze she was slurring

her words. "I know he is with you!"

"Your husband would not be here!" Grace said angrily.

"You were his lover!"

"I have never been in bed with Charles Marshall. And frankly I can't see why any woman would." God, Grace was in her nightgown standing at an open door, loudly arguing with an unreasonable drunk.

Katherine shoved past Grace. "Charles! I know you are here!" **Come out!**"

Outraged, Grace grabbed her car coat from the closet and slipped it on to cover her nightgown. Katherine had glanced in the kitchen and was opening the bathroom door. Finding it empty, she was now headed towards Grace's bedroom.

"Your husband is not here!"

"Then where is he?"

"I have no idea!"

"You've slept with him before!"

"I have not!"

"He's slept with all his research assistants. He's told me!"

"Told you?" Grace couldn't believe that.

She actually smiled. "Oh, yes. He tells me all about it–when you come up with some new sex trick he passes it on. You girls enhance our sex life."

"You put up with that?"

Katherine changed her tone to a firm. "All I want is my husband. He admitted publically that you were lovers in the past..."

Now it was Grace's turn to be angry. "There was never any affair! You're husband's a liar! "

The finality in Grace's tone seemed to stop Katherine. She reached up to pat her graying hair and stiffened her back, as if suddenly realizing what a scene she was creating. In a lowered voice Katherine continued. "It's late..."

"After 3 a.m."

"And Charles's not back. I...I just wanted to know where he was?"

"I would take that up with him."

Katherine still looked about with unfocused eyes. "Being–sleeping with my husband is an honor..."

"Not to me. Not to any woman who respects herself!"

Marshall's wife focused now on the dark glass of the sliding door leading to the balcony.

Grace considered suggesting Katherine go check it out, but decided against it. Katherine looked at the daybed Grace used as a couch. She seemed to want to look under it, but glancing back at Grace's hard face, decided against it.

Pulling herself together, with as much dignity as she could muster, Katherine walked to the door. "If Charlie comes..."

"He will not."

With a last look around, Katherine opened the door and walked out. Grace locked it behind her. She had forgotten what living around the eminent Marshalls was like.

Chapter 4

When Grace had a problem she couldn't work out, she kept it in the back of her mind, but also looked for something she could solve. The famed genetic pioneer Barbara McCormick had always been fascinated by the central dark colored bloom of a Queen Anne's lace. Why was it always in the center? Why was there only one purple red? Her own 'Popcorn Gene Switch' theory should be able to explain that placement–did it? Those were questions that fascinated Grace, not what lab she would be running to. She'd get some work done today.

The sun was rising, painting a yellowish sky. She didn't have the energy to start her usual morning run down in Oyster River Harbor, instead she let herself out the sliding glass doors to the balcony with its small table and chairs. This neat, little two bed room apartment was worth, what, back in her hometown of Island Pond, Vermont? Maybe forty thousand? Here this condo, in this exclusive area with its water view, was worth maybe three million dollars. She would miss it. Deeply breathing in the salty air, Grace sat down and let the tea cup in her hand cool a little as she stood gazing out at the smooth harbor water.

The Japanese language had a word, what was it? Grace pictured it in her mind and then said it out loud in a soft voice, 'Arigatai'. A sense of appreciation. A sincere recognition and realization for what one has. How often had she allowed the beauties and comforts of her life to be taken for granted?

She loved this home, only it wasn't her condo. It belonged to the Oyster River Research Institute. Now where would she go? How long before she could find a new place to live? This place came as part of her contract, but without it she would need to buy a house. Only with no savings, she couldn't afford to buy one, since for years all her money had been poured into new equipment for her research.

Grace would have to get accepted at a research institute or university. Most universities would require teaching and she wasn't any good at dealing with masses of students. How long before she could set up her own laboratory? And then what, how many years to find new friends–if ever? She sipped from the teacup. The green tea tasted bitter.

A sea gull flew at her balcony, then veered off. Beyond in the bay, she watched as a man rowed a red boat out, probably one of Neptune's rentals. Stowing his oars, he unsteadily started to stand up in the rocking boat. Stupid idea–must be a landlubber. Standing, he was pulling off his shirt, too distant to see his age, just a man with a stocky, wiry body. A newbie taking a fishing skiff out to go swimming in the North Atlantic, in October?

He was pulling off his trousers. Did he have a wet suit to put on? Scuba? She didn't see any. The water in the deep harbor would be too cold to swim. He had a short, white bathing suit, no, that must be his underpants and he was pulling them off too. Grace felt vaguely voyeuristic watching this guy, but he certainly had picked a public place to strip. He seemed to be taking his time pulling his clothes off, trying to balance on the rocking boat, as he folded his underpants and neatly put them down on the seat.

With a definite feeling of unease, Grace looked about the harbor. Somebody should go out and talk to the guy. There were a few boats moored, two sail planers were in the distance but no one near him. *Nobody to say, hey buddy, before you go in maybe you ought to sober up?*

Should she call the Coast Guard? What was Kurt's cell phone number? The naked man stood tall, theatrically putting his hands on his hips and scanning across the bay, looking in her direction. Could he see her staring? No, of course not.

He looked down at the water. Up at the clear sky, then

he jumped, kicking widely from the boat. The guy quickly sank under the dark water. His head bobbed up. He flailed about wildly, as if trying to reach the boat but it wasn't anchored, and his frantic windmill threshing caused waves that pushed it away. He went under again.

Grace ran inside for the phone, desperately dialing 911. Through the sliding glass doors, she could see him rise to the surface one more time. As Emergency services answered he went back down under the water. He didn't come up again.

Following instructions, Grace stayed on the line until the white police boat arrived. They quickly tied a line to his drifting boat, then followed her unhelpful, relayed directions as to where he disappeared. "Left. More. The other way–I'm sorry." She hung up as the fire department's boat was arriving with not much hope of finding the guy. Feeling sick, she just put on her light jacket and running shoes and headed downstairs.

As she walked, she could hear the fire boat's bull horns echoing over the water. She looked toward her lab, feeling too upset to go in, so instead she kept walking down to ORR's docks. For research purposes the Institute kept several small, bright yellow, motorized rowboats, more for teaching the summer students than anything else. Should she take one of them out and join the search? That probably wasn't a good idea.

She stepped off the gray decking onto a perforated steel ladder that rose and felt with the tides. It was now at about a fifty degree angle. The steel with its wooden cross tiers bounced underfoot, always making her feel off balance.

The ladder ramp ended on to an odd tree of floating docks, the farthest one out was where Dr. Kurt MacKay moored the thirty-six foot Cabo Rico Cutter sailboat he lived in. It had a nice, white curved sail boat hull, only spoiled by the blue tarp roped over the damaged bow that someday Kurt was going to rebuild.

Now he was working in the slip next to it, on the deck of a thirty-eight foot lobster yawl which was the diesel he used for his harbor research. Kurt was hauling up two, big metal buckets, but he had stopped to study the police boats, as black wet-suited divers were jumping off the fire boat. Noticing her approach, he reached up and offered a steadying hand for her to climb on to the yawl. "Pretty Lady, welcome aboard."

Grace stepped down and tried to adjust to the bobbing boat beneath her. Next to him, were several metal buckets holding writhing clumps of lobsters. "You doing research, a lobster bake or both?"

Kurt looked down. "Not with these. " He lifted a three pounder up, its spindly legs clawed air. It was the usual mottled black-green and orange shell, but when he turned it right side up she could see ovals of bright turquoise colored scum on its segmented abdomen.

"Is that a cross with some of those blue lobsters?"

"Nope. Some sort of growth on the shell."

"Parasite?"

"Might be a lobster parasite, might be benign, something I haven't seen before." He frowned with concentration. "Rub your fingers on it."

Brilliant idea. Some unknown fungal infection, smear it on your finger and see if it grows on humans. But ever driven by curiosity Grace rubbed her fingers on the turquoise mottling as the lobster curled his tail. "Feels slippery. Is it going to turn my fingers blue?"

"Don't seem to have that effect on human skin. Leastwise not mine, but it's real softening of callused skin. Stays on for most of the day."

"Is it harming the lobster?"

"Don't know. These are moving okay, don't seem to be bothered." A helicopter loudly whirled above them. Kurt looked up. "Blue--State police. What's going on? Those cop boats are about where those marine archaeologists should be finding the *Siren*."

"The what?"

"1820's Whaler–sunk right over there."

"Inside the Harbor?"

"Yhep. That was part of the curse. The widow wanted to see the ship sink, just half a mile from safety. Drowned the three cursed brothers and the rest of the crew."

"And the marine archeologists haven't found this site yet?"

"Nope."

She gave him a sharp look. "But you have?"

Kurt smiled slyly. "Maybe." He looked up as the police helicopter circled over them, headed toward the police boats. "But why all the cops?"

"A man. I saw him, he took a rental boat out, stripped and jumped in."

"Suicide?"

"What else could it be?"

"Don't know. Got my own problems." He looked toward the yellow Captain's Roost building. "You know this supposed new boss of ours?"

"Marshall?"

"Yhep. You didn't look too happy to see him. He was bragging he was the man who gave you your start?"

She ignored the last. "I have no influence with him, if that's what you are asking."

"He was down here, with his lady assistant looking things over. Doesn't think my 'dinky boats' fits with his idea of Institute crafts."

"Can you get dockage elsewhere?"

"Sure. If I want to pay over five figures for two slips, and if I can get past five year waiting lists."

"I'm sorry." She looked back at the Captain's Roost. "It looks like I'll be looking for another laboratory myself and a condo."

"Why?" He didn't look happy. "Marshall's talking like you're his beloved protégée. He certainly won't be lusting after your little condo. Hear tell Fritz's mansion wasn't good enough for Marshall, he's looking across the harbor, to all those old money estates on the water."

"The Greenfield's?"

"Naw. I heard he made an offer on 'Red Rose Cottage'."

"Steward and Joyce Brewster? That house has been in her family since Revolutionary times. Have they put it on the market?"

"Nope, but Marshall made a low ball offer through a real estate woman."

Grace gazed across the harbor, she could barely see the rambling white clapboard house, with it's silly old Dutch windmill. She knew Steward sat there in the garden on his wood glider, looking over at the Oyster River Harbor Research Institute that he pretty much created. When Stewart started working here ORR was doing research on everything from early germ eradication to electric boxes for healing. Becoming Head of the Institute, he brought to it the strict scientific discipline that marked Oyster River today. He made ORR what it is, then years later, the institute condemned his research and hid his name from their lists. "The Brewsters won't sell."

"Hear tell Steward politely turned him down. Marshall told the realtor to go back and keep badgering them. Said he had reason to believe they would be changing their minds."

Grace remembered the great man's tactics of dirty tricks and blackmail. "Marshall used to take pride in his ability to force others to do what he wanted."

Kurt calmly looked from the Roost to her. "Maybe he's going learn some of us don't fold."

"Where is Marshall living? Certainly not at the Shoreline motel?"

"Adam put them up in the guest speakers' suite, over the boat house. Wouldn't have thought it would be big enough for them."

God, he was living just down the road from her? Shit. "How did Marshall know about the Brewsters and their house? They've been retired from Oyster River for years, and that house was never Institute property."

"Apparently Marshall's been paying secret calls here, as part of his hiring. Been sneaking around on Sunday nights, checking out the labs, learning the lay of the land."

His legendary secret lab snoops. That certainly sounded like Marshall. "What he goes after he usually gets and the Brewsters had that old scandal."

"Nobody cares about something that happened that many years ago."

"Marshall may make it front page again, if they don't sell to him."

"Nice guy." Kurt was looking to the commotion in the bay. "He also says the Wilshusen mansion is going to be open for whom ever he brings in. Hinted it might be open to you?" Kurt raised an eyebrow.

Grace could guess how Marshall phrased her possible cooperation. "I'm leaving. Do you think he can get Fritz out?"

"Adam seems to think Marshall is next to God."

"Maybe Fritz can retire?"

"On what? That wife of his is always spending next month's check. At his age, the best he can get is a part-time job teaching undergraduates at some junior college."

"They'll be without a house, without Margey's gardens." Grace shook her head. "And my condo. The eminent Dr. Marshall won't want me around watching." She thought a moment. Grace needed time to prepare, plan. "Don't say anything about my leaving." She couldn't look at what was going on out in the bay. "If Marshall's talking like he's not too happy about your qualifications..."

"Whal, seems I've got a contract for five years, with two, free boat slips guaranteed."

Five years? Grace's current contract only ran three years. So much for her negotiating ability and Adam's '*vast appreciation for her unique talents*'. "Then there's Bobby and Sara. With Eric gone, if Marshall doesn't pick Bobby up as an assistant..."

Kurt eyes were hard. "They'd better start looking. When Marshall was on that inspection tour, he had Bobby in tow. Ordered Bobby to go get him coffee. Bobby wouldn't and he spouted off to Marshall. They're fire and gasoline from day one." Kurt was looking out to harbor as an orange pontooned Coast Guard cutter joining the town boats. "When Marshall came down to look at my 'garbage barge', he had a assistant with him, Diandra something or other. Big boobies."

"That would be Marshall's idea of a lab assistant."

"I'd like to get in those tight pants." He leered.

She ignored it. "Let me know if you hear of a decent condo for Sara and Bobby."

"A place around here among the millionaire estates? With lots room for a kid, a dog and new, screaming baby? Cheap enough for an underpaid graduate student? Sure."

"Is there any chance you could take Bobby on as an assistant?"

Kurt seemed to be considering it, then said regretfully, "Bobby's a good worker. Be proud to have him–but the money's been running thin. Gotta get another grant soon just to pay my motorcycle gas. Can't take on another assistant now, jes had to let Herald go."

She understood the feeling. Grace turned to climb back onto the dock, Kurt reached out to steady her elbow. "Uh, lady. There is something I wanted to ask you."

With her foot in the air and the boat and the dock bopping, she looked back to him. "What?"

"I got this invite for free food."

Grace shook her head. "Not now. Not with everything..."

He persisted. "This is a fancy do, a formal dinner in New York City. Should've asked you sooner. I need an escort."

"What about that blonde always hanging off your motorcycle?"

"Tanya? Nope. This is a high end invitation. Need a classy lady on my arm. First Saturday in November. I'll keep yer pot full of healthy lobsters?" He added hopefully.

Kurt was a colleague, admittedly an abrasive one, but a fellow scientist, maybe even friend. She was certainly talking more of her private business to him than anyone else. He was never an official lover, but they had gone out a bit, until she started worrying that their going to bed together might damage their work relationship. She would like to oblige him but not now, not with everything ending so suddenly. "I can't.."

He looked away, out a the water. "You don't owe me anything, still it's a free eating. Few speeches. Fill yer full of sushi and have ya home before yer turn into a pumpkin."

Normally he would've just dropped it. This seemed to mean something to him, but she felt so tired and beaten. She just shook her head.

He nodded and half lifted her on the dock. For a short, scrawny looking man, Kurt was unbelievably strong. He was still looking out at the boats in the Harbor. "They got something." The black, wet suit divers had converged alongside the Coast Guard vessel. "Must've found your boy." Kurt said quietly.

Chapter 5

Grace looked and saw men onboard the ship reaching down. From the dark choppy water, darker arms of wet suited divers pushed up a flash of pale white. "Oh, my God."

"Good thing you saw him go in." His face carefully neutral, Kurt said, "If they didn't get him before the tide turned, he'd been flushed out to the Sound. Curse of the widow."

But if she had called sooner, would he still be alive? Feeling sick, Grace nodded and walked away. Why would any one give up his life like that?

Slowly she walked to her laboratory. Unsettled, Grace sat at her desk, she had her timetables and her heavy workload, she must get something done. She opened up a current spreadsheet, tried to concentrate but again felt terribly tired. As usual, she'd left her hand bag back at the condo, but she had her extra key ring with her. Just sitting here was getting her nowhere, moving was always better than brooding, she headed out to her car.

Driving out of ORR she decided to turn right, away from the road that led toward the town of Oyster River. Grace didn't want to drive that road that curved around the harbor, where they laid that naked man's body on the deck. She wanted to get away from all of that.

Not paying attention she just drove, turned off the main road, picking random side roads. Eventually found herself driving past long lawns of smooth grass and expensive houses. Finally she started thinking rationally, the car was low on gas, she'd left her handbag with credit cards and driver's license back at her condo. This was really not a day to be just aimlessly rambling. Still, she didn't feel like going back to her lab and working. There was a stretch of meadows on both sides of the road that ended in trees with no house in sight. Only wild flowers and woods. Maybe if she just parked here and walked a bit.

Where she pulled off the road was bordered by white-boarded horse fences, but the field beyond was knee high in wild meadow grass, obviously not grazed. At the edges of the meadow were clumps old growth trees. Some wealthy person's estate–so wealthy, Grace couldn't even see the house. Leaning her elbows on the fence, she focused on the meadow with its fascinating, overgrown mix of seeding grass and wild flowers, with tall stalks of Queen Anne's laces waving above them all.

Ahead was a car gate, leading to a dirt road. She walked over, but it was locked, with a bold orange 'no trespassing' sign. Still, if she just walked about a bit, nobody could mind. Grace found herself climbing on to the bottom board of the fence, balancing precariously, then swinging her legs over the top and finally jumping down.

All around her were hundreds–thousands--of wild flowers. Genetic daisy chains that reproduced from their wild parents. Grace walked to a large bloom, the perfect Queen Annie's lace. Each wide bloom composed of tiny white florets on fragile stems and then that passionate, single, red-purple bud in the center. Was there only one? Or was it like the bunches of four petaled lilac flowers, if you looked closely, you could always find a floret with a three, five and six petaled mutations? Could you find multiple of the red buds in the center of a Queen Annie? Grace started across field, studying each bloom. Was the red the stamen?

Only one central, single purple-red bloom in the first fourteen heads she studied. As she bent down to study the fifteen, Grace was vaguely aware of a heavy drumming sound growing closer. With her attention totally consumed by the flower before her, the drumming stopped behind her.

A creak of leather, then a man's voice. "Dr. Farrington?"

As if surfacing from deep waters, Grace blinked her

eyes and looked up at a massive, golden hunter, ridden by a man with wheat colored hair and sun freckles. Oh, lord. She was on private property. Probably his. "I'm sorry," She started.

"Dr. Farrington, do you remember me?"

"I am so sorry....I'm terrible with names." She looked about. "This is probably private land."

"It is. Mine." He easily dismounted from his tall horse, and held out a hand to shake. "I'm David Gardiner. We met at the reception Monday."

God, was it only two days, since her world started to crumble? She shook his strong firm hand. "Oh, yes. I'm so sorry. You're the man Adam is trying to rope into..." had she really said that? "talk you into being on the Board."

The man's slight smile widened wickedly. "Adam generally phrases it as a '*great opportunity*' that he might be able to obtain for me." His light blue eyes were twinkling.

Grace tried to apologize again. "I've been preoccupied."

"With the genetics of my meadow flowers?"

She turned away from him. "Actually, yes." Grace automatically relaxed, studying a question related to genetics. "Wild flowers are fascinating, each individualized structure, optimized for obtaining nutrients and reproduction." Reality intruded again. "But I shouldn't be trespassing."

"Again, this is my property. You're to consider yourself my invited guest, when ever you wish. But, pardon me, your face is streaked with dirt."

Oh, she must look a sight. Outside of lipstick, Grace never put on much makeup. She took her coat sleeve and wiped a cheek. God, Adam would be counting on her to represent Oyster River. Not stand in some potential patron's field looking like a looney. "It's been a terrible day."

"You seemed distracted at the reception?"

She did not want to go down that route. "I saw a man

die today."

"I beg your pardon?"

"A suicide. I have a condo that overlooks the harbor and I was standing out on my balcony. I called 911, but it was too late."

He looked at her in seeming sympathy as he asked, "Have eaten anything lately?"

"What?"

"My mother's British forebears always said that it is easier to maintain a stiff upper lip on a full stomach."

He looked over the fence. "Is that car yours? That gate is for the back road to my house. If you could just follow me."

Her mind was still not operating. "The gate's locked."

"It can be opened." He hauled himself up into the English saddle of his tall hunter. The golden horse tossed its head, and eagerly pranced sideways, obviously joyful to be moving again. She wondered why they couldn't just walk to his house? But she found it was easier not to argue and to just follow him.

In an area that had five acre zoning minimum, he apparently had quite a bit more. Driving her car slowly after the horse, she passed neatly fenced fields, mowed paddocks and two horse barns. Near the barns there seemed to be a large dog kennel, with beagles that barked to see him. For the main house she expected something with tall pillars and a Tara like porch. Instead they stopped at a cobble stone courtyard, behind a long, rambling, gray-wood shingle two story. There were other low buildings squaring the courtyard–a five door garage? Servant's residences? A sandy haired teenager was coming out from the stable. As he dismounted and gave the teenager the reins, David rubbed the horse's neck. Watching him being let away, David commented, "That's Raj–a good hunter."

Grace followed David up a flag stoned path to what must be the back of his house. Most people in this world didn't seriously study genetics and certainly didn't know her, but of the few that did know of her achievements Grace was used to a fawning deference that made her uncomfortable. This man was different. He obviously did know her work, and he seemed to be honored by her company, but certainly wasn't over awed by her presence.

Inside she stepped down to a wide blue slate floor. The hallway was dark, with old timber beaming, the bones of an colonial farmhouse, obviously added to many times. As they walked to the front of the house, the ceilings got higher. In a wide foyer, light was coming in from small bull's eye glass windows set aside and above the double doorway, striking a full length portrait of a woman in white satin. Grace stopped to study it.

David joined her. "My paternal grandmother, Helen. Painted in London by John Singer Sargent.

"Magnificent–the painting."

"So was she." He smiled. "You don't know who Sargent was, do you?"

"He's obviously a great painter."

"Some people say that." That impish smile again. Not mocking her, just enjoying a private joke. "I also have some Audubon bird prints you might be interested in." He lead her into an open, very masculine room with a high, wood mantled, square cut stone fireplace; deep, brass studded leather furniture; and walls of bookcases. "Now let me get you something. Coffee? Tea?"

"Tea." She sank down on a strangely comforting chair.

"Sandwiches–anything you can't eat?"

"I should be helping you." She started to get back up.

"No need. Caine's about. I'll be back in a moment."

He left and suddenly she felt abandoned.

Chapter 6

It was quiet here, reassuring in a room that smelled of books and old money. Grace should pull herself together, she was representing Oyster River Research to a possible patron, but why should she worry? It was going to be Charles Marshall's new empire. He was taking over ORR, while she was running, again.

Oyster River had meant so much to her, first, a place of refuge, then a focus for her research. But surprisingly what she would miss the most were the people here, the first real, close friends she'd ever had. Now Fritz and Margery Wilshusen would be kicked out. Bobby was probably next. Kurt would stay. He had his contract and he needed his dockage. Kurt was just contrary enough to supremely enjoy fighting the great Charles Marshall. That would have been a fight she would have loved to see.

Strangely in this quiet room Grace felt her strength returning. Why should she run? Not without fight! Marshall or no Marshall she would be staying at Oyster River! Suddenly that all pervasive tiredness drained from her body. She had two more years on her contract, if anyone was getting kicked out, it would be him!

She couldn't get the laboratory keys from Marshall and Security, but she could transfer all her data to her personal laptop. All her work she would carry safe with her. If Marshall sneaked into her laboratory and "borrowed" her DNA analyzer, well she would by-pass ORR's security and call the police.

Drop in all poor Mac's lap, Marshall would find out the local policeman was her best friend's son. Have Freya go after Mac and Mac go after Marshall. Yes. This time Grace would be the one with friends on her side! This time Grace knew all Marshall's slimy tricks and could deal with them.

With restless energy, she stood up and walked to the

fireplace mantle. The bookcases on either side held not the usual leather bound masterworks but instead well worn books on horses, gardening and travel. Over the mantle, she saw a huge, yellowed varnished decorative map of the world. The legend read 1931 and it was marked with red lines going from England to New York and different continents. Another label in the Pacific Ocean read 'Travels of the Prince of Wales'.

She was studying it when she heard him coming back.

David nodded approvingly. "You're looking better."

"I'm feeling better, Mr. Gardiner." Grace said returning to that deep leather seated chair.

David sat in the one opposite her, across a brass topped coffee table. "That man who died, was he a friend of yours?"

"No, at least I don't think so. I don't know. I was out on my balcony and I saw a distant figure in a boat, I really couldn't see who it was, I might have know him..."

"Perhaps it was accident?"

"No, he stopped rowing, stood up, undressed and jumped in. He seemed to struggle, trying to get to the boat, but he certainly wasn't able to swim."

"Sad. Some fight so hard for life, others throw it away." He seemed to effortlessly change the subject to one she was comfortable with. "What did part of the Queen Anne's Lace flower were you studying?"

"The central, red stamen..."

"It isn't a stamen." Apparently Mr. Gardiner knew his flowers. "The white florets contain the pollinating apparatus. The single, central red bud is sterile."

"What is its purpose?"

He looked surprised. "I don't really know, perhaps you, Dr. Farrington, with one of your Farrington Fusions, you can puzzle that out."

"Grace. Please."

"Only if it's David."

A balding man, dressed casually, carried in an elaborate silver tea tray. Grace noted gold trimmed bone china, a cup for her and mug for David. On it were also two plates: a crystal platter of neat, quarter cut sandwiches and another of fancy cookies. Well in this house, they were probably were the British 'biscuits'. Who was the man with the tray? Too old for a son. Servant? Boy friend?

"That looks very good, Caine. I'll serve." David said.

The man withdrew and David picked up the tea pot. "Do you like it with cream and sugar?"

"Black, with lemon." She noted even a small crystal bowl of freshly cut lemon slices, as he poured her a cup of spice smelling tea. Grace wasn't hungry, but if she was going to stay and fight Charles Marshall, having a well-to-do friend who might wind up on the Board of Directors would be to her advantage. She reached for a sandwich and found herself eating salmon salad. "With a British high tea, I expected cucumber."

"Never liked those green veggie bits myself."

She took a tentative sip of the hot tea, the fragrant blend of orange and anisette and other flavors there were too subtle to fully puzzle out. "Delicious."

"It's special order from London, 'East Indian Sunset'. The Cheese Shop in Oyster River stocks it for me. If you would like, I can have Caine put some up in a tin to take back with you?"

She nodded. "I'd love it." She drank more. When she got back, she would have to set up a meeting with Adam, outline her case. If she continued at ORR, her lab was going to be sacrosanct with locks that Marshall couldn't enter!

David wasn't drinking. "Perhaps you can explain a genetic question for me."

"I'll try."

"A mule is know for its hybrid vigor, yet a hinnee isn't?"

Grace turned that over in her mind. "A mule is the offspring of a male donkey and female horse. A hinnee is the offspring of a male horse or pony with a female donkey. The mule's hybrid vigor you are probably referring to is its strength, size and physical well-being that mule crosses often exhibit. Vigor that seems to be greater than either of its parents."

"The hinnee doesn't have hybrid vigor."

"It doesn't have the general attributes of a mule. True. But a hinnee may have distinctive inheritances of their own." Grace nodded. "I've never studied them."

"Mules and hinnees are sterile."

"As an interspecies cross. Yes–like lion and tiger mixes. However there is a case that I have heard of, but not studied, where a least one mule bore a colt."

David cocked his head. "Isn't that impossible?"

"I wish I had the genetic work up on that case, but I don't. Still, there are few theories on that. One is that during chromosomal meiosis, that in a very rare event, both parent's genes completely remained together during the homologuous recombination stage, say the horse's genes all migrated over to form the embryo which would become the mule. Another theory, is that the mule, instead of being the expected half horse half donkey hybrid mix was say 60% horse."

"How can that be? A child is 50% one parent and 50% the other?"

"Humans should receive 23 chromosomes from each parent. The male sex chromosome is a "y". It's shorter, with less genes on it than the female's 'x'. That's why problems like hemophilia are usually passed from a carrier- mother to son."

"Females can't get hemophilia."

"Actually they can, but it is very rare. A female hemophiliac would have to have a father with hemophilia and mother who is a carrier, has hemophilia herself or has genes that spontaneously mutate. Sadly possible, if a woman takes her father for hemophilia treatments and meets her husband-to-be in the doctor's waiting room. "

"Go back to the mule, who is 60% horse. Could you explain that in lay man's terms?"

Grace took a chocolate covered biscuit and chewed it giving her time to think. This why she never liked teaching undergraduates. You had to explain everything in their terms. "All right. You are working in a factory. They give you plastic bags and four trays with colored beads, red, yellow, blue and green. The first two plastic bags have two strands of beads in them, with distinct multiples of beading, containing all four colors.

"You take one strand from each bag to place together in the third bag–this is your new organism, that you will now copy. As the proto "embryo" develops, you will start trying to accurately copy those two bead strands patterns from the third bag. Soon you are doing more and more of them. You probably will probably make mistakes, in threading the beads–changing their color order. Or incorrectly putting three strands of beads into one bag, when you should only have two. "

He was following her. "Chromosomes, with genes in the wrong order..."

"Might give you a mutation. In most cases a mutation that will be a fatal one for your embryo."

"Do you think there are many mistakes in the gene copying?"

"When Yale's In-Vitro Clinic started closely monitoring infertile women, they found that often the women did get pregnant, but lost their babies within the first month. Researchers theorized that in the normal population pregnancy loss was as high as 50%. People don't realize it's that high, because the embryo self-destructs before the mother even realizes she's pregnant."

"But in the pregnant mule's case..."

"If you keep throwing bead strands into the bags, you might toss in an extra, incomplete strand. Your mule will have a complete set of the genes it needs to live, but that extra strand of horse may allow the mule to reproduce. It would be fascinating to know if that mule's off-spring could be successfully mated. I should Google it."

"Do you look up a lot things on the Internet?" He asked in a surprised voice.

"Of course." She focused back on him. "That's pretty much what makes a scientist. An endless curiosity that can't ever be satiated."

"Ever study horses?"

"I've looked at some of the nineteen century and twentieth century records of thoroughbred horse matings."

"The Stud books." He nodded.

"They are invaluable for following traits like speed, color, size, temperament, in a controlled mating situation."

"I have a rather extensive library of those here, some originals, others copies of records aristocratic British families kept with their horse matings."

They spent the rest of the hour speaking about David's horse breeding and at the end, she left with a tin of tea and directions for David's front driveway. It was asphalted, long and curving through more forest, finally coming out to the road, landscaped with mounded banks of manicured azaleas. No imposing security gates or name signs, or any indication of the huge estate behind it, just a small, neat bronze plate set on the hillside with the house number 936.

With new resolve, Grace drove back to ORR. She would fight Marshall, and this time she would win! He was on her home ground. And if he ran true to form with his sexual harassment, dirty tricks or sloppy science, there would soon be enough evidence to get him kicked out of Oyster River!

But when she turned off the main road into ORR's

peninsula, she could see the entrance to the first parking lot was blocked by flashing police cars. Three cars, one red and blue from local police and two rotating yellow lights from the Institutes' own private security. With a feeling of dread Grace parked on the road and hurried over to the knot of curious bystanders.

Chapter 7

It was worst than she thought, Adam Greenfield had apparently just arrived and the local tan uniformed policeman stood beside him, while two green uniformed security guards were holding Bobby, with his arms tightly handcuffed behind his back.

Adam was rapidly talking to the policeman, unfortunately not Mac or Ben. "Please, we do not want the publicity! Dr. Marshall said he's not pressing charges, this whole thing is a mistake."

The policeman was getting a call over his radio. Luckily, he had a parkway accident to run off to. "All right, sir." He said before leaving.

Adam then hurried to ORR's security guards. "Get him out of those handcuffs. I didn't know we hand any!"

Grace pushed through the knot of rubber necking students, she couldn't believe this was happening so soon!

Adam looked to the growing crowd. "Please, people. Go about your business! This is over." Adam turned to Bobby. "Go back to your condo."

Bobby started to explain. "He..."

Adam cut him off. "I'll talk with you later!"

Grace was at Bobby's side. "What happened?"

"Nothing." Bobby answered sounding beaten.

Adam angrily corrected. "He punched out Dr. Marshall!"

Grace looked to Bobby. "Why?"

Bobby wouldn't meet her eyes. "I didn't punch him, I jut clipped him."

"Why did you hit him?" Adam asked.

"He said something."

Grace implored Adam. "I'm sure it wasn't Bobby's fault."

Adam looked to Bobby. "You're to stay away from Dr.

Marshall!"

Bobby suddenly seemed to realize the extent of his 'little clip'. "How can I stay away when I'm working as his lab assistant?"

Adam glared at him. "Not any longer."

Bobby looked down toward his ORR condo, where his daughter and very pregnant wife waited. "My teaching..."

After clearing the crowds, the security guards were coming over, but Adam waved them off. "I'll take care of this." He looked dismissively at Bobby. "I'll talk with you later–just stay away from the labs!" Adam headed off in the direction of Eric's–no–now Marshall's lab.

Bobby's shoulders slumped, as the full weight of what he had done seemed to register.

"Why did you hit him?" Grace asked again.

Bobby shook his head. "He said–it doesn't matter." Turning his back on her, Bobby walked away.

Grace started to follow him, then decided to hurry after the departing Adam. Having to lengthen even her long strides to catch up beside him. "Bobby wouldn't have hit Marshall without good reason."

Adam looked harried. "This has gotten so out of hand."

"You're firing Bobby?"

"Charles Marshall won't work with him."

"But who will teach Eric's students?"

Adam rubbed his forehead, as if in pain. "When I interviewed Dr. Marshall he seemed excited about teaching. I remember him saying those young minds would invigorate him."

"But after you hired him, it was different?"

"Now he says that he's not teaching, even with Bobby doing most of it."

"Bobby's taught the courses dozens of times. Under Eric, he wrote the syllabuses, corrected the test papers and counseled the students. He could do it all."

"Bobby Jamison doesn't have the credentials we require for our course lecturers."

"But he can work for ORR somewhere else? I may be able to pick him up on one of my grants."

"You already have two part-time student assistants. Are you going to let them go?"

Inger and Nick, they needed their salaries to stay in college, so she couldn't do that. "No. I'm–I'm trying to get another grant."

He looked down at her. "With the financial turndown, there doesn't seem to be much out there."

She continued, "The condo. Can Bobby and Sara keep their condo? "

"Dr. Marshall wants it for his assistant, Miss Hollings."

"That's not fair!"

"While Eric Larsen was here, he allowed the Jamisons to live in his housing allowance. With Eric gone, I can't justify leaving a graduate student living for free on Institute property. One who is not even employed here anymore."

"You need someone to teach."

"Charles Marshall wants him out. Dr. Marshall is a great asset to Oyster River."

"Is he? Marshall hasn't done a bit of important research in the last twenty years..." *Or at lease stolen any worthwhile research.* "Dr. Marshall apparently doesn't like Dr. Fritz Wilshusen. Or Kurt–Kurt MacKay's currently bringing in almost as much money in grants as I am." She hated pleading but said, "Adam, if you lose Kurt, Fritz. Bobby and myself, is pleasing Marshall worth all that?"

Adam truly looked torn. "When we were negotiating with Marshall, he was fantastic. He loved ORR's set up. He said to keep it a surprise, but that you would be delighted to see him. He didn't want changes..."

"Then you signed a binding contract with him and now its all different," she finished bitterly.

Adam nodded his head. "Some of his demands are way beyond reason."

She wanted to bring it back. "If Bobby had a job with ORR, could you find them some other place to live on the campus?"

He ignored that. "Half Bobby's salary was for assisting Eric with his teaching schedule."

Grace stiffened. She knew where this was heading. "I don't teach. It's been written into my contract."

Adam could be tough. "I can't keep Bobby on, unless you pick up Eric's classes. Look, Eric rarely showed. All you would have to do is a few short appearances. If you took over Eric's full Fall schedule, half of Bobby's salary could still be paid from the teaching budget. No condo, no benefits, but that might give them a semester to work something else out."

"Sara's pregnant. If she loses her insurance..."

"They'll have COBRA. ORR will pay six months of that."

"Where would they live?"

Adam shrugged his shoulders.

As much as she wanted to help Bobby, Grace shook her head. "I find teaching too draining. Too much time away from my real work."

He sighed. "Then Bobby and his wife have no job and no condo."

"With Sara's pregnant?"

"That's not my problem."

"You've got to get someone teaching this week..."

He hesitated, "If I could put your name on the catalog as instructor for the rest of this year--no promises–but I would try to work out some temporary living arrangements for the Jamisons."

If she wanted the boat, she was gonna have to steer it.

Stiff with anger and frustration, Grace said nothing.

Adam waited, when she didn't speak he said, "You'll have to let me know--shortly. Now, I've got to go and try to pacify Dr. Marshall." He turned away and hurried off.

With some gawking students still staring, Grace moved her car into the parking lot before her lab and went in. Eric Larsen had thrived with teaching, listening to the students' fresh perspectives, and soaking up their eager energy. Teaching for Grace took precious time away from her work, left her feeling drained and inadequate. She couldn't do it!

She tried to concentrated on cell slides, but was too upset to work. Finally, Grace picked up her laptop, locked up and slowly walked back to her condo building. In the lobby she found Sara struggled with some cartons balanced against her huge stomach.

"Hi, Grace." Sara gave a crooked smile. "Got any extra moving boxes?"

They both knew Bobby would explode, but Grace just hadn't figured on it happening so soon. "Sara, has Adam officially told you to move?"

"Actually, after Bobby left this morning, this little snip was knocking at my door, announcing herself to be Diandra Hollings. She claims she's Dr. Marshall's Associate and she wanted to measure the condo for her furniture."

"My God– she didn't."

"Yhep. Pushed her big mammary glands right in past my ballooning belly. I explained the condo comes furnished. She just looked disdainfully at our things and said *'I'm not living with this rubbish. They'll have to buy something decent.'* "

"Does Bobby have any kind of lease or contract? A letter of intent from Eric?"

"No. We always knew that the condo was really Eric's. He just let us live in it."

"Has Adam or any other official of Oyster River informed you in writing that you have to move?"

"No, but my charming husband just smashed the mouth of their new, prize Director of Research."

"Why did Bobby hit him?"

Sara looked down. She knew, but she wasn't talking. "You know Bobby's got a short fuse."

"What did Marshall do? Please, I need to know...to help you both."

Sara shook her head. "Bobby'll never tell you."

"Then you tell me. Please!"

Sara looked away from her. "Marshall was bragging that he sleeps with all assistants. That you and he..." She stopped, not meeting Grace's eyes. "Bobby was really trying to keep the promise he made me about not blowing up, but Marshall said something crude about you. Bobby didn't even tell me what it was, but I would have hit Marshall too!"

Oh, God. "All of it is lies! I never let him touch me!" Grace forced herself to calm down. "How is Bobby taking the news about the twins?"

Now Sara looked down her belly and seemed ashamed. "I haven't told him. It just seemed one more rock on his back..."

Grace nodded. "Okay. The important thing is we'll get through this! I'm staying. Keep Bobby inside and quiet. Don't pack at all! Wait until you are officially told to leave and make them put it in writing first. Then Adam will have to give you time to pack. In fact, if he comes to talk with you, get off your feet and look big, sick and helpless."

Sara ruefully looked down at her swelling belly. "That won't be too hard."

Grace had to do something. "I may be taking over Eric's classes."

That surprised her. "You're teaching? Oh, Grace, you hate teaching."

"If I do, I'll need Bobby as my assistant, doing the same thing he did for Eric. That means ORR will pay half his salary. It's not a done deal, but it might work out. Maybe Oyster River can get a grant for the rest of his salary. If you can't keep this place, there might be something else on the Institute's campus. But I need time! You and Bobby have got to stall. Okay?"

Finally looking hopeful, Sara nodded.

Grace hurried upstairs to her condo, as she turned her door handle her hand slipped. She looked down at her fingers. They still had that silky feeling from Kurt's blue lobster gunk. Grace went into the bathroom and scrubbed at her fingers, trying to wash it off. Still, even after stiffly rubbing with a towel, she felt an annoying soft slipperiness. She went back into the living room and plugged in her lap top.

If she taught, then the Jamisons needed the second half of Bobby's salary. It was 3:30 Wednesday, she might still get someone in a corporate office someplace. Even trying for grants for just herself had been hard lately, with the financial downturn, money was tightening up. She'd been calling all her sponsors, but no one was renewing. Where else could she get a patron? Grace pulled out an old address book, with pages slotted with business cards. She went page by page. Brian Kancir, *Affiliated Technologies*, nice young guy, engineering type, tall she thought, always chatting her up for a possible business linkup. Had she ever gotten a grant from *Affiliated*?

Yes, years ago, not with him but with his predecessor, Mrs. what was her name? Grace thumbed through book, Marsha Totem. Marsha had been Brian's boss, but Grace had the vague feeling that Marsha retired. Okay. What possible project would appeal to *Affiliated Technologies*?

Grace started googling *Affiliates*' website. What were they into? *Norfolk Chemicals. Bruno Pet food. LeVeck Pharmaceuticals. Madame Celestine.* Military research–would a civilian company be doing antidotes for germ warfare? She had done generational work with small pox vaccines. No. Probably not. *Affiliated* was into water purification. Might there be a match? Gene splicing to create a super-oil-clean-up bug?

Nervously Grace dialed the Brian's number. This was ridiculous. She didn't have a project, much less a proposal, and she was calling a man she briefly knew for a lot of money.

A woman answered with a bored voice. "*Affiliated Technologies.*"

"This is Grace–Dr. Grace Farrington. I was wondering if I could speak with Brian Kancir for awhile." God, that sounded like she was asking for a date. "It's about a grant proposal."

Apparently the woman recognized her name, because her tone instantly changed. She took Grace's number and said Brian would be calling her back shortly.

Nervously, Grace stood up, wiping perspiration off her forehead. Her fingers were silky and slippery. Did that lobster shit ever come off? She'd kill Kurt the next time she saw him. Grace tried to calm herself as she sat before her laptop and began roughing out a proposal for an e-coli based splice project. She'd need what, fifty pages? Thirty? She had barely starting typing into her laptop when the phone rang.

At this point she almost wished it wouldn't. She deliberately let it ring three times, before she picked up and answered formally. "Dr. Farrington."

"Grace, this Brian Kancir."

"It's good to hear from you." Of course, she was hearing from him, hell, she just asked him to call her.

Brian was continuing. "I was at Dr. Marshall's reception. I wanted to say hello to you, but you left so early."

Oh, shit. Would Marshall be getting all her grant people too? "I'm sorry about that. I really wanted to talk you."

He kept on enthusiastically. "Having the renowned Dr. Charles Marshall in our area is fantastic!"

This wasn't going the way she wanted. "For awhile now I've been thinking about a possible research project *Affiliated* might be interested in."

There was a short, telling silence, before he spoke in a very slow voice. "Grace, I know the company would be honored to be working with you, but with the recession, we're pretty much out of funding pure research. I'm sorry."

"It is tight right now," she agreed.

"Of course, *Affiliated* once talked with you about sponsoring a worldwide series of symposiums on your Popcorn Gene Switch theory. Have you given anymore thought to that?"

Speaking around the world might actually help her. With *Affiliated*'s lavish corporate budget she wouldn't be boarding at the usual college dorm rooms, she'd have four star hotels and first class flights. It would get her out of this mess and give her time to find a new laboratory. She'd have to drop her research for a year, but she needed a rest. It might actually aid her work, but it wouldn't help Bobby or Sara. "Would *Affiliated* be interested in maybe a super-bug that might clean up oil spills? A possible gene splice with practical applications?"

"We're already working on that. Of course, your expertise would immensely add to the project." Still he continued in a regretful tone. "But budget wise, I don't think they'll go outside of the company right now."

While holding the phone, Grace was studying *Affiliated*'s web site on her laptop. Pet foods. Madame Celestine? "Brian, *Affiliated Technology* owns something called *Madame Celestine*?"

"It came to us when we purchased *LeVeck*, a French chemical conglomerate. *Madame Celestine* sells women's beauty products for the high end market."

Grace saw a possibility. "Can I have your word that you will consider this call confidential?"

He sounded interested. "You know you can trust me."

Since his livelihood depended on a symbiotic relationship with the scientific community, she knew she could. "I'm going to discuss research that's not mine. It's being done by a colleague."

"I won't even take notes."

"My colleague is doing a study of a natural occurring organism, that might lead to a long lasting skin softener. It's a recent discovery and of course, he can't promise that it might not have side effects or be dangerous to humans, however," she looked down at her smooth finger tips. "I have never seen such an interesting, raw secretion. "

"Who is this colleague?"

Since she was dumping his research, she might as well go all the way. "Dr. MacKay."

"I don't think I've heard of him."

"He works here at Oyster River. He's brilliant, but with a very practical bend. He's working with sea creatures from the bay..."

"Wait!" He cut her off. "You don't mean Kurt MacKay? That guy in the fisherman's sweater, at the Dr. Marshall's introduction party? The guy who rides a motorcycle? Tells all those racist, sexist jokes?"

Her hopes sank. "A bit risque."

"I think he restrains himself around you. The ones I heard, I wouldn't have repeated in a Marine barracks."

"Kurt MacKay is washout a character model, but he's a really good scientist," she finished lamely.

"What are his credentials?"

"He's had several discoveries."

"If I'm going to sell him to the Financial Appropriations Committee start with his educational back ground. Does he have any University affiliations? Awards?"

"I don't think his work can be sold that way." How could she sell Kurt?

A pause on the line. "Could Charles Marshall be persuaded to co-author this sea organism study?"

"No!" Her vehemence sounded extremely unprofessional. "I don't think that Dr. MacKay would be willing to share credit for a possible discovery of this magnitude with a scientist he hardly knows. "

"The Committee will never do a grant to him alone. But with a strong, commercial outcome in the balance, Dr. Farrington, would he do a co-authorship with you?"

He changed from 'Grace' to 'Dr. Farrington'. They'd gone from Kurt's research to putting her total scientific reputation on the line. She didn't answer.

He repeated. "I might be able to sell a grant proposal with Farrington–MacKay on it."

She sighed. "When could this be done?"

"The next open Financial Appropriations Committee meeting will be November 15th."

"No."

"That's when it is, and the agenda is already firmed up for the meeting. I probably can't insert another project. I will try, but the earliest I could promise a discussion slot would be on the February docket."

"That's too late. This is a study that must be started immediately. The organism we will be studying is a rare find. It may be a single mutation, that will fail to survive the winter water temperatures or it may have just been washed in to the Sound by some non-reproducible fluke. If we don't go after specimens now we may never find them again. "

There was silence on the end of the line and Grace held her breath until Brian answered, "There might be some people I could talk to. Could you e-mail me a proposal tonight?"

"Dr. MacKay hasn't written a full proposal yet. That'll take a few days..."

"This isn't the academic world. My Committee wants

to know what *Affiliated* can expect to get out of your study, a reasonable projected time-frame and a rough budget. Two pages should do it. But it has got to be a Farrington-MacKay study. Can you do that tonight?"

"I've got to contact Dr. MacKay. Tomorrow?"

"E-mail me."

She verified his e-mail, then got off of the line. By wedding herself professionally to Kurt MacKay, she would be linking her academic prestige to a contrary man, who would do anything for a chance to shock the establishment. Great. In trying to get a salary for Bobby and a home for Sara, Grace might dump her own reputation. If she lost to Marshall again, there might not be a laboratory that would ever have her.

Grace slowly walked to the sliding glass door, pushed the drapes aside and let herself out on to her balcony. She looked out over the quiet green harbor. In her mind she still could still see that man jumping and struggling in that freezing water, then being hauled out dead. Grace came back in and pulled the curtains closed. He had suicided because he was too afraid to live. She wouldn't be.

Grace dialed Kurt's cell phone. Of course, she got no answer. He was probably out with one of his many girlfriends. She left a message. "This is Grace. I must speak with you immediately regarding a possible grant!"

Chapter 8

Not able to sleep much, Grace was up before dawn. No time for running today. She showered then began typing the *Affiliated* proposal into her laptop, doing two paragraphs on the skin softening results and commercial possibilities. Then she concentrated on the budget: salaries for Kurt and one assistant; rental for his boat and gas; to house the affected lobsters, they'd need laboratory fees for ORR, maybe new specimen tanks? How environmentally sensitive were lobsters? Well, they kept them alive in open tanks in restaurants for a limited period of time.

    Kurt's laboratory space at Oyster River was smaller and shared with students so they would have to store their subjects in her laboratory. She'd have Nick clean and reactive the salt water tanks on the East wall. She would have to help Kurt find out what this blue mottling was? How did that stuff stay active on your fingers for so long? Could they grow it in captivity? She added genetic testing fees to the budget. Chemical breakdowns of secretions would also be needed? She rubbed her first two fingers against her thumb and still felt a faint slipperiness to finger tips. Unbelievable.

    At her lab she found Kurt had left a message on the phone, he'd meet her across the Harbor at noon, at the outdoor snack bar attached to *Neptune's Grotto*. Apparently he no longer wanted to talk business at Oyster River Research. It was good they were going to be off ORR's campus, oh, God, she was getting so paranoid! Marshall wouldn't be bugging her lab–or would he?

    Yeas ago, when she was just starting out in Pasadena, there was a big hope for a Hepatitis C vaccine. Marshall was bragging he'd get there first. Two other researchers had their own line of cultures that looked promising. They made the mistake of announcing their results at one of Marshall's directional meetings. The great man just smiled benignly. That was the Monday before Thanksgiving. That Friday, when Joe and Duwon were home, eating turkey left overs with their families, the great Charles Marshall had the cleaning crew dump all their cultures.

At 11:50, Grace drove her car over the main road that encircled the harbor, parking in *Neptune's* lot. She stayed in her car, didn't see Kurt's truck or motorcycle, but he never was on time. At 12:20, smelling the roasting franks, she was getting hungrier, so she walked over to the open snack bar window and ordered breaded clams and fries.

Here the salty wind was chilly, but the mid-day sun warmed her. She squirted tartar sauce into a folded cup and took her paper wrapped feast over to a weathered gray picnic table, overlooking the bay. The grinding of a motor boat caught her attention and looking out to the water, she saw a curtain of blue smoke rising. Grace stood up and walked to the edge of the pilings. Below her, Kurt was expertly maneuvering his diesel yawl alongside *Neptune's* dock, that now floated low with the tide.

Grace went back to her table. There was a straight ladder on the pilings, which Kurt was soon climbing. He blew a kiss to her as he went over to the counter to put his order in. When Kurt finally joined her with an order of crablegs and onion rings, he chose to sit on her side of the table, rubbing his thigh against hers. "Hi lady, you rethinking that fancy dinner do of mine?" He asked hopefully.

She ignored that. "Marshall has dropped Bobby Jamison as his assistant. I was trying to a grant from *Affiliated Technologies*, so I could pick him up in my lab."

Kurt started cracking crab legs. "Aaup."

"They weren't interested in anything I could come up with. Too pure researcy, not enough commercial application. No deal, until I mentioned a colleague of mine might have a new discovery that could translate into a pharmaceutical skin treatment."

Kurt looked up. "Who discovered that?"

"You."

"Discovery? What discovery?" He thought about it. "That juice from those moldy blue lobsters?"

"Maybe a long, long lasting skin softening cream?"

He didn't look happy. Giving away another's research was a definite no no.

He started sternly, "Grace,..."

"I just mentioned your name! That you were doing underwater research. Stuff anybody could find on Oyster River's website. I didn't mention lobsters or blue mold. And I'm sorry, but Bobby needs a job!"

"*Affiliated* wants to give me money?"

"Well there's some complications. At Marshall's coming out party, you made an excreteable impression on their representative."

Kurt swelled up with pride. "Must've put on a good red-necked show."

"More purple necked." Grace took her plastic fork and stabbed a fried clam. "Why do you do something so dumb? Marine Science is the livelihood you've chosen. You're good at it..."

"I'd say great."

"They want a co-written study. With my name on it."

Using his fingers, he dipping the crab meat into the paper cup of melted butter. Chewing a bit, before he spoke. "First, if we're doing some negotiating. I want quid pro quo."

"Job for Bobby and grant money for you isn't enough?"

"Nope. You agree to be my escort to that awards dinner."

"You're winning an award?"

"Nope, but a friend from overseas is going to be there. Corresponded with him for years, but we've never met in person. He's studies minnows, into some fascin..."

A complete definition of the parameters of his friend's studies could take all afternoon, she cut him of. "I go to the dinner and you'll agree to the study?"

"Nope." He cracked two more legs. "First you promise to go to the dinner with me, then I promise to **just talk** about this research project with you."

That irritated her. She was trying to save Bobby's job and get Kurt a grant, now he was using it to twist her arm. That was Kurt MacKay alright. "When and where is the dinner?"

"First Saturday in November. In the City, at eight."

"Get me the address. I'll meet you there."

"Naw, I'll come pick you up at seven o'clock."

"In your pick up truck?"

"Truck's down, until I can get the bucks for a new transmission."

"An hour into the city on back of your motorcycle? How about the train?"

He paused. "I'll borrow Tanya's car. Make it six o'clock in case of traffic. I pick you up at your condo. You **got to** be on time for this one!"

This formal dinner started as an evening time waster, now she would be tied up all afternoon too. "Okay, I'll do it. Now the study. Do you still have the lobsters?"

"Nope. Didn't have extra tanks and didn't want them contaminating my other specimens. Didn't want to throw them back in the bay, either. Got rid of them."

Shit. Their miracle samples were gone. "Do you think that secretion might be like ergot to humans, hallucinogenic? Or poisonous?"

"Hope not. I got rid of them by eating them."

"Can you find more?"

"Know where I was diving. Could look there."

"I've told Brian Kancir that this study must be done before the winter sets in."

"Aaup. Won't be freezing in a wet suit in December. Now, I took some close up, color photos of those lobster abdomens to send to a Duon at Woods Hole and to Skipper in Japan."

That was good! "Maybe we could attach them with the proposal?"

"We got a proposal?" He sounded surprised. "You had time to whip out twenty pages of jargonese?"

From the pocket of her jacket, she handed him three sheets.

He studied it critically. "Farrington–MacKay?" His face had that lowered drawbridge look. "Like MacKay–Farrington a lot better."

"They want Farrington-MacKay."

"You gonna be freezing yer balls off diving in that cold, black Sound?"

"They'd be happier with Dr. Nobel Prize Winning Charles Marshall–MacKay."

"Never!" Kurt cracked some more crablegs, took a few bites, then said resentfully, "Seems like I do all the work, and you're gonna claim the orca's share of the credit."

She sighed. "When my current grants run out, I've got nothing and with this economy, all my usual sources are all cutting back. Is it any better for you?"

He chewed a bit, then said. "Nope and my pick-up needs a transmission and my yawl engine could use an overhaul too." He thumbed through her proposal. "Three pages? That's all?"

"All they require."

"Like working with these guys. You got a pen?" She handed him one and he started scribbling over her papers. "You want a sell this thing?" He put a line through '*seems to smooth skin*' and '*might be long lasting*' before printing above it '*miraculous skin rejuvenating treatment. Lasting days.*' '*Smoothing away age wrinkles*' That'll sell it."

"We don't know it will do that..."

"Grace, it's a scientific proposal, not a sworn affidavit!"

"We have to offer them something we have a chance of producing...if we plan to work with them again."

He smiled broadly. "Oh, we will."

A thought occurred to Grace. "If Marshall finds out we've got a miracle in the test tube, he'll claim it."

Kurt looked up from the proposal. The dark eyes that stared her with were colder than the sound's black depths. "Let him try." He looked back down at the proposal, made a few more changes and then looked up at her with an uncharacteristically somber expression. "Grace, I am what I am. Ain't changing for you or Bobby or the Lord High Executioner. We do this study together, even after its done, you'll be connected to me. Could be some day down the road, I'll do something that will make me and you total poison to the great Scientific Community, jes like the eminent Dr. Steward Brewster."

Grace nodded. "Then you'll catch lobsters and I'll cook'em for the tourists."

Kurt nodded, with small smile. "Like I said, it'll be nice to have a classy lady on my arm at that formal do." He started studying the budget spread sheet again. "Well, you got money down for me. Too low." He raised the figure. "And if it's going to be a Farrington–MacKay study we need money for you."

Grace noted that the figure he wrote for her, the supposed eminent, senior study member, was exactly the same as he proposed for himself. Well, this proposal was a starting point, for negotiations with *Affiliated*.

Kurt was continuing. "Bobby will be our assistant–he's a scuba diver?

"Bobby swims." She remember their Sunday beach picnics at the Point. Sara cooked the sausages over driftwood,

Grace studied seaweed configurations, while Bobby treaded water just past the breakers, holding a giggling Ginjer, as they bouncing up and down with the waves. "He's never mentioned doing scuba." That might be a deal breaker.

"Well, he works with me, he's gotta. I'll train him, but we'll have to include diving gear for him. He can use Herald's old tanks, but he'll need a wet-suit big enough for him. You didn't put in any tank re-filling costs, those add up fast." He scribbled more figures down. "The rest of these request figures look okay, but double them." He thought a moment and then started scribbling an additional paragraph. "If this thing becomes commercially viable, we'll both want ongoing royalties."

"For work under hire, they won't do that!"

"Lady, you've got a platinum reputation. *Affiliated* is gonna consider itself lucky to be getting the eminent Dr. Grace Farrington's name on a project of theirs."

"If we ask too much, we may lose them."

"No guts, no glory." Kurt handed her back the proposal. "Write it like I say or no deal. If I find them, I'll e-mail you the lobster photos. Too bad we didn't take any skin shots of our fingers before and after. Reactivate at least eight of your salt water tanks."

"I'll have to buy more salt."

"Save the salt. Use water deep dipped from the harbor at high tide. Have Nick dip his buckets off the end of my dock, not closer, less sediment. Can your tanks cool?"

"Yes. Should I start them?"

"Not until we get something. Then they'll have to be kept at sixty-nine degrees. "

She looked up, questioningly.

He continued. "That's, oh, 20.6 Celsius, for you scientific types. Ph levels at 7.3. What do your tanks usually have for salinity?"

"About 3.5 %."

"That's fine. If our lobsters reach molting, additional calcium will be needed. If we get anything, I want to keep'em alive as long as possible to see if there are adverse effects of that blue gunk." His smile widened into that familiar leer. "Hey, since we are now wedded as MacKay–Farrington..."

"Farrington–MacKay." She pointed out firmly.

"Okay. Farrington–MacKay, want to go to bed to finalize it? Leastwise I'll get to be on top one time in this partnership?"

Grace glared at him. "Good try. E-mail the photos by 3 p.m. And don't spend your 'royalties' yet."

He was up and gone, leaving Grace feeling better than she had in days. Fighting Marshall would be pure pleasure to Kurt and this proposal had a definite chance.

She wanted to just go back and work, but since the grocery store was down the road she might as well do her weekly shopping, then she could get back to her data.

Unfortunately Grace was reaching for a grapefruit when she was waylaid.

Chapter 9

"Grace? Dr. Farrington."

Grace turned to see a red-haired woman, medium height, standing there with a pen and notebook in her hand and an oversized, leather handbag hanging from her shoulder. That damned reporter. Serena? Sandi?

"I'm Sam-Samantha Carson. Reporter for *The Sound Times*. I've tried to interview you before..."

"And when I said no, you wrote that hatchet piece on me!"

"You read it?" asked a surprised Samantha.

"People as far as San Francisco sent me copies. You made the big time."

"It was country wide, but not in *the New York Times*." The reporter said regretfully.

"Too bad for you."

"Look, ..."

She started, but Grace cut her off. "Because I didn't have time to dictate some puff piece, you made me out to be some sort of reclusive hermit. Anti-feminist! Anti-scientific community!"

"I didn't mean it that way, really. You know publicity could help you get the Nobel, maybe."

"Not your kind."

"Look. This is my job. Please, five minutes, this is not about you your fight with Charles Marshall."

"About what?"

"Early in your career you claimed he cheated you out of your research and as a newly graduated student you were brave enough to challenge him. Then he claimed you were his spurned lover, trying to get back at him. You lost your case."

Grace said nothing but felt sick at the thought of this being paraded in the newspapers again.

After a moment, Sam continued. "I'm not writing

about that, I mean, I sort of am because he has come to ORR, I'm researching Dr. Marshall. You weren't the only one he screwed–No, I don't think you had an affair with him! I don't think you lied to that discipline board, from I've learned about him, I think he did. And I won't be writing about you and him now." She stopped, then tried again. "But that article I wrote about you, it wasn't intended as a hatchet piece. I needed the money and I got an assignment on you. I had a deadline, I tried to talk to you, but you kept refusing."

"Did it ever occur to you that I was struggling with my own critical deadlines, and I didn't have time to waste on you?"

Sam bit her lip. "I didn't say anything about you that wasn't true. I wrote about your pioneering work. I knew about this Marshall thing then, but I left it out. I did say that you refused all my interview attempts. The editor rewrote some more of it, pushing the 'recluse, non-feminist, non--sisterhood angles'."

"I am not anti-feminist. I am anti-lolling in the past and blaming all your procrastinations and failures on the great male establishment's barrier reefs."

"You can't just keep avoiding me," said the reporter.

Grace shifted her food basket to indicate she was walking. "I think I can."

Defeated, Sam stepped to the side to let her pass. "I'm not doing the present article on Dr. Marshall. This one is on your witnessing of Miakos' suicide."

The man in the boat had a name? Grace turned back to look at her. "Miakos? The man who jumped?"

"He is–was–a famous artist. Founder of Grotesque Animalism. He's currently got a show at the Gull's Eye Gallery in Oyster River Harbor."

"Why did he kill himself?"

"It was a suicide? You're sure?" Without even looking down, Sam was scribbling on her small notepad.

Grace sighed. "There was nobody else about. He just rowed the boat out to the center of the Harbor. Got up, undressed and jumped."

Sam nodded. "The Gull's Eye Gallery owners said he couldn't swim. He hated the water."

"Then it must have been suicide. Are you doing an article for *The Sound Times*?"

"Yes. A straight news piece. Can I quote you? I won't if you say no."

She was just trying to do her job, but, regretfully, Grace shook her head. "Please, I just want to be left alone."

"It's a straight news article. Your name is already public on the police blotter as the person who called it in."

The woman had to make a living too. "Okay. Quote me about just what I told you."

"Did you know him?"

"No."

"Did you know he was an artist?"

"No."

"You called the Coast Guard..."

"911." Something she wanted to forget. If only she had called earlier?

Sam fished into her handbag and pulled out a small camera. "If I could just get a picture of you." Sam had switched it on and was lining up a shot of Grace holding a grapefruit in front of a stack of chicken soup cans.

"No!"

"Please. I get paid extra if I've get photographs."

Grace shook her head. "I'm sorry, but no."

The reporter had lowered her camera. "You're a public figure so I could take it, but I won't, unless you'll agree. There are pictures of you all over the Internet. And you've been interviewed on so many t-v shows...the editor will probably just print one."

That was certainly true, and it would probably be

unflattering. Annoyed Grace put her basket down and moved to a solid wall for a background. "All right."

Sam snapped two or three times then put the camera away. She was fishing in her handbag for something else and she looked embarrassed. "I'm also trying to sell another piece. Under the pseudonym of Kit Samuels–it'll be on Miakos' death for the tabloids. I won't use your picture, I promise. There are some people saying that Miakos might have been lured to his death by the Curse of the Widow?"

"What?"

Out of her huge shoulder bag the reporter pulled out a blue book with black line drawings on the cover. With a sinking feeling, Grace recognized Freya's *Hauntings of Oyster River Harbor*". Sam opened to a page marked with a torn notepaper. "The cursed three...the Smith brothers."

Oh, God, was Freya behind this? "That hardly looks like a historically credible reference."

Sam started to copy that down...

"Don't write that! Please!"

The reporter shoved Freya's book back into her handbag. "There's a wreck out in that area, an 1800's whaling vessel, the *Siren*. State University archeologists have been looking for it and they might have disturbed the spirit of the widow."

"The widow?"

Sam quickly flipped through pages in her small notebook. "The Widow O'Reilly. Supposedly she was betrothed to one of the three Smith Brothers. They were Captain Benjamin, Lemuel and Wardell Smith. They were cursed by the Widow Noreen or Maureen O'Reilly. Allegedly, because of that curse, an unholy, unnatural Northeastern hit Oyster River Harbor in June 1838 just as the *Siren* returned. She sank, killing the three brothers, and most of the crew. The Widow rented rooms from a Mrs. Greenway. Today, that's the house on Main Street that has Abe's Bookstore in the basement."

"The Widow Noreen or Maureen?"

"The *Hauntings* book and several sources gives her as "Noreen", but another period source names her as "Maureen". I've got to research this more. Going over to Whaling Museum today."

"To research an 1800's witch's curse?"

"It sells."

"Where did you get this bunk from?"

She had the dignity to look slightly ashamed. "Dr. MacKay..."

"Kurt?"

"He told me the story of the disgraced widow, who cursed the *Siren's* Captain and his two brothers for what they had done to her."

Oh, God. ORR did not need this! "I am sure a man as intelligent and scientific as Dr. MacKay doesn't believe the spirit of a century dead widow influenced a suicidal man!"

"He didn't say he believed in it. He just told me the legend and that the wreck is probably out there where Miakos went down. And that the brothers drowned within sight of their home port in an unnatural storm. Can I say that Dr. Farrington thinks there is nothing to the story?"

"No! We'll both sound like cretins! I really don't want to be quoted in any 'curse of' story. Further more, if you persist in quoting Dr. MacKay, I believe Adam Greenfield and Oyster River Research's law firm might take action."

As Grace pushed past her, Sam called out. "I won't mention your name in the ghost one. I promise!"

Grace had her doubts on that one.

Chapter 10

Back at her lab, Grace checked the mail, phone and e-mails. No word from Brian Kancir at *Affiliated*, should she call him about the grant? No, she didn't want to sound desperate. Finally she managed to get through her load of e-mails and return some calls, but her mind kept returning to Bobby's problems. Was Bobby still teaching? It was 2:30. Gail took a late lunch and Grace might catch her now and find out.

At ORR's small cafeteria Grace picked up a tea and coconut muffin then walked outside, down the grassy lawn to the picnic tables by the water. Three others were taken by groups of laughing students and the one closest to the water was occupied by Gail Travinski, Oyster River's long time temporary secretary. She was deep in some over sized paperback.

Walking over, Grace asked, "Mind if I join you?"

Gail looked up. Dark blonde hair, full figure and sky blue eyes, Gail billed herself as a 'Polish doll', always friendly and always helpful. Four years ago, when their last secretary retired after thirty-six years, three new secretaries proved unequal to the job. Gail was contracted from a temporary agency to clean up the back filing and answer the phones until a new person could be hired. She immediately took on the full duties and straightening out everything, soon they all relied on her. But when Marshall comes in, he was known for wanting a clean sweep. Soon only his people would be in key positions and with Gail as a temp, it would easy to get rid her. Why had Grace never pushed Adam to give permanent status to her? As Grace sat down, Gail warmly smiled, as she shoved her book under her handbag, almost as if she was hiding it.

"Grace."

"Has it settled a bit since?" Grace didn't finish with 'since Eric's sudden death.'

"Adam has me shuffling classes. Bunch of

withdrawals, more than usual, all because a Nobel winner's name is no longer on our courses."

"That's so stupid." Grace said. "Bobby taught all Eric's classes. He can teach Marshall's."

"Well. Dr. Marshall isn't teaching. Off the record, I don't think the great Marshall ever planned to teach, but..." Shrugged her shoulders.

"But Adam thought he was?"

"Adam had me set up the printer's proof of the new catalogs, with Dr. Marshall's name as Chief Instructor. Then, in front of me, Dr. Marshall said Adam 'misunderstood'. Actually, his assistant, Diandra Hollings would be..."

"Teaching?"

"Well, collecting the remuneration."

"But not teaching? She's his assistant."

"Ms. Hollings wishes to be referred to as 'his associate'."

"Do you know what her credentials are?"

"I asked if Miss Hollings if she had a curriculum vitae she wanted me to input. She said no. I asked if she had taught previous classes for her biography in the new catalog, Ms. Hollings said no. So I asked about what hours she wanted to set aside to counsel students? She just glared at me. "

"Is she Dr. Hollings?"

"Before I dared ask, she blew up. Ms. Hollings was highly incensed as being questioned by a peon."

"But you'll need to get a new catalogue printed."

"Adam came over and quietly told me to hold the print run until he could get things '*worked out*'."

"Is Bobby Jamison teaching? Or is Adam appeasing Marshall?"

Gail shrugged her shoulders again. "I don't think even Adam knows who's teaching what." They finished eating and started walking back towards the buildings across the road. Narrowly missing them, a speeding red car pulled into the handicapped spot close to Administration building. "Speak of the devil." Gail said in a undertone.

A trim, but well endowed woman climbed out of her sporty, Miata convertible.

Gail pointed the a sign, but she spoke kindly. "Miss Hollings, that's a handicapped spot."

Grace clarified. "Dr. Wilshuen has a bad hip, and he has trouble walking, so he takes his car from his house. We usually save that spot for him."

Diandra Hollings turned to stare at Grace. "Oh, another 'temporary' who thinks she runs things about here? You're lunch buddies? Lovely. You can eat together and soon you might be out of work together."

"Actually, I am not in Administration. I'm a researcher, Grace Farrington."

"Yes, I should have recognized you." That seemed to confuse Diandra. "An internationally recognized scientist and you eat lunch with a clerk?"

"Administrative Assistant." Grace corrected.

"But you eat with the staff?"

Grace sweetly smiled back at Diandra. "Gail has low standards."

Diandra changed her tone. "Actually, Dr. Farrington, I have been interested in your work. I would like to talk with you some time."

"Perhaps when Gail is unavailable." Smiling slightly, Grace walked away. She had to still think about moving, could she find another lab over on Long Island and bring Bobby and Gail along with her? Nice dream but not practical.

But what did seem practical was the e-mail she got from Brain Kancir the next morning.

Chapter 11

Brian had arranged a meeting in three days at *Affiliated's* Headquarters. Good, she immediately shot out an acceptance, then e-mailed Kurt. He'd better be able to attend. Full of energy Grace headed down her condo stairs at 6:30 a.m. and as she crossed the foyer, she heard a soft voice calling, "Bobby?"

Sara was coming around the stairs, carrying their three year old. Ginjer's skinny legs were awkwardly straddling Sara's growing belly.

Sara's eyes were red, probably from crying. Seeing Grace she said, "Oh." in a disappointed voice.

"It's only me. Sorry."

"I thought it might be Bobby." Sara looked like she was about to cry again.

"You okay?"

"Yes. No. Not really." She put the baby down and little Ginjer immediately started toddling off. "Back pain's really bad. Can't sleep in any position. Yesterday, Bobby bought me flowers–flowers! We're losing his job, and we should be saving every penny, and he brings me a bouquet of yellow roses!"

"He was..."

Sara cut her off. "We started fighting. He walked out...he didn't come home last night."

Grace thought fast. "He probably was watching t-v in the student lounge and fell asleep again."

Sara nodded. "It's so hard on him, being penned up in the condo. Worrying about money..."

"Is Adam going to have him teaching today?"

"If he comes back home, so I can tell him."

"He will." Grace smiled and left Sara, not feeling as confident as she tried to sound. She had her running shoes on, maybe stretching her legs might help. Heavy clouds coming in. Getting her own car, she looked for the Jamison's van, but didn't see it, Bobby must be driving it. Grace pulled out on to the main road, turning left again, following along the marshes from Oyster river. Reaching the old town, she parked behind the stone cottage looking library, its grass and sand beach park fronted on the Harbor. It would be good to run a bit, think things out and plan how she would get Kurt to put in a respectable appearance at the meeting with *Affiliated*.

Grace stretched her leg muscles against the car. *Affiliated* would expect a public announcement of their grant at the Roost, with Nobel Prize winning Charles Marshall in attendance. Maybe she could get them to hold off, at least until they had some study results, or any blue mottled lobsters to study. Maybe she could get them to announce the grant at their Headquarters? The less time Marshall knew about their research, the less time he had to spike it.

She started up the slight slope from the library that gave out to Barrel Path. It was a dead end road that curved along the Harbor up to the gas tank farm. Usually, she just took off at a run, but today she really didn't really feel like it. She had to get past this weakness, this desire to just lie down, curl up in a ball and forget everything. Well, if she didn't run, at least she could walk.

Ahead was a small bridge, under it ran the overflow from a dammed pond. She stopped on the bridge, resting her arms on its wood railings. The foaming water continued past the sand and the Library park as it ran out to the Harbor. With the Harbor on one side, the other was someone's manicured lawn and a large, pond. Still with no energy to run, she turned and faced the pond.

Above it, a beautifully landscaped house was set back. What a nice, quiet place to live, but unless they were retired, the wealthy owners probably only used it as a weekend house. Grace looking past the black, flat rock dam to the large pond, with it's flashes of silver, gold and red-orange carp roiling to the top of the thick pea soup water. What a view the owners must have of that quiet pond.

The morning was growing more overcast as she stood there, the coming storm seemed drain the color out of her life. Nothing seemed worth trying, even thinking of fighting was futile. Grace was trying to get a grant that she had to hide from ORR. That wasn't the way to keep working, this was not the way she wanted to spend the rest of her life. A propane delivery truck headed toward her on the other side of the road. Slowing before the tight bridge, the friendly driver waved and Grace managed a small wave back. She didn't know his name but most mornings that driver passed her and they waved.

God, she was so exhausted. Grace shook her head, she was here to run or at least walk. Then she would have to go back and work; pushing, she forced herself to walk to the tank company's chain link fence. Heading back a little of that relentless tiredness was gone, as if something was over.

Walking cleared her mind of anything but the screaming gulls out on the Sound, but when she reached the bridge again, she stopped. She still wasn't ready to go back to her lab. Take the longer run through the Oyster River town and into the small hills? No. She just stood on the bridge listening to the dam spill gurgle, again feeling betrayed, being overwhelmed by a desire to just give up. Finally, she just headed back to her car. Feeling as worn out as she did, she'd better hoard what energy she had left for her research.

Driving back into the ORR parking lot, Grace parked near her lab. A State Police Detective had called and wanted to meet with her. Well, it turned out to be two. A Detective Noonan and someone with an 'U' name. They just asked about what she had seen when that man jumped in. They only stayed a brief time, but recalling that man's deliberate, almost resplendent suicide, Grace couldn't settle back into her computer work. How could a successful artist just throw away his life?

She did need to speak with Adam Greenfield. Grace called the administration building.

Gail answered promptly with her professional. "Oyster River Research."

"I need a few minutes with Adam."

"He's here now, but will be running out shortly."

"Try to hold him for me!" Determined to catch him, Grace hurried from her lab to the glass windowed Admin building, intercepting Adam as he was just hurrying out.

"Grace..." He looked besieged.

She had the distinct feeling he had been hurrying to avoid her, but she quickly blurted out. "I will teach Eric's classes."

Apparently Adam hadn't expected that. "You?"

"Well me and Bobby, if he's kept on."

"At half pay only for him!" Adam explained. "Eric taught without pay, as his donation to ORR. There is nothing left in the budget to reimburse you for this semester!"

"I'm working on a grant that might cover the rest of Bobby's salary. For the teaching, my name will be in the catalog, but I'll just do the same amount of classes as Eric did."

Not looking too happy Adam said, "Dr. Marshall wants Bobby fired."

Grace looked at the tall, harried man. "I can't help that. I can tell you, that if Marshall continues here, I may have to leave. I know we have contract..."

Adam looked terrible. "He said he was your mentor! That it would be a happy surprise for you."

She cut him off. "It wasn't. I don't want to go into the details. If Bobby teaches with me, can they still stay in the condo?"

"Dr. Marshall needs that apartment for his assistant."

"How about the rooms over the boat house, the guest lecture's suite?"

"They're mostly booked. When the Marshall's move, we'll have the guest lectures for our Cell Series coming."

"Could the Jamisons stay in the student dorms?"

"With a child and a baby on the way?"

"Just until I can find somewhere else for them to live?" She held her breath.

Adam looked trapped, but said, "They will lose the apartment, but if you take on Eric's courses, I'll get Bobby half his salary and maybe someplace to stay for this semester only!"

"Agreed."

He looked away. "You know, being president of ORR is just a volunteer job. I'm spending half of my week over here! I have a construction company to run."

"Things will settle down," Grace coaxed, not believing it herself.

Adam took a deep breath, then repeated, "I'll tell Gail to redo the catalogs with your name as professor, but that means you can't leave until the summer sessions starts."

That would be two full semesters of living with Marshall. "Only if Bobby Jamison stays teaching!"

Adam tightened his lips. "Your deal is only valid, if you can keep Bobby from physically assaulting someone."

"I can," She lied. "When do the Jamisons have to move?"

"I'll stall as long as I can. And I will try–but I'm not promising--to find them rooms somewhere else."

"Then I will teach. Thank you, Adam," she said, knowing that Marshall would be doing his damnest to throw out Bobby, along with Kurt, herself and anyone else he considered 'disloyal'.

Teaching would reduce her work output, but knowing she done her best for Sara, she actually felt better when she walked back. The ORR grounds smelled of salt water and were still brightened by white mums and lavender butterfly bushes. No frost yet, but more of the tree tops were yellowing. She could hear the lapping of waves as she neared her lab. Where had Bobby gone last night? Grace decided to check down at the docks.

From here, it looked like both of Kurt's boats were in. Strange, he usually took the diesel out at dawn to check his experiments and trap lines, even in this threatening weather, he loved being out on the water. Maybe he'd found some blue infected lobsters?

She saw Kurt awkwardly working on his lobster yawl; hearing her footsteps on the dock, he looked up calling out softly. "Lady."

"Find any blue infected lobsters?"

Kurt shook his head regretfully. "Gonna have to widen my search pattern. Do we have a grant?"

" I sent you an e-mail. They want to meet both of us in two days at three p.m., we've got to make a professional, competent impression."

He grinned at that. "Maybe you should start contacting a few of your other sources, try to sell our miracle drug to them?"

"Without blue tailed lobsters?"

"Optimism pays dividends." He was awkwardly trying to wrap a oily rag around his left arm, as sort of a sling, trying to tie it one handedly by holding the cloth's end in his teeth.

She climbed on board to help him. "What happened?"

"Wrench kicked back. Hurt my right arm."

"Need a ride to the doctor?"

"Naw." He looked out at the water. "But I got to haul some pots in before it starts raining–see if we got any blue tailed lobsters."

"And you had to let Herald go."

"Course now with this arm, I'll have to try to hire somebody, but Herald's got a better paying job dealing cards for the Injun casino." He looked out at the dark water. "Lady,

I could really use some help."

She was surprised. Kurt asking for help? That arm must be worse then looked. "Want me to cast off?"

"Need a bit more than that. Could you spare some time to haul in pots for me?"

Chapter 12

The diesel yawl chugged and belched blue smoke as they pulled away from the gray dock and a rainbowed oil slick followed them. Beginning goose bumps from the cold dampness, Grace wished she'd worn a warmer jacket. She reached for his work gloves, but they smelled fishy. She put them back on the deck and stuck her hands in pockets her light car coat. The distant harbor town was misty with fog. It was one of those days when she could almost see the square rigged whaling ships at anchor.

Shouting over the engine, Kurt broke her reverie. "Grace, remember that dinner we're going to?"

"Of course." Actually, she had forgotten.

"It's at an embassy."

"Nice."

"Gonna be black tie."

"You're gonna wear your black blue-jeans?"

"Nope, rented me a genuine monkey suit."

"Good." She was starting to shiver from the wind's wet chill. How long would this good deed take?

"Well, seeing as its formal, you got an evening gown?"

Oh, boy. "I could get one."

His face relaxed into a smile. "Good." He swung the throttle, and they picked up speed. Steering with one hand Kurt again shouting above the engine. "Grace, get that pole hook, over there and put on those gloves! My specimens can chop a finger. Besides looking for the blue tails, we're taking a census. Ratio normal lobsters to twisted shell ones."

"Twisted shells are infected with our blue stuff?"

"Don't think so." He winced as he forgot and moved his arm. "Them twisted shells been bedeviling lobster men in the Sound for years." He cut the engine expertly, letting the yawl drift towards a faded yellow buoy, bobbing in the harbor.

Wrinkling her nose in distaste, she pulled on his fish

smelling, heavy gloves. "Makes the lobsters uneatable?"

"Eating's fine, but don't look good in a tank at *Red Lobster*, so the fisherman have to sell them for a cheaper price. Poor bastards–those guys work like hell on the freezing water, so some hedge fund guy can order surf and turf. Then they lose money cause of some fungus or virus or water pollutant twists the shell a bit." He was looking deep in to that unfathomable water endlessly searching for the lobster man's enemy, one he fully intended to vanquish.

As ever, she was curious. "Do you think the twisted shelled lobsters have an inherited weakness?"

"DNA problem? That's your department."

"Have you done any work ups?"

"Lady." He sounded exasperated, "You get the big grants. On my pittances I can't afford to test even one of them."

She thought about it. "Get me a healthy one and one or two deformed ones from the same area and I'll start doing some preliminary sequencing."

"Can't pay ya."

"Well, we'll consider part of the *Affiliated* grant, if we get it."

He nodded. "Hook that rope under the buoy and haul it in. We're doing a measure and tag."

"If we find blue tails?"

"We'll collect any blue tails in those buckets over there.""

She awkwardly hooked the first pot and started hauling in. Lord, she was strong for a woman, but it was hard work, made harder by the cold water. Slowly she pulled that pot up through the heavy, dark gray water. Finally, she was rewarded with a bread box sized, netted lobster trap writhing with crabs, bait and, unfortunately, one healthy looking dark black and orange lobster. She measured him, while Kurt threw the crabs overboard and rebaited.

Under Kurt's direction, they motored to two more marker buoys. Grace hauled pots, measured and weighted lobsters, and tagged several. Kept two, a healthy one and a deformed shell for her DNA testing, while the others, undersized, she tossed back in the salty water. "You know, with your arm hurting, you should get Bobby out here to help you."

"Til we get a grant, ain't got much to pay him with."

"I'll speak to Sara. Point out you're a friend in need and since he's out of his morning job, I think it would be better for all of them, if he just wasn't stewing around the condo."

"Thought after he punched out Marshall, he was outta here?"

"I'm temporarily picking up Eric's teaching schedule, with Bobby as my assistant."

"You teaching?" Kurt sounded surprised at that, while he was changing the direction of the bow. "Gotta pick up some data from the Octagon. I've been running deep Harbor temperature studies." He headed towards the bright yellow, eight sided research house boat, bobbing in the harbor. Its flat roof was covered with weather instruments and radar antennas and inside ORR's marine station were counters along the bulkheads, set up as computer terminals. There was a small generator, closet toilet and, centered on the floor of outdoor carpet, was a glass viewing box, allowing scientists to look down into the great, green depths below them.

It really would have been simpler to just outfit a wide boat, but the Octagon was a big favorite with the student classes. And ORR's budget survived with researcher grants, student fees and donations. Grace often took visiting researchers out here and most seemed impressed.

As they got closer, she yelled over the diesel's loud pounding. "How many more lobster pots to haul in?"

He yelled back. "Jes a few." From a New Englander

that could be five or five hundred.

When he expertly maneuvered in close to the three foot decking around the Octagon, Grace jumped on to the houseboat and tied the stern line to cleats set in the decking. Kurt had cut the engine and was now getting ready to throw her the bow line. Without being able to use his arm, he awkwardly jumped on to the platform instead.

"Need anything from inside?" he asked, making the most of the opportunity to rub bellies as he pushed past her. Grace shook her head and jumped from the bobbing deck back on to the yawl. While he worked she would take the time to warm her hands in her jacket pockets.

She heard him thumping on the door of the Octagon. With one arm, Kurt was at a disadvantage, but that door should have opened easily inward. She called out. "Need my key?"

"Need two good hands. Seems to be jammed." He started to put his right shoulder to it, then winced. "Damn."

"Don't make your arm worse." Grace scrambled up, waiting a moment to catch the rhythm of the boat's bobbing, then she jumped back on to the house boat decking. When she reached Kurt he was pushing the door with his good hand. It was open a crack but still stuck. When it closed, the door was rubber sealed, with a foot and a half of thresh hold up from the deck to keep out high waves. But the door should have swung inward easily.

Grace looked in the crack. "Something must have fallen inside. I didn't think there was anything that close to the door." She put both her hands on the door and shoved with him. It held solid. "Was it locked?"

"Aaup. Had to use my key."

"Wonder if some teenagers got in and partied again?" Grace was putting her shoulder against the door. Kurt had his good hand above her, pushing. Slowly the door gave inward inch by inch.

Then the smell of bad meat overcame the fishy seawater. Even with the door just a foot and a half open, Grace could see what was behind it. A body. A man. A big man. Stiff and dead. She couldn't see the face, but she knew the bloodied silver hair. Charles Marshall lay inside the octagon houseboat. Very dead.

Chapter 13

They didn't push their way in, just retreated to Kurt's diesel yawl, keeping it tied up. By the urine smell and stiffness of his body, Marshall was obviously long dead. Her cell phone didn't work out here on the Harbor, but Kurt raised the Coast Guard on his yawl's radio, leaving them to silently wait aboard his boat, bobbing in the low waves.

Grace sat, not talking, with arms wrapped about her chest, as if it were some kind of protection. There was a time when she was an undergraduate student that she had looked up to Dr. Charles Marshall as a distinguished looking, paradigm of the questing scientist, an authoritative, fatherly figure. That was before she worked in the University Lab and heard the rumors, then had to push his hands off her body. That was before he stole her discovery. Grace began shivering uncontrollably and not from the cold.

Heavy, stiff folds of an old jacket descended on her shoulders. Kurt's jacket. She looked up at him, standing there is just his blue-plaid flannel shirt. "You're cold."

"Naw. Men are warmer." He sat down beside her and put an arm over her shoulder.

She looked away, trying not to see the Octagon. "If you had some liquor aboard, I could use a bit."

"Got a bottle of moonshine stowed right under that seat there."

She looked toward it, but he regretfully shook his head. "Got the pol–lice coming. Don't want alcohol on our breaths."

"Yes." Grace agreed. She didn't demur when Kurt pulled her close to him. He smelled reassuring male. And alive.

An orange pontooned Coast Guard zodiac arrived first, with two uniformed officers who were business like. Not hostile, but definitely not friendly–maybe not sure of their jurisdiction? The house boat was at sea, but... One officer stayed on the Coast Guard boat, while the other balanced on the houseboat's deck. Kurt joined him, talked for a bit and then came back to sit with her.

After what seemed like an age, she recognized the town police boat plowing through the waves. She felt her spirits lift a little, Mac was piloting it. He motored past them, swinging to the back of the Octagon. She couldn't see his boat from where she sat, but could hear him climbing on board the houseboat and see that deck rise a bit, counterbalancing his weight. He carefully came around the side, carrying a capped styrofoam cup, his 6'5' frame just two feet from the roof.

Mac walked to the Coast Guard officer at the Octagon's door and the dark blue uniformed officer moved a bit to let Mac look inside. They talked in low tones, both looked over at Grace and Kurt. Finally, Mac nodded, then carefully brushed past the Coast Guard man on the narrow deck and came over to where Kurt's boat was tied.

Nimbly for such a big man, Mac hopped on board Kurt's bobbing boat, then he moved to sit on her other side. Ever Freya's son, he came bearing a capped, styrofoam cup of steaming tea, which he handed to Grace. "Damp day." He said.

Grace gratefully took a hot gulp and then passed it to Kurt for him to share.

Mac continued. "When the Coast Guard patched in to me, I alerted the State Police and the Corner. The Corner gets badly sea sick when he just looks at water. He's at the pharmacist, getting Doug to call to his doctor for an emergency anti-motion prescription, then Ben's bringing him out on a dock tender ship." Kurt passed the tea cup back to Grace, who just used it to warm her icy fingers.

Mac finally asked. "So what happened?"

Kurt nodded to Grace. "I hurt my arm this morning, engine kicked back. The Lady was helping me pull up my pots and I needed some data from this houseboat."

Mac gave an encouraging nod.

Kurt continued. "Was gonna get a computer readout of the water conditions from underneath the Octagon. The door seemed stuck. Grace came and helped me push on it."

"Was it locked?"

"Aaup. Had to use my key."

Grace interrupted. "After those kids broke in and partied, security installed a lock that automatically kicks in when the door closes."

Kurt nodded. "Pain in the ass. Gotta keep unlocking it when yer're working about."

Mac looked toward the door. "So you used your key to open it?"

"Only it didn't open much." Kurt stopped, seeming to remember. "Felt stuck. Figured there was something fallen behind it, a chair maybe."

Grace felt she should say something. "I came over to help him. We both pushed. It opened enough to see..." She just stopped. She wasn't crying or upset or even sad, but she just felt like she no longer controlled her voice.

Mac looked at her with concerned eyes. "It's okay. I've seen him. Now," He looked to Kurt. "You have a key to the houseboat?"

He nodded. "We both do. Everybody does. There's also extra keys hanging in a cabinet in the Security booth at the dock.

"Is that locked?" Mac asked.

"No." Kurt smiled "Boat booth too small to party in. Course there's a lock on the booth door, but don't think anybody's seen that key since 1942."

"Great. That narrows it down to every one in Oyster River." Mac looked to her. "Do you know who the victim was?"

Victim. Grace suddenly realized that bludgeoned head

was probably unnatural. Maybe he died in the throes of an epileptic fit? No. He died blocking the door and his boat wasn't tied up to the Octagon. It wasn't natural causes. Probably not a suicide. Why was her mind working so slowly? "He's–I really didn't see his face--but he looks like Dr. Charles Marshall."

Mac looked surprised. "Dr. Marshall? He's a visiting lecturer at Oyster River?"

"He's the new Head of Research. Replacing Eric."

"Then he's new to Oyster River?"

"Yes."

"Do you know where he lives?"

Kurt nodded. "He's staying over the boathouse. The Research Institute keeps a fancy suite above there for visiting lecturers on Institute property."

Mac turned in his seat and pointed to the two story, brown shingled building on the water at ORR's Point. "That one?" Kurt nodded and Mac wrote it down.

Kurt continued almost regretfully. "He's got a wife and kids. Kids grown and ain't here. But the wife is..."

Oh, God, but someone was going to have to tell her. Grace interrupted. "Her name is Katherine. Somebody is going to have to tell her...not by phone..."

Mac managed to sound professional, yet kind. "We'll take of that. It will be in person. Do either of you know of any threat to Dr. Marshall? Any enemies?"

Other than herself or anyone ever unfortunate enough to have worked with him? No, she didn't want that mess brought up again. "I don't know of any enemies he'd have here." She looked to Kurt. He had put his big hands around hers, but even his fingers couldn't warm her frigid body.

Kurt was looking up at Mac, appealing to him. "Look at her. This Lady's upset. Her hands are freezin'. She shouldn't be bobbing out here in the sound. Might be going into shock."

Mac looked back at Grace, not just as a police officer, but as a long time family friend. "You need transport to an emergency room?"

She shook her head emphatically. "No!"

Mac looked to Kurt as he stood up. "Take her back to her condo. Grace, do you want me to call Freya?"

"No." Freya would be working.

"The State Police will probably drop by wanting to ask their own questions, but you get her warmed up first."

From the Octagon's narrow deck a voice yelled out. "Wait a minute–they're witnesses! Maybe suspects!" The Coast Guard officer was protesting, but Mac had nimbly jumped off Kurt's launch and was moving to untie the stern line. "I know where they live."

Kurt's engine kicked to life. Looking unhappy the out-classed Coast Guard officer found himself throwing off the bow line as Mac pushed them clear.

On open water, Kurt opened the throttle wide and headed across the choppy bay. Grace just looked down at the deck boards. She hated Marshall, but how could anyone kill him? Whether he deserved or not?

"Here." Kurt yelled above the waves slapping the bow. He was handing her a flat pint of liquor. She took too large a sip and choked as it burned down her throat. It hurt to breathe again, but felt some feeling coming back to her fingers. After that she just stared ahead, not really seeing anything.

When they finally reached ORR's dock, Kurt jumping out and tied up the boat himself. Grace just sat huddled on the wooden seat, until he came back for her. Using one hand, he literally lifted her to her feet and walked Grace to the rail, but she just stood there. He put both hands under her arms and lifting her up on to the dock, like she would pick up a pack of soda. She'd forgotten how strong a man he was for such a slight looking build. Walking arm in arm, they walked past her lab. She should be working; would she ever be working again? They walked to her building and climbed up the stairs. At her door she just stood there.

Kurt was talking. What was he saying? "Grace? Honey, the key?"

Clumsily she fished into her pocket. Finding her key ring, she held it out before her and just stared at her keys. Kurt took them, opened the door and walked her to the couch. There she could look out at the bay. Out where the Octagon gently bobbed, out to where the Coast Guard and Police boats flashed their yellow, blue and red lights. Kurt crossed the room and tugged at the long, seafoam-green drapes. First trying the cords, then just yanking them across, to shut out the horror in the harbor.

Grace just sat there, hands folded in her lap. Charles Marshall was dead. Ding dong, the witch is dead. How could he have died on the Octagon? Why would he go out there? The door was locked–was he alone? A suicide? But the skull looked crushed? Could he have done that to himself? Beat the back of his head against the bulkhead? Was the killer still in there? There was only one big eight-sided lab room, with that small chemical toilet closet.

But they hadn't looked inside.

Only how did Marshall and his killer get out there? There was no boat tied to the Octagon deck. Swam out in a wet suit? Charles Marshall certainly wouldn't have done that. So there must have been a boat and the killer left with it, or two boats if Marshall came with one and the killer had the other?

Kurt was coming over with a bottle of her plum brandy and a juice glass he pushed into her hands before he poured several ounces.

"Grace, maybe you should call your doctor?"

"Why?"

"Whal you look like a beached fish. And if a doctor puts ya under sedation, the cops can't question you."

She shook her head. "Gotta talk to them some time." She took a gulp of plum brandy and as her tongue numbed, she set her glass down. Getting sloshed with a male holding her was not the greatest strategy; that went double if the male was as instinctively predatory as Kurt MacKay. If she did anything, with anybody, she would be in full control!

But Kurt surprised her. He just held her against him, as he shared her brandy and she closed her eyes, listening for the police at the door. After what seemed like hours, Kurt got up and from the sounds and smells, Grace realized he was frying some eggs. Must be lunch? Dinner?

They ate in silence. Why hadn't the detectives come? Grace looked to the phone and was surprised to see Kurt had unplugged it. There was a buzz from her door, Kurt moved to the intercom and pressing it. "Yes?"

"Detective Uri. State Police." Grace was shocked to see that the clock registered four-forty in the afternoon. Where had the time gone?

Kurt was not pressing the door opener instead he was looking to her. What did he plan? They were going to barricade the doors? Fight the police off as Ma and Pa Barker? "Let them in. The front door is probably open anyway."

Grace went in to the bathroom to prepare herself. She decided not to put more lipstick on, she just splashed water on her face before coming out.

The two state police were standing in her living room, introducing themselves as Detective Uri and Detective Noonan. Were they the same ones who had questioned her after Miakos death? These guys seemed taller. Why with all her supposed genius, could she never recognize people, unless she had known them for years? Freya said it was because she was afraid of people. Gail said she was totally uninterested in most people...

"Dr. Farrington?" The first detective began. "We spoke with you about the suicide yesterday."

Yes, these were the same guys, but a little less sympathetic this time? Were they more guarded today?

"Dr. Farrington." The second detective started.

"Just Grace." She felt comforted to have Kurt coming over to sit beside her.

Following Kurt's move, Detective Uri looked to his partner. Grace had the feeling that they wanted Kurt out, but couldn't demand it. "Perhaps, Mr. Mackay, Grace might feel more free to answer if you stepped outside?"

Grace sat up. "No. I want him here!"

Again the two partners exchanged looks. The other one nodded, Uri turned back to her.

"Did you know the victim?"

Had they decided he was definitely a victim? Not just another suicide? Could the Octagon's interior roof have collapsed crushing his skull? "I didn't see his face."

Uri watched her closely. "Then you have no idea who he is?"

Kurt stiffening beside her.

Grace continued. "I assume, from looking at his size and hair that it is Charles Marshall."

"You know Mr. Marshall?"

"He's the new Head of Research at Oyster River Harbor. He and his wife have just moved here from Colorado."

"Then you never met him before?"

"Charles Marshall is a Nobel Prize Winning Biologist. He's known internationally in the scientific community."

"Why were you and Mr. MacKay on the Octagon?"

"It's Dr. MacKay." Grace corrected. "The Octagon houseboat is Oyster River's in harbor lab."

"You do research on a party boat?"

"It's not a party boat," she said firmly. "Inside are computer stations and Sound monitoring equipment."

"Battery run?"

"There's a solar lighting set up on the roof, but there's also an unwater, electrical cable from shore for the computers and a gas generator."

"An electric cable to a boat?"

"It's permanently anchored for on site research. " Grace looked to Kurt for back-up. Why was he being so quiet? When he said nothing, Grace continued. "The computers on board keep recording temperatures, wave heights and wind pressures from the bay. Occasionally we all go and download data that is relevant to our research."

"So early in the morning?"

Kurt finally spoke. "Actually, it was kinda late for me. Had some engine trouble."

Noonan looked to Grace. "Was it Charles Marshall's job to go out to the Octagon?"

"No. I have no idea why he was out there."

"Do you know anyone who would want to harm him?"

They looked at Grace, but it was Kurt who answered them. "Don't see as how we can help you any more. We just found the body and called the Coast Guard."

The police finally left. Kurt stayed. Eventually, he got up and half lifted her into her bedroom. He pulled back the sheets and took off her shoes. She laid down and then he laid down beside her. Yes, he was going to want something, but tonight she didn't want to be alone.

Yet Kurt her only kissed the top her forehead and snuggled next to her. Staying the night, holding her gently, as she drifted off to sleep. And to Grace's great surprise, leaving early the next morning, without once trying to take advantage of the situation.

And too her greater surprise, she found herself very disappointed about that.

Chapter 14

Three days later, Grace briefly considered putting on her single black dress for the memorial service, but she wasn't part of the family. And although she never would have wanted Marshall murdered, she certainly didn't mourn his loss. Still one must respect a mourning family's feelings so she put on a navy pantsuit and cream blouse and wondered if this service wasn't going to end with a drunken Katherine Marshall screaming across the church at her, "You harlot! You slept with my husband!"

The memorial service was being held at the Congregational Church up on the Lake. Grace grabbed up her handbag and jacket. She considered taking her car, but she glanced at her watch and realized there was enough time to walk from the condo, past her lab, up to the Captain's Roost Headquarters. That old wooden mansion was built along the main road across from the State fish hatchery.

Traffic through the fish hatchery and up to the dead end at the Congregational church parking lot was surprisingly heavy, so it was good she didn't bring the car. After crossing the main road, she walked into the fish hatchery. In the 1800's, part of Oyster River had been routed to feed several circular current tanks, now filled with Speckle trout fry sorted by size. In front and to her right, was an artificially raised, grassy berm that held a long pond where the big breeder fish were kept under the shade trees. She just walked past this and followed the road headed upwards to the church.

Far to the left on a small hill, Oyster River had been damned to form a large lake, where alongside it, a white board church had stood since 1782. She was surprised at the number of cars in the lot. It had filled up and was overflowing down to the fish hatchery's parking. It was doubtful the Charles Marshall had that many family members to fly in–perhaps the draw of a Nobel Prize Winner? A murdered Nobel Prize

Winner? Maybe if she ever won a Nobel, she too would have someone show up at her funeral.

There were people on the Church's wide, white boards steps, talking. She passed a bronze plaque giving credit to the founders–the Smiths, Gardiners, Jones, Scofields–all the old families, settling this land before Revolutionary War times. God, lets get this over with.

Inside the old church, Grace smelled dust, funeral flowers and a discordant mix of too strong after shave lotions. With so many strangers, she felt her throat constrict at being trapped. But she was relieved that this was just a memorial service, not a full funeral with an open casket. The widow was sending the casket back to Colorado, after the police released it, there was a murder investigation after all.

At the door Grace saw that red-haired reporter enter and stand within the entrance, so far the woman had the good taste to not be questioning people during a memorial service. Grace started down the central aisle. A woman was looking at her, whispering to her husband; this part of notoriety always disturbed Grace. She decided just to take the nearest seat in back and get out as soon as she could. The pews were filling up and it looked like there was going to be standing room only.

Dressed in black, Katharine Marshall and her grown children were seated in the front row. Also dressed in black was Marshall's lab assistant, Diandra. She was seated in that front pew, so either Katherine had been gracious enough to invite her, or Diandra just took it upon herself to intrude on the family. As president of ORR, Adam Greenfield sat with his wife, Rachel, across the aisle from them. On his head Adam wore a black yarmulke. Fritz and Margery Wilshusen sat alongside the Greenfields and beside them, filling up the pew was Kurt. She was surprised to seem him come. She didn't see Freya or the Stewart Brewsters. Mid-way in the church, sat Bobby with Sara. In the aisle, Ginjer played with a prayer book, while their central pew was filling up with others.

A discordant ringing and Adam answered his cellphone. Behind him, Grace could make out David Gardiner quietly talking to a shorter, dark haired man alongside him. A hush settled on the crowd, as the minster entered and slowly walked to the pulpit in his white robe and gold prayer stole. The reverend gave a dignified eulogy, speaking as if he had known Dr. Charles Theodore Marshall his whole life. Talking about his marvelous discoveries, his kindness to young scientists, his innate sense of fairness and honor. Grace wanted to vomit.

There was a woman loudly crying in the front. His wife, Katherine? No, his research assistant, Diandra.

Grace expected that Adam Greenfield would get up and say a few words on behalf of ORR, but he didn't. And the minister did not do the normal request for anyone who wished to speak of the departed, that must have been a decision of the widow's. Just a short, simple, dignified service, and then Katherine and her children were leaving the church. The Research assistant stayed seated, softly crying, until Adam awkwardly went over to her. Others were getting up so Grace could leave. As she walked out the back, Samantha stood back, while another reporter's with pad poised started questioning Grace. "Dr. Farrington, weren't you privileged to work under the renowned Dr. Marshall?"

Pretending not to hear, Grace brushed past both of them. Outside she took a deep breath of watery smelling air and mentally erased the packed people around her. She always loved field research, being out in the sun, maybe today she should get outside, Grace mused as she headed down the wooden steps. Below her she could see Mac in his tan police uniform and a State patrol officer in gray, standing alongside him. She kept climbing down, but the officer in gray stepped into her path. "Dr. Farrington?"

"Yes."

"Could you come with us please?"

Ahead in the parking lot was a police car, double parked and empty, with its lights flashing.

Mac was whispering to the state policemen urgently. "Couldn't this be done across the street? She isn't going to run."

Chapter 15

Grace stood there, shocked. "Am I being arrested?"

A third man in plain clothes cut in. "No, we just wish to talk to you."

The State Trooper coldly added. "Now...please."

Another voice, faintly familiar, yet different, now cold and commanding. "Grace." She turned to look into the concerned pale blue eyes of David Gardiner. "Grace." He repeated with a gentler tone. "Do you have lawyer?"

She looked about, confused. "No."

David looked to the suit next to him. "You do now. Alan go with her. Drive her."

"Actually, she'll be in the patrol car," the State trooper said.

Oh, my God! In front of everybody, she was being taking away in a police car? In the doorway Samantha and that other reporter were rapidly scribbling on their note pads as Grace found herself reddening as the crowd gawked at her. Okay, she the found the body, that made her a witness and they just wanted to talk with her. But, Kurt was in the crowd. Why weren't they bringing him in?

David wasn't cowed by the taller Trooper, as he firmly demanded. "The address of where you are taking her?"

The officer modified his tone. "She's not under arrest. We're just talking."

"She requests a lawyer be with her. That is her right, or she doesn't speak to you! That is correct, isn't it, Alan?"

Alan didn't say anything, but Mac in his official police uniform did. "We will be taking her to the station at the Main road intersection. Just to talk."

David nodded. "We will find you." He turned to Grace. "I want you to confer with Alan on your rights, before you speak with these men. Do you understand?"

"As a witness I don't have the right not talk..." David

and Alan exchanged a look of frustration and Grace gave in. "Don't say anything until I've talked with Alan."

Alan nodded, then Mac was reaching out to guide Grace over the hill, down to the police car. As they drove her away, the last person she saw was Samantha, still scribbling on her reporter's pad.

At the station, Grace was lead to a small, bare room with a table and chairs and left alone. What more did she have to tell them? Mac soon returned with a cup of tea, she looked up eagerly, wanting to talk, but the State Trooper had followed him and was standing in the doorway, staring at them grimly.

Grace opened her mouth, but before she could speak, Mac cut her off. "Your lawyer is here, talking with us. He'll be with you shortly."

The State Police officer glared at him as they walked out.

Grace drank the burning tea. Wondered when she could go. If she could go? Then Mac came back in. "You're going into the conference room down the hall."

Robotically she followed Mac. He closed the door behind her, leaving her in a room with only that short, fiftyish, dark haired man who had been with David. He politely rose and shook her hand. "Ms. or Mrs. Farrington?"

"Miss. Just Grace."

"My name is Alan Silverstein. I'm a corporate lawyer and very good friend of David's."

"I don't really need a lawyer, but how much do you charge per hour?"

"Right now I'm doing this as a friend of David's. If this runs over an hour, you'll owe me a steak dinner, okay? Now about this..."

This was overwhelming her. "I'm geneticist and I don't usually need a lawyer."

"That's good. Again, I am not a criminal lawyer...."

"I need a criminal attorney?"

He raised his hand. "I don't think so. If you were under arrest they would have had to tell me. They say you aren't, which means if you don't want to talk them you are free to go. But if you have nothing to hide, I would advise you speak to them, because as a witness if you refuse to talk they can go to a judge and subpoena you. Of course, you can invoke your fifth amendment right to not incriminate yourself..."

It was getting so ridiculously complicated. "What is this about?"

"Apparently you found Charles Marshall's body?"

"Yes. I told them everything I know."

"Dr. Marshall has just moved here, is that correct?"

"Yes."

"But you knew him previously?"

"I was student of his and later I worked in a laboratory he was head of. But I haven't spoken with him for years, before he came here Monday."

"Any grudges or unsolved problems between you?"

What was in the past was over and best forgotten. They would never know, if she kept her mouth shut. "I've told them all I know about his death."

The lawyer's eyes sharpened at her evasion. "If you allow them to question you as just a witness, you have to tell them the truth or it is a criminal act, obstruction of justice. If you think any admission might be self incriminating then you can refuse to speak. In that case, that would be what I would advise."

"Can you stay with me?"

"Technically, they are only questioning you as a possible witness to a crime, so you aren't entitled to a lawyer. However, if you agree to talk with them, I will just walk in with you. It's worth a try."

Grace nodded, Alan rose and she found herself following him. Mac was waiting out in the hallway and led them to a larger conference room, with two other men in plain clothes and that grim Trooper. She was relieved to see no two-way glass mirror, but the first inquisitor announced. "This session is being video taped."

Alan nodded and sat down at the table and Grace sat right next to him.

The second plain clothes man smiled in a friendly fashion. "You really don't need a lawyer."

Alan looked to her and Grace tried to smile back at the officer. "I would be more comfortable." Grace looked over at Mac too.

The friendly detective's lips tightened as he briefly nodded to the uniformed officer, who turned and indicated the door to Mac. Mac gave one last look to Grace and then reluctantly left the room with the other uniform.

The smaller man started. "I'm Detective Ahern and this is Detective Noonan."

Grace looked up. "You both questioned me about that suicide?"

Her lawyer seemed to stiffen beside her, and too late Grace realized she should not be volunteering information.

The bigger man spoke up. "That was myself and Detective Ivan Uri. But there was something strange about that suicide. You said you saw him drown out in the harbor, yet no one else seemed to have seen that?"

Her lawyer gave her a quick glare and Grace didn't respond to the opening.

Detective Noonan persisted. "Funny, being out in the open like you claimed and nobody seeing it? Do you know why that is, Grace?"

Grace wanted to tell him to call her 'Dr. Farrington', but she didn't dare. "No, I don't."

After a brief silence, the other plain clothes man asked. "You found Charles Marshall's body?"

"With Kurt–Dr. MacKay."

"Why did you go out to the houseboat?"

"Dr. MacKay had to download some data from an experiment he was running."

"He carried out a laptop with him?"

"We just use a flash drive, it's small, about the size of a matchbox."

"You always go with him?"

"He had hurt his arm, and I was helping him bring up his lobster pots for his research."

"Have you ever been to the houseboat before? Would your fingerprints be there?"

"Yes. Two weeks ago, I was out downloading data."

"You still have an experiment going?"

"Not now. Dr. MacKay does."

"Kurt MacKay, I understand he's a member of a biker gang?"

"I know him as **Dr.** MacKay, a fellow scientist at the Oyster River Research Institute.

"You knew Charles Marshall previously?" It was asked in an almost uninterested tone.

If she stayed calm, it would all be okay. "Yes."

"He was your mentor?"

"**No!**" God, she had better get a hold. "I was his student for a few classes–years ago."

Her new lawyer looked at her sharply, but the detective was continuing. "Later you worked in his laboratory?"

"No, I worked in the University Laboratory. He was Head of Research there, but actually I was working with Dr. Johnson."

"And you had no problems with Dr. Marshall?"

How would she answer that? "My knowing Dr. Marshall was years ago. I haven't seen him since I left Pasadena to take a position here."

"But you had a personal relationship with Dr. Marshall?"

"I did not."

"Didn't you have an affair with him?" They were all just staring at her.

"Most certainly not!" Her feeble attempts at calm researcher was gone.

"That's strange–I understand there was an inquiry and Charles Marshall admitted to the affair?"

Chapter 16

Alan Silverstein stiffened and her lawyer was putting out a hand to restrain her, when Grace just blew it. "There was an inquiry because I accused him of stealing my research. The 'affair' was a lie he made up to defend himself." She should have realized Katherine Marshall would be spilling all the garbage to the cops. After all these years, Katherine couldn't seriously believe Grace would kill her husband? Was Katherine trying to deflect suspicion from herself?

The interrogator continued. "But the Board believed him."

"A bunch of male chauvinistic pigs–his friends, all of them!" She finished angrily.

Alan put a firm hand on her arm. "That's enough, Grace."

She turned to him. "I didn't kill him! That was all over years ago!"

Alan glared warningly at her. Grace shut her mouth and sat back. Then the lawyer looked to the two police detectives. "I think you have enough."

"Actually we have more questions."

"That's unfortunate, because Grace has finished answering your questions. If you wish charge her, do so. Otherwise we are walking out of here."

Frustration was written on the two officer's faces, Grace said nothing and her lawyer said sat silently.

"Excuse me," said one detective as they both got up and left the room.

Grace turned to Alan. "I should have..."

He raised his hand and pointed a finger towards the camera hung from the ceiling. "I think very shortly we will be talking outside of here."

In a few minutes Mac came in and led them out of the conference room. "I'm sorry about this, Grace."

Grace started to talk, "You can't believe I killed him! I haven't heard about Marshall for..."

From his six foot plus height, Mac looked down at her saying firmly. "You have a lawyer. You talk to him, not me, not Freya, not anybody else. Understand?"

She nodded and looked away. As they walked outside she realized her car was back in ORR. The police had driven her here, didn't they owe her a ride home? Alan was talking to David, who was standing by a black Mercedes Benz. David looked up. "Can we drive you home?"

Grace looked back at Mac, who said, "We'll drive you. Or him. Which ever you want?"

She didn't really want to be seen riding in a police car again. "I'll go with David." Mac nodded and turned away.

When Grace got to Alan, she had to say, "I didn't do very well in there. I should have..."

"You should have spoken more candidly to me about a possible motive, as ridiculous as it is. I think they're on a fishing expedition, because they obviously do not have anyone else to pin this on. If they talk to you again, you **do** need a lawyer."

"You?"

"Unfortunately, my expertise is in corporate mergers. I think you should employ someone with a criminal law background."

God, what would that cost? "Well, thank you."

David persisted, "You are going to put someone on retainer, just in case?"

Grace shook her head. "I don't think you gentlemen know what a researcher's budget is like."

Alan nodded. "Yes. That can be a problem." Alan looked to David, who gave him a 'solve this' look back. After a moment, Alan continued. "But I might have an answer. I have nephew, Mark Silverstein. Graduated from Yale, top of his class, worked as a D.A. for five years, and he's now starting out in my firm. He's very bright, but so far not too many clients, a celebrity such as yourself might be a very good way to get his practice kicked off. He might be willing to do it pro-bono..."

David looked unhappy. "She's being questioned in a murder case. Is an untested attorney the right way to go?"

"At this moment, she is a witness only. Mark would scrupulously protect all her rights. And if it ever came to a court case—I don't think it will–counsel could be decided upon at that point."

A concerned David looked to Grace.

Grace shook her head. "I didn't kill him. I didn't like him. Hell, at one time I hated him, but that was years ago! At the worst, I was just going to move on to another lab. That's a tremendous inconvenience, but not reason to kill somebody."

The lawyer looked at her. "Does anyone else know that?"

Grace started to say no–then saw visions of Katherine and Marshall's buddies on the Disciplinary Board on some witness stand. And she'd told Kurt and who else at ORR that she was leaving? Oh, God. "Yes."

"Then the person you speak to is my nephew. This is my card, call that number and my secretary will refer you to Mark. I want you to have a sit down with him as soon as possible."

David warned, "Do not speak to the police again without him or Alan." Then he changed to a cheery tone. "Now where shall we go for lunch?"

Grace looked him in bewilderment. "Lunch?"

"Remember the British, food, stiff upper lip. Besides we owe it to Alan."

"Yes." The lawyer beamed. "And if my time is to be reimbursed with a steak dinner, and David is the host paying for it, I can order at bottle of St. Henri Shiraz."

"St. Henri?" Grace repeated.

Alan smiled benignly. "A divine wine with a hint blackberry, plum and currant spices." He looked triumphantly at David.

Who wryly smiled back. "Yes, I've heard that. A bit pricy so I've never had any myself." He looked to Grace. "We will make sure Alan shares the bottle with us."

It was should have been a good meal, a fancy restaurant, with candles and heavy, cream colored linens on the table, but to Grace everything tasted like sand. Charles Marshall was dead, and he was still poisoning her life!

Returning to ORR, she asked David to let her off at the Administration building where Gail had her desk in the center of that glass and ceramic tile lobby. Sitting in a virtual fishbowl, Grace wondered how she could get anything done, much less everything.

Concerned sky-blue eyes looked up at her. "Well, at least you're not under arrest. Adam was really worried when the police took you away."

Ignoring the opening Grace said, "You left a message you wanted me to sign some papers?"

Gail lifted a folder from her desk. "This is your teaching contract and your authorization for Bobby to be your assistant. The catalog blurb I wrote for you..."

Automatically, Grace just started to sign everything handed her.

"No!" Gail protested. "You should always read it first! At the least the catalog blurb." She stopped and then continued regretfully. "The contract doesn't specify that you are teaching only as long as Bobby remains assistant. I couldn't get Adam to put that in, but you have his word. As long as Bobby doesn't punch anyone out..."

"What about the Jamison condo?"

Gail was carefully fitting each signed paper back in to her file. "Adam didn't say anything about that, but he did say

Ms. Hollings is not moving in. Apparently her contract was with Dr. Marshall directly, so she is not going to be picked up on ORR staff."

"Can we get Adam to give Bobby some kind of lease?"

"I don't think he'll do it. Especially after Bobby punched Marshall out." Gail was methodically filing each paper signed. "I think you should just let the matter rest for now, I'll work on Adam in the Spring. And we'll have to see who is the new head."

Grace nodded, pretending to glance over the next paper she was signing, with her mind spinning in so many directions she couldn't concentrate. Finishing, she headed back outside, walking towards her lab, finding herself relaxing at the thought of immersing her thoughts in mouse fur inheritance patterns.

The door to Eric's old lab was open, well, it had been Marshall's laboratory for a few days. Several half filled trash cans stood out in front of it and a group of students had gathered on the sidewalk. Now they were muttering among themselves.

Stopping, Grace heard angry shouts from within the lab.

Chapter 17

"**Don't!** You shouldn't touch that! " A woman's voice pleaded.

A determined Katherine Marshall marched out of the lab, carrying a box of files. Those files she just dumped unceremoniously into the nearest trash can. A terribly upset Diandra was helplessly trailing her. "You can't do this! That is Charles' legacy!"

Still holding the empty box, Katherine turned back to the lab, but Diandra blocked her path forcing Katherine to stop. Katherine screamed at her. "**Our legacy!** My husband's and mine! I am Mrs. Charles Marshall, his widow! Everything of his is now **mine**! To do with as I wish! And I wish to dump it all!"

Grace could see an ORR security person in the distance, watching but pointedly staying away. Diandra looked to the crowd for some sort of support, then she fixed on Grace. "Dr. Farrington. Please, stop her! Dr. Marshall's papers should be donated to some library. Perhaps here, Oyster River Research could be turned into a monument to Charles Marshall's heritage!"

Grace said nothing. Not being able to force Diandra to back down, Katherine pushed around her and stalked back into the lab building. Diandra was actually crying, as she ran to Grace. "Please! Stop her! He wouldn't want this! His work must be preserved!"

A big, shiny red pick-up truck was pulling into the lot with Adam 's Construction Firms logo. Security must have been told to contact him in case of another problem. Grace was relieved to see Adam hurrying over, to Diandra she said, "That's Adam Greenfield, he's President of Oyster River. He would know of the importance of Dr. Marshall's work. If you go talk to him, he might have the trash containers saved."

Probably happy to be appealing to a male, Diandra

turned from Grace and rushed to Adam. Grace quickly walked past both of them to the quiet sanctuary of her lab, vastly relieved to be out of it all.

But of course she wasn't. The question was who would want Charles Marshall dead? She was the one they were questioning. That made her the chief suspect, so the police would concentrate on building a case against her and not look anywhere else. If the murderer had to be found, she better start looking.

Grace opened up a new document on her laptop, she'd do this murder investigation the same way she researched the DNA of an a tiger's white fur mutation. She set up a spread sheet, titling it 'Murder Suspects'. Then Grace started labeling columns. "Murder of Marshall", under that heading she labeled sub-columns: 'Motives', 'Means', 'Opportunity', and one 'To do' for her research. She inserted two columns for possibilities: 'Pros' for why it did happen that way, and 'Cons' for reasons it couldn't have happened that way. Thomas Alva Edison had always kept rigorous notes of his experimental failures, because he knew, in years ahead he would recall his successes, but forget the 'whys' something would not work.

The Motive, Means, and Opportunity columns could each be given subjective percentages, that could be totaled and using the final 'Total' percentage, she would weigh her range of possible hypotheses. When her spread sheets revealed a hypotheses, with a high total of clustered interest, she would arrange experiments to prove or disprove that particular assumption. By presenting possible alternate theories, studying them and disproving them one by one, Grace would finally whittle them down to one supposition that stood out as the correct assumption.

She decided to add a second main heading: "Miakos"–suicide? Accident? Murder by Witch's curse? She knew nothing of the man except she had watched him die, but the police questioned her as if she was one of their fledgling hypotheses. She had better fully study Miakos' death. Under the heading for Miakos, she added the sub-columns for 'Motive', 'Means', 'Opportunity', 'Pro' and 'Con' and 'Total' percentage columns.

Before all the columns, she set up one labeled 'Suspect'. In the first row she typed 'Miakos'. Under his Motive column, she typed: 'suicide'; Means: 'boat rental'; Opportunity: "There"; Total Percentage Miakos killed Miakos, "100%".

The 'Pro' column, of course, she typed 'G.F. witnessed him doing it'. Still in the "Con" column she had to type: 'Why?' Why would a successful artist suicide?'.

In her end "to do" column she typed 'Learn more about Miakos'.

Marshall's death was harder. Seeing his bloodied, caved in head she assumed it wasn't suicide, but she typed a row for suicide, as a possible long shot anyways, 2%. Along with Epileptic Fit? Collapse of Octagon roof structure? The neat thing about computer spread sheets was you could always insert another row, column or active cell.

The corner may be sea-sick, but Dr. Jensen would rule out accidental death she was sure. No, this was murder. Leaving she and Kurt as the last known people to have seen the victim, and from the police's stand point, maybe alive. Still, she was a witness that they couldn't have done it, so she didn't even bother adding a row for murder by "G.F. & K. MacKay" as a hypothesis. Let the police worry about that one.

Who knew Charles Marshall well enough to kill him? Anyone whose work he had spiked or stolen, so she could think of a few names right off. But of those, who could have been in Oyster River Harbor, been able to get a boat or even known of the Octagon? None of those names could have gotten a key to the research ship and moved about unnoticed? She made a note on the spread sheet to under 'To do': Speak to Mac re: alternate murderer suspects and possible witnesses?

Although the detectives might not be looking for somebody from Marshall's past, Diandra Hollings had come with the Marshalls. Obviously she had a job with him and might have been his lover, in fact, knowing how Marshall worked, probably was his lover. But if she killed Marshall, she'd be out a mentor, employer and someone she might actually have cared about giving her a weak 20 %.

Katherine Marshall should resent the relationship with Diandra, but she had put up with many girlfriends in the past, so why get upset over one more flaunted affair? Motive: "Jealousy" Percentage: 20%. Was Charles going to divorce her? Probably not–he never had before. And with children and decades of marriage, Katherine would have walked away with a good chunk of his assets.

The Wilshuens, Fritz and Margery? Their motive was being thrown out of their house and Fritz's job. Means? Fritz knew about the ORR boats, but with his bad hip, it was unlikely that he could have managed to climb down to the docks. Margery never learned to swim, she said she was afraid of the water and that night they probably would have been hosting their weekly string quartet rehearsal at their house. When she subtracted the "Cons" from the "Motive", Grace put the Wilshuens down for an overall total of -10%.

Who else? Kurt could have killed him without her, and then gone back to 'discover the body' with her. She give him 15% for means. Kurt MacKay was strong enough to take down a bigger man, add another 10%. Opportunity: He lived alone, so didn't have to account for his time. Kurt had Motive: Marshall was trying to get him fired, maybe another 20 %? Still, to Kurt, Marshall's threat would have been a challenge, something he would relish fighting. No, Kurt's motive leaked like a sieve, a weak -5 %, although, the police might not see it that way. Still, she gave his overall total as 25 %

Now Adam Greenfield had hired the eminent Marshall

and was discovering the great man's wormier aspects. In a few years–actually months--Oyster River's President would've wanted to kill Charles Marshall, but probably would never have done it. In the motive column she typed in "Too weak" or a 2 %. Adam got an overall 10% for means.

Then there was another person, with motive, physical strength and a lamentable lack of self control. Bobby Jamison. Marshall had ended his job and condo, Motive: 30%. There were mitigating Cons, Bobby's situation was not that hopeless. He'd been temporarily fired at Oyster River, but he and Sara could have gone back to the mid-west and lived with Sara's family. He had friends. Yet, the strongest 'Pro' was Bobby's black-powder temper that could smolder or explode. Sara said they had a fight and Bobby stormed out and he didn't come back that night, Opportunity 25%. Means: his physical ability, he was smaller than Marshall, but younger and more athletic, so means 20%.

Not wanting to go home, did he take out a launch and motor to the Octagon? Did he moor it on the seaward side, so it wouldn't be seen, because he had plans to sleep in the houseboat that night? Did Marshall take a launch out to check one more possession in his new domain? On the Octagon did he find Bobby there and did they fight? Maybe Bobby didn't realize how badly Marshall was hurt and he just left? As he was dying did Marshall block the Octagon's doorway to fend off another attack?

Grace stopped typing. Many times in her years of research the data had gone a way she didn't want it to. Then she had two choices: Grace could ignore the deviations, or she could follow the facts to a conclusion that she may not want. Throughout her career, Grace always followed the data's true trail. On Bobby's row in the 'To Do' block she typed: 'Find out time Marshall died?' How? From Mac or Freya or the newspapers? In another cell under 'To Do': Talk to Bobby, where did he go that night? Alibi? See how he answers. Under

'Motive', Grace reluctantly added "20%" for temper, but however angry as Bobby was she could not picture him actually killing Marshall. And under 'Con', she also couldn't see Bobby killing someone and then running. She could put a -10% in that block.

So back to her Suspect column. Who else? Did she know anyone in the Denver academic community, that might know gossip about the state of the relationship between Marshall and Diandra? And what about Katherine? Wives have killed faithless husbands, but in the Means column Grace had to admit 5'5' Katherine would have had little chance against 6'2' Charles Marshall.

Still, if she hit him for behind? But how did Katherine get to the house boat? She couldn't picture stately, portly Katherine sneaking down to the dock, casting off a launch, starting the engine, and piloting it out to the houseboat lab, then tying it up, all skills not usually done in high heels. Did Katherine have any boating experience? Definitely, negative numbers for Katherine's "Means" column.

Surveying the entire spreadsheet Grace only wished she could put some more notes in the 'Con' column for Bobby, more negative percentages in his row that was totalling so positively high.

Chapter 18

Finally she finished her Murder Suspect spreadsheet, then she had to go to 'Help' to figure out how to put a password on it, since this was one document she didn't want anyone else reading. Then there was something she could do. Putting on her car coat, Grace locked up her laboratory and headed towards the entrance of the peninsula and the main docks, where a bitter, damp wind hit her. The downside of living just off a New England harbor in the colder seasons.

Orange looking porthole lights were glowing in Kurt's cozy sailboat home. Grace was wearing rubber soled shoes, so she just padded on board, knowing he still must hear her above him. At the cabin's swinging doors she stopped, having no wish to walk in on him and Tanya or Cindi or Jo-Anne or whoever. He really didn't have a doorbell, so she primly knocked on the stripped teak trim around the cabin doors.

In a moment the two hatch halves swung opened and Kurt looked up at her. He was in green plaid flannel shirt and jeans, with a meatball sandwich in his hand; seeing her, his face lit up. "Hey, wanna screw?" He asked invitingly.

"No." She took his offer of a hand down the steep steps, really a ladder, to the warm cabin that smelled of garlic sauce and maleness. Surprisingly neat, the cabin bowed out with its polished teak trimmed build-in table and benches, with more wood trimmed lockers for maps and such, beside a small but well laid out kitchenette. Overhead an electric lantern swung as the boat bobbed on incoming waves. Grace knew up in the bow there was a built in double bed. "Did you find any blue mottled lobsters?"

"Nope."

"Are we going through with this?"

"*Affiliated*. Sure. If they pay, I'll find blue tailed lobsters, if I have to paint them meself. Now lets get back to the important things–how about I rub you a bit between yer legs?"

He was reaching to do just that, as Grace firmly pushed his hand away. "Actually, I always expect to have to take a number at the door."

He smiled widely. "Things aren't quite that good. With grants down, I take you ladies out to dinner less."

"All us heartless sirens are after your money."

He managed a leer. "And me other treasures."

"Kurt, you still have that long distance lense you were photographing dolphins with?"

"Somewhere around here." He looked about the cabin. "Haven't hocked it lately."

"At Marshall's funeral, how did you think Katherine behaved?"

"Like any good WASP wife, sad-eyed, but tearless. Standing tall. The true mourner seemed to be that sexy Diandra Hollings."

"She's a young girl, obviously seeing Marshall as some sort of scientific god, yes, she probably was in love with him. But I was wondering more about Katherine. If you took your sail boat out, just beyond the point, and you anchored there tonight you'd have a good view of the boat house windows."

"I'm to be sort of a sea going peeping tom?"

"Yhep."

"What am I looking for?"

"A boyfriend."

"Katherine would be pretty stupid to have him around here, so soon after her husband's murder, but they say most murderers do some really dumb things. Okay. You cast off the lines and jump back on board and we'll go voyeuring. When we aren't peeping through the port hole, maybe we can rub your thing against my thing and start a fire?"

"No." She was in no mood for that tonight.

His hand had carelessly landing high on her hip She

could feel it trailing down her stomach and on to her inter thigh, pressing hard on her jeans. Actually it was a bit arousing, but she reached down and gently took his hand away. "Doing that you couldn't keep your mind on business."

"Ah, but if the Coast Guard sees my sailboat out in the middle of the bay, out of my snug harbor, having you aboard will explain it all. Those guard boys understand a man and woman would need some privacy out where ya can't hear the shouting."

"You'll be shouting?"

"No, you lady, with thanks for the oversized gift I'd be giving ya!"

"No thank you. Actually, I have dinner engagement."

"Too bad." He didn't look all that disappointed.

"Can I cast you off?"

"Nope." He looked at the brass rimmed clock. "I'm expecting someone. Tanya should be here soon."

"You had a date coming? And you're propositioning me? What if she got here and we had departed?"

"Tanya's got a great respect for me work. I would've told her I had a report of a rare white whale. That as a scientific type, I jes had to motor off and check it out."

"Tanya? Isn't she the biker, barmaid and ex-carnival knife thrower?"

"Aaup. May have some connection to the Russian Mafia in Bayonne, too."

"Tanya, the jealous one?"

"Yeah. She is a bit put out about you going with me to the Embassy dinner."

"Don't you think having a jealous girlfriend who throws knives is a bad idea?"

He smiled ruefully. "It's occurred. But I jes don't know how to put it to her to break up."

"Maybe you could tell her that you've had a life altering vision of the Virgin Mary and you're joining the

Catholic priesthood."

"Me? Celibate? Tanya'd never believe it."

"Right now, we both have to find someone that the police will believe murdered Marshall other than ourselves, so I suggest you start peeping as soon as you can!"

"Only for you fair lady."

Chapter 19

If the police arrested her, she would never again have her regular Monday night dinners with Freya. Grace shook her head, she had to get off this morbid train of thinking. As she drove to the Library parking lot, Grace's mind should be working on problems with mice fur and breeding a mold resistant strain of rice, yet she constantly felt compelled to think about her Murder Suspects spreadsheet.

She couldn't see Katherine stealing a boat and killing her husband on the Octagon. What if she had a lover? Not somebody she had met at Oyster River, there wasn't time. Could he have come here from where they last lived? Denver? A lover that followed her here, stayed at a motel somewhere? A male strong enough to overcome Marshall? A male familiar with boating?

He then what—rented a boat? She could check with Neptune's rentals, but the police must have done that or did they bother? He could've stolen one of ORR's boats? A stranger walking about the Oyster River campus might not stand out with new students registering all the time, but why would he have returned Marshall's boat to the docks? It would have been to Katherine's and his advantage to have Marshall's body discovered as soon as possible? Why hadn't Katherine reported her husband missing that night? Did they have another fight? Was she embarrassed to report his absence? Or was she used to his leaving and not coming back for a day or so? Of course, if Katherine was hitting the bottle again, could she have been in a drunken slumber from that night to all the next morning? Another 'To Do' for the sheet: ask Mac what condition Katherine was in when the police broke the news of her husband's death?

Grace started walking up toward Main Street. As a town, Oyster River had peaked in the early eighteen hundreds, when its small fleet of whaling vessels harbored there. Then, like a penny poor spinster, the town just shut its doors, shuttered its windows and dried up. It was the poverty of its townspeople that actually preserved Oyster River's lovely colonial and federal buildings. In the early 1900's wealthy couples found the Harbor was a nice bit of rural beauty, only a short train ride from New York City. Those classic buildings were reborn as small, exclusive shops, catering to the well off. Grace kept walking on slabs of old cement side walk, that slanted crookedly from the big tree roots sneaking under them.

Mid-way she inhaled smells of cedar and savory and went into the Cheese shop. The one story shop was crammed with gourmet candy, edible delicacies, spices, fancy aprons, specialty cookware. In front to her right was a wall of exotic teas, perpendicular to a refrigerated case with home made apricot crepes and an abundance of quiches. To her left were the gourmet chocolates and Italian "veggies" fashioned from almond paste. In a central area the cash registers were ensconced in a square of high counters, displaying fancy pot holders and platters of food samples. Grace tasted several dips with cracker slivers and decided to buy a nice champagne cheese puree and thin lobster crackers for Freya's tonight.

The back the shop was also divided into two sections: The right half was steel cooking tools, cook books and copper bottomed pots and the left side was a small deli with a refrigerator case for sandwich meat. Grace added some roasted, butter-scotch almonds to her hand basket, and then decided to pick up some cheese stuffed salami to take home.

While her husband sliced Italian salami in the back, Terri rang up her order. "Try some of the red caviar. You'll love it."

"Not on my budget, might like it too much."

Terri smiled, totting up the almonds.

Grace looked about. "A friend mine, David Gardiner, gets a special order here from England?"

Terri's face brightened. "Oh, David. He has a lot of

special orders. Was it the Welsh clover cheese? Or the Bristol smoked Kippers ?"

"No. A tea, an odd spice tea."

"Cinnamon Burst?"

"That doesn't ring a bell. It was orange and star anisette, and some other herbs..."

"East Indian Sunset? Orange Pekoe based with flower herbs. Actually more Asian than Indian, it's a bit pricy, but a little goes a long way."

"That's it. I'd like a..." She thought about it, this was not the time to be spending extra money but her quiet tea drinking and thinking periods were when she got her best work done. "Let me try a small tin."

"I don't have any now, but I can add it to the current order. Should be in at the end of the month. Do you want me to call you?"

"Thank you." It was always such a pleasure to shop there.

Oyster River's Main Street was relatively short with only a few smaller, narrow old roads branched off for board homes that once housed seamen's families. Leaving the Cheese shop, Grace turned left, towards a tall, dark green, two story building, with a small patio area in front of it. On the side there were steps that lead down to the new age store in the basement, Freya's *Haunts of Wôden*. Grace headed down to a magical world of crystals, tarot cards, lightning struck oak branches and Hindu spirit bells.

Ensconced by the door was a nearly three foot tall pink quartz crystal, on a lighted base stand. New. Grace looked at the price tag, who would spend over two thousand dollars for a pretty pink rock? Grace certainly didn't believe any of the minerals on sale here gave a person "energy" or "purification" or "better karma", but she had to admit, being around Freya was like being plugged directly into all the surging energy of the earth's core.

Only five inches shorter than her policeman son, Freya stood six foot tall, with the chest and build of a Wagnerian mezzo-soprano. With her hair hung down in one thick, long, yellow braid, Freya looked every inch the Viking Witch persona she assumed. Now she was wrapping thin, leather stripping around a rod, topped by a large, pointed clear crystal.

Hearing the high, door bell tinkle, Freya turned around. "Grace." Hurriedly she put down her Wiccan wand and pushed around the counter, reached out and enveloped Grace with a great, comforting bear hug. "You haven't been answering your phone."

They usually didn't hug when they met but it seemed just what Grace needed. Freya looked down at her. "How are you doing? Mac said you looked terrible when saw you on the Octagon, he was so worried for you. He held off notifying the State Police for as long as he could, to give you more time to adjust."

"Thank him for me."

"Why didn't you answer my calls?"

"I haven't been picking up any of my messages lately."

Freya understood, "After you saw Miakos jump?"

"Did you know Miakos?"

"He and several of his ex-wives shopped in my store."

Grace needed more of an answer. "But you didn't know him?"

"I know he's an artist. Founder of the 'Grotesque Animalism' school of art, it's a bastard off shoot of Abstract Expressionism, highlighting homo sapiens' basic bestial nature."

"Why would he suicide?"

She shook her head closing out the cash register. "He was at the top of his game–hadn't heard he was sick. I don't know. Couldn't it have been an accident? He was always pulling crazy stunts to get media attention. He's got a show just opening at the Gull's Eye. Publicity would have been helpful." Freya tossed on a rainbow knit cape and turned the lights off as she and Grace headed outside.

As Freya locked up, Grace mused, speaking almost to herself. "Even for a show's publicity, a non-swimmer jumping into the harbor is a little extreme."

"I'll agree with you there."

They started walking, past the Seamen's Church. Down a short side street and on to a parallel street, where Freya and Mac lived in a two story wooden house that backed out on to the harbor. Freya had inherited it, now she rented out the upper story and Mac had his apartment in the basement. On the front porch, Freya fumbled for a key.

"You finally locked it?" A surprised Grace noted a shiny, brass lock on the door.

"My son 'The Cop' has been after me. Expects there's a mass murderer stalking Oyster River." Freya's tone betrayed total contempt with the idea, but Mac must have really laid down the law to get his mother to start locking up. "Couldn't find the keys, so Mac bought new locks for all the doors, a ridiculous waste!"

Actually Grace agreed. On her spread sheet for her murder theories, she hadn't even included a hypothesis row for a crazed, random murderer loose in Oyster River Harbor. Should she include it? Where was the nearest State Mental Hospital? They went inside to a parlor decorated for Freya's tarot reading clients in dark cranberry-purple velvet drapes and heavy Victorian furniture.

On Freya's horsehair couch there was a UPS box open with a massive, three foot long wooden handle sticking out of it. Grace walked over and studied the iron topped tool. "Is that an adze?"

"Working reproduction of a tenth century Norwegian trimming axe. With this we may be able to lay the keel by February."

Grace looked up with interest. "You and Mac are

building a long ship?"

"Maybe someday, but now it's just a faering."

Freya was always doing something interesting. "What's a farring?"

"F-a-e-r-i-n-g. A Norse boat for fishing, approximately the size of my row boat out back."

Grace looked back at her in surprise. "You're building it out in your backyard?"

"With snow coming? Nope, the Whaling Museum keeps up that old Boat wright barn on conservation property by Harbor Park. Made a deal with them."

"What is that costing you?"

"Nothing. They let us use their barn and then we will let them exhibit the faering during winter months."

Grace was following Freya into her dining room. The rest of the house was Swedish modern furniture, in light blond wood. Almost as much at home here as she was in her own condo, Grace just walked through into the kitchen and put her salami in the refrigerator to keep until she left. Enveloped in a cloud of steam Freya was checking the contents of her crock pot as Grace smelled a hardy Beef Bourgogne.

While Freya poured red wine in to three goblets, Grace opened the dip and crackers and carried them out of the kitchen onto the old wood, fire-escape back porch, which had enough room for a small kitchen table, tons of hanging plants, and Freya's collection of wind chimes. Sitting here listening to brass, glass and pottery chimes, they could watch the sparkling of the last sunlight on the Harbor. As usual, while they waited for Mac to get home and join them they would sip wine and talk quietly.

"Freya, what do you know about the *Siren*'s curse?"

"It's in my first book *Oyster River Harbor Hauntings*."

"You don't believe in that stuff?"

Freya hesitated, then carefully replied. "I report what others say they have seen. There was a Widow Noreen

O'Rielly. She did get pregnant out of wedlock, and there are court records that she sued the three Smith brothers for paternity."

"Didn't she know which one?"

"Well, they didn't have you and your DNA testing machines in 1837."

"And the Smith brothers?"

"Captain Benjamin and his brothers, Lemuel and Wardell. They're in the records at the whaling museum. All were on board the *Siren*, when she sank here, during an unnatural June nor'easterner."

"Because of Nora's curse?"

"No, actually, I think the hatred needed to sink that ship came from Jersillda."

"Jersillda?"

"Wife of Captain Benjamin, a very strong minded woman, know locally as a herbalist and a healer. Benjamin brought her back from one of his whale hunts, she was white, but raised in the Caribbean and supposed to be well versed in Hoodoo or Obeah work."

"What?"

Freya took a sip. "Today they might call it Voodoo or Santeria. African slaves brought their religious pantheons, mainly Yorba, to the Caribbean with them. These forbidden religions were fused with acceptable Catholic Saint worship."

"Could Marshall been bludgeoned to death as some sort of cult sacrifice? Is there an active Santeria cult around here?"

Freya shook her head. "They'd be sacrificing chickens and rabbits. Oh, I get purchases of the Saint candles and the sacred oils they would use. That section is in the back of the store, but it's a faith where they're praying for grandma's health and their boyfriend's love. They don't do human sacrifice, except in the movies." Freya took a deep sip as she watched an orange sail board maneuver. "Yes, your real interest should be in Jersillda. Some of her books are still in your old Administration building library, the Captain's Roost was originally the house Benjamin built for her. The night of the fatal storm Jersillda was seen on the beach watching as the *Siren* foundered."

"And this 1800's tragedy has some relationship to a murder today?"

"Two men have been found dead. Miakos was a known womanizer. Your Dr. Marshall?"

Grace had to admit. "Yes, he fits the pattern, but I thought the curse was to kill three unfaithful brothers. Not two unrelated deaths?"

A frown crossed Freya's face. "Spiritual powers can't be aimed like a gun. Give the lady a break, it's been nearly two centuries and it's hard to focus hatred that powerful."

Grace knew better than to probe as to whether Freya actually believed all that nonsense. There were sounds coming from the kitchen. Mac must have come up from his basement apartment. Freya rose to go back in. "Time for dinner." Grace followed her back into the kitchen.

Mac was inside, ladling himself a huge plate of beef stew.

Freya asked. "You have any news for Grace?"

Mac wasn't even making eye contact with Grace. "Ma, I'm eating down stairs...I've got to study for my sergeant's exam. Excuse me." He started to hurry off.

Freya called after her son. "Don't you want any bread?"

To Grace, it looked like the only thing he wanted was to get away from her. Mac couldn't possibly think she had anything to do with Marshall's murder? Could he?

Looking annoyed and embarrassed Freya ladled out two more plates, then carried her stew back out onto the porch. "Well, I guess my son, the cop, won't be joining us."

Grace added a slice of Freya's home made, braided-bread to her stew plate, then joined her on the porch. As the sun set sank lower it was cooling off, but the tart wine and stew warmed her.

Freya continued. "Both Noreen and Jersillda and the wreck of the *Siren* are in the town history books. Perhaps the diving archaeologists are disturbing the spirits?"

Grace wanted to escape the Halloweenie aspect. "Freya, what else do you know about Miakos?"

"I went to the opening reception for his show at the Gull's Eye last Sunday."

"Did you see him?"

"No. He never goes to his openings. His ex-wife and his agent were there and of course, the Ingersols–Elise and Gunnar--it's their gallery. Wasn't too big a turn out, still, Sunday we had that driving rain."

As they were cleaning up Grace asked. "Would Miakos' show still be open tonight?"

"The Ingersols stay open until nine."

"Instead of the book store, can we take a look at his art?"

"We can do both."

They left Freya's and walked up another short lane to come out on the side road that ran past the library.

As they walked Grace asked. "Do you know a man named David Gardiner?"

"The Gardiners are an old, local family. One of the founders with the Jones, Scofields and Smiths. A lot of Gardiners are buried up at the Congregational church yard."

"I was at his house, Route 8, in the hallow. I wish you could see it. Quite an estate. All old British Empire leather and brass studs."

"What were you doing at his house?" Freya sounded interested.

"Adam Greenfield is trying to get him on the Board of Oyster River."

"Must have bucks." Freya sounded very interested.

"He's got acres of land and raises horses." They were walking out on to Main street.

"Is he married?"

"That's what I was going to ask you."

"David Gardiner. .." Freya mused.

Grace looked away. "He's probably married. Or gay. Or..."

"Or he might just like you? Did he ask you out?"

Grace thought about it. "Not really. We did go to dinner, the three of us."

"Three?"

"He lent me his lawyer, when the police were questioning me about Marshall's death. That's not really a date."

Freya tightened her lips. "Well, for a hermit like you, that's something."

"I'm not a hermit, I just work long hours." Freya gave her 'the look', so Grace continued defensively. "I had lunch with Kurt the other day."

"MacKay? I don't know how you stand him! He was in my store, buying incense once, '*to get the ladies in the mood*'. Gave me a business card. Read it after he left, it said, '*you've just been patronized by the KKK'.* "

"Kurt gets a kick out of shocking people, but he's actually a very nice guy. He's got black friends, too. And with his research he's an open minded scientist..."

Freya only looked at her, then said. "I'll ask around about Gardiner. Doug was it?"

"David."

"I think I've heard that name, but with our luck with men, he'll probably be out on parole for the ax murder of his last girl friend."

Chapter 20

The Gull's Eye Gallery was a white-painted, wooden store front, with two plate glass window bays that over hung the sidewalk, sandwiching a central door set back three steps. Inside the gallery, almost all of the first floor had been opened up to free-standing, textured beige fabric covered partitions standing on a highly buffed, wide-boarded chestnut floor. There was also a small office and framing shop in the back. When they entered Grace noted that, even with Elise's cinnamon potpourri boiling at the entrance, the whole gallery had a unpleasant city street stink to it.

Immediately ahead on the partitions were five foot by five foot collage canvases in black, blood reds and dingy whites. A thin, fortyish natural blonde, Elise Ingersoll was placing a large, red "sold" dot on the card next to the first massive upchuck of paint, shattered garbage and rusted razor wire. Freya leaned over and said in a low voice. "There were only two red dots when I was here on Sunday."

Elise looked up and smiled proudly. "We're almost sold out. We've just got this deposit in an e-mail from Greece. Our web site is paying off."

Grace couldn't see why any of it sold. Miakos's 'Grotesque Animalism' work reminded her of the graffiti scarred walls of abandoned warehouses. As she and Freya walked about, Grace said in an undertone. "Looking at this stuff, you almost feel dirty."

Freya smiled and whispered back. "That was supposed to be his genius. Smell it?"

Grace concentrated on an odor she had been trying to ignore. Freya nodded. "Each piece of art has a sponge built into the collage. The gallery owner has to refresh the urine every day before displaying any of Miakos' art."

Oh, God. "Would you buy any of this?"

"If I had a few hundred thousand to spare?"

"If you had it?"

With the gallery owner's back to them, Freya shook her head. "But he's obviously got a market."

There was a discreet, matted and framed sheet at the back of the gallery with titles and prices that blew Grace's mind. If Miakos could get six figures for what was obviously his old t-shirt stained with paint, then lacquered to a piece of discarded cardboard, he certainly didn't have money problems. One less motive for suicide on her spread sheet. At Grace's signal, Freya finished her conversation with Elise, and they headed outside.

It was a relief to breathe clean air again. Across the street beckoned the cozy lights of Abe's Books, another basement store, set in a whitewashed stone foundation, opening at street level. They stepped inside a wood beamed space crammed with bookcases, set around a central area where you could sit on over-stuffed sofas and drink Abe's free coffee.

As they walked in, Freya bend her head down and said in an undertone. "Feel for vibrations here? This is the basement of the house the Widow Noreen O'Reilly rented her rooms in."

"The witch in your book, who cursed the Captain of the *Siren*?"

"Unless it was the scorned wife."

Thin, dark goateed Abe sat behind the central counter, reading a book not even bothering to look up when they came in. There was a couple already browsing in the cook book section, as Freya moved to his counter, softly calling out. "Abe?" He still stared at his book, as Freya gently sought to bring him back to this dimension, by speaking a little louder. "Abe?"

At last, blinking behind his thick lenses glasses, he looked up. "Freya?"

"Is that *Viking Ship Building* book I ordered in yet?"

Looking out of it, he glanced around. "Yes, yes, I know it is. It's here somewhere, you'll love the photos of the wood working tools. I have it right here...someplace."

With Abe's book piles that could mean it wouldn't be found until after Christmas. Belatedly Abe looked about his store seeing if there were any other patrons about and probably reassuring himself that the whole place hadn't been stolen while he was immersed in his book. When he saw Grace he said in a carrying voice. "Good evening, Dr. Farrington. How's the Popcorn Gene Theory coming?"

Usually, if there were no one else in the store, it would have just been 'Grace', but when he spoke, the woman shopper looked in their direction and gently poked her reading husband. Grace just smiled at Abe, she really didn't like being put on display but Abe was an old friend. That had been the strange thing about her dinner with David Gardiner. He didn't introduce her to anyone, he didn't seem to be looking about to see if anyone noticed he was sitting with the world renowned 'Dr. Farrington'. David just seemed to be enjoying her company.

In a quieter, more personal voice Abe continued. "So sorry you had to see Miakos make his last stand."

"Do you think it was suicide?" Freya asked.

Abe was still searching stacks of books, all with rubber banded papers showing the names of their owners to be. "What else could it be? Nick at *the Crab Claw* said Miakos was alone when he just got up and hopped off."

"Nick saw it?" Grace said eagerly.

"Nick had taken out the garbage and was stealing a smoke on the pier." Abe was studying yet another book that caught his interest.

"The police said that I was the only one who saw it." said an offended Grace.

"Naw. Two college kids were also out sailing. Didn't understand what they saw until later."

"The cops aren't checking hard enough," said Freya grimly. Grace was sure one policeman would be hearing about that!

But Abe was looking at her. "You found that new research head bludgeoned on the Octagon too?"

"Charles Marshall." Grace added. If you want information, you've got to give some, so Grace gave a full description of finding Marshall's body. She was aware Freya was listening intently.

Freya had obviously been curious, but would never have made Grace go over it again. To both of them Freya started asking. "Dr. Marshall had an assistant?"

The encyclopedic Abe answered. "Diandra Hollings. She's still registered at the Shoreline motel down by the town beach." He was digging deeper through the stacks of books that fortified his position. "Ahh! Freya, here it is." He handed her a oversized volume with a half built Viking craft on the cover.

As Freya studied her treasure, Abe talked more. He felt that Miakos was definitely a suicide, but no, he couldn't understand why a successful artist would kill himself. "He was just divorced, but that will–would--have only make him happier." And, no, Abe hadn't heard of any escaped maniacs in the area.

The tourist couple brought up several books to buy, and as Abe completed their sale, he continued talking to Grace and Freya. "Adam Greenfield has been in looking for a directory of scientists, trying to find a new Head of Research. He's in a blue funk." They talked for quite awhile, but Grace did not bring up the question of David Gardiner's marital status. Abe would know, he knew everybody, but maybe she just didn't want to know for sure right now.

When Freya and she finally left the store, Abe was buried back in his book. You could pass the store at two a.m. and sometimes the lights would still be on. Usually they parted here, Freya to walk home, Grace to go back to her car at the library, but Grace felt compelled to ask. "Freya, maybe we should pick up my car and I'll drive you back home."

"Why?"

"Well, there has been two deaths." Grace couldn't say the word murder.

"You sound like that fool son of mine! I do not need a babysitter. And neither do you." Freya drew herself up to her full six foot of height. "Anyone out there is going to be afraid of me. We took that women's defense course and we can both walk our selves home, quite nicely."

She started to turn away, when Grace put out a hand. "Freya, I like to know more about Miakos. Didn't you have a friend, that retired art critic for the *Times*?"

"Linda Hartz?"

"Could I meet her?"

"We hold Power Circles at Alma's house every third Tuesday of the month. That's this week. She's usually there. It would be a good way to meet her."

"Can you get me invited?"

"Of course. I'll pick you up at your condo, at six thirty tomorrow. Do remember this time."

Chapter 21

Rather than go right back to her condo, Grace stopped off at her lab. She was working longer hours but getting less done, with having nightmares of being arrested and obsessively thinking about her Suspect spreadsheet. Her famous concentration was suffering. Normally she would be pulling up her e-mails, instead her mind flooded with images: Marshall's bludgeoned head; Diandra's desperation; Katherine's cold determination to throw out her husband's work. Had Katherine killed her husband? Why now?

Grace pulled up her Suspects spread sheet again and added in the Pro Column several cells of her suppositions about Katherine. She added another row, 'Santeria Practitioners', then she felt like of fool for even putting that down. 'Motive', sacrificial need? 5%?; 'Means', local 5%. Could they have had some sort of mental control over Miakos? Forcing him to suicide? She put a weak 2 % in their 'Means' column. This was getting her nowhere, so she closed her Suspect spreadsheet.

She pulled up some minnow embryo experimental results and found she didn't have the patience to decode them. Closed that data spreadsheet and opened up her e-mails, quickly scanning the list. Something from Brian Kancir, she pulled it up. He had managed to arrange twenty minutes on next Monday, during a scheduled financial review at 10:25. Twenty minutes, that's all she and Kurt rated, but twenty minutes was a chance. She forwarded the e-mail to Kurt. She'd have to follow up to be sure he bothered to read it and hadn't hocked his laptop again.

Why had someone returned the boat that Marshall used to get to the Octagon? Were they in the same boat that took him out? If so, it was probably someone he knew and trusted. Grace gave up and pulled up the Murder Suspect's sheet again. No one theory popped as a viable premise to test, much less prove. When that happened with a line of study, she was forced to look farther afield, she must do that now. Widen the net.

Was Marshall killed because he interrupted a thief on the Octagon? Then why take his boat back? Enemies of Charles Marshall at his last position followed and killed him? There must be someone she could contact. His lab in Denver? Pasadena? She'd have Gail get her a copy of Marshall's biography. Grace looked down the Suspect spreadsheet of ORR people dealing with Marshall, there was someone–two someones-- missing.

Grace inserted two rows, for Stewart and Joyce Brewster. Motives: Marshall wanted their home and he had some secretive way of getting it. They had the Motive and Opportunity, but physically, was it possible? They were both in their eighties? Their total percentage was weak, but she should at least talk to them. She had to look their telephone number up. What would Grace say? *Last week did you guys skip the Golden Age Club to murder Dr. Marshall?* Grace remembered the three of them deep water fishing last summer. Stewart hauling in a fighting swordfish, stabbing it and fileting it and later Joyce firmly lifting the huge platter of fish steaks to the grill. These people were aged, not helpless.

You do not ignore data, no matter how improbable it may initially look, but she needed a reason to talk to them. Joyce was descended from an old, local family, and she volunteered at the small Whaling Museum. Joyce knew as much of local history as anybody, Grace could say she was researching this 'curse of the *Siren*'.

She called and the sweet voice of Joyce regretfully told her coffee at three Thursday was the earliest Grace could drop by. There was the bridge club, the church social, Strewart's golfing, Boater's lunch at the Neptune, Joyce's floral society. It seems two eighty year olds had a busier social schedule than she did. "Thursday it is. Thank you."

Again Grace returned to her Suspects spread sheet. She upped both Stewart's and Joyce's 'Means' by 5%. They certainly were getting around, but still thinking of them as murderers was ridiculous. She should head home.

A pinging noise and she checked her e-mail again. Kurt saying he would pick her up for that meeting at *Affiliated's* headquarters, Monday at 9:30. With the threat of Marshall gone, should they just forget about this sit down with Brian's people? Did they still need to go through with a study on a lobster anomaly they didn't have? Yhep. Bobby and his multiplying family needed a job, their laboratories needed funding, so she sent a confirming message to Brian Kancir.

But she still stared at that Suspect's sheet. Would the grant money come through before she was arrested for murder? Two murders? No witch's curse killed Miakos. No Santeria practitioner killed Miakos or Marshall, but it was too, too convenient that both Miakos and Marshall died on the Harbor that same day–or was Marshall the next day? He was found the next day but probably died the day before. When she found the body, why hadn't she had her wits about her and touched his skin to see how cold it was? The day Miakos died, Kurt had seen him alive on the water but, dead before Kurt returned to his house boat . She put a note in her 'To do' list: try and pin Kurt down more on timing.

At noise made her look up. She suddenly realized how dark it was getting, so much earlier. Her lab windows showed total blackness outside and the campus would be virtually empty now, but more foot falls outside in the foyer. Somebody outside her laboratory door. The foyer was dark, but she could see a figure–man or woman? Why at this time of night? Maybe they were going to another lab? No. The handle was turning on her door, someone was coming in and Grace found herself stiffening.

Chapter 22

Trying to remember Freya's empowering self defense courses, Grace grabbed for her car keys. Slipping each one between the fingers of her fist, for a makeshift weapon...

But a woman walked in–Grace breathed out in relief, no mad killer, only Diandra Hollings in a pale yellow jacket. With her characteristic hip swing, Marshall's assistant was walking over.

"Dr. Farrington."

"How you do?" That sounded silly, but Grace couldn't say she was happy to see Diandra. Why was she here?

"I've been interested in your work...for a long time." Diandra explained.

"Thank you."

"I've read your papers..." Diandra stopped, seemingly at loss for words. "And you do have books?"

"Yes, I do." Did she want a book signed? Diandra didn't have a book in her hand and she was just standing there awkwardly. Finally Grace continued, "My papers pretty much cover my theories."

"Well, actually I was wondering if you needed an associate–an assistant?"

That's what she was here for. And it must be hard for someone as proud as Diandra to have to beg for a job. "I'm so sorry. I have presently have two assistants." She thought of Bobby. "Actually three and that's about all my present grants will allow."

Diandra moved closer. "But I'm very good, I know you think I was just Charles'–that Charles hired me because of what I look like..."

"No. No." Actually, that's exactly what Grace thought but. "Being an attractive woman is not incompatible with being a good scientist."

"I've got a resume." She took a folded paper out of her

jacket pocket.

"But I'm not hiring at this time. I'm sorry." But since she just stood there, Grace relented and took what was three pages stapled together. "I'll keep it on file. If I run across something—I guess you are at liberty now."

Diandra twisted her lips. "Actually Adam persuaded Katherine Marshall to keep me on for three more months, to sort and pack Charles' papers. They do owe me something. Charles didn't give me a contract, but when I agreed to move here, he promised me employment. There's some talk of a library dedicated to him. I could curate that, but his widow doesn't really seem to be interested in financing his legacy. Katherine wanted me fired immediately, but Adam pointed out that donating her husband's papers might be some sort of income tax deduction."

Diandra stopped talking, Grace realized she had to say something. "Well posterity will make its own judgement on Charles Marshall's legacy. Now I think you have to focus on where your life is going." Grace briefly scanned Diandra's resume. Good schools, not bad grades, of course, Marshall liked his sex toys smart, but maybe she was doing Diandra a great disservice, thinking of her as the mistress? What if everyone believed Charles' lies about herself? Grace turned another page. The resume was well written and on heavy, ecru paper, bet Gail typed and printed this. But, outside of Diandra's graduate studies with Marshall, she really had no laboratory experience to offer, no publications and a single B.S. degree.

Diandra was watching her anxiously. "Perhaps if you let one of your assistants go?" She was really pleading–certainly not caring at all about whoever would be 'let go'.

"There's going to be nothing with me in the foreseeable future." Diandra's face looked so worn, Grace had to add, "But I am in daily contact with a number of laboratories, if I hear of anything, I'll let you know." She looked down at the resume. "You don't have an address here."

Diandra looked embarrassed. "It's the Shoreline Motel. I left it off."

"Ask Gail if you could use ORR, and she could forward it."

"Could you give me a letter of recommendation?" She looked hopeful.

"I haven't worked with you." And I think you're a bitch, Grace thought but amended. "I could say that I knew you as Dr. Marshall's assistant in the short time he was here."

She looked a little disappointed, but said, "That would be very kind."

"I'll drop it by Eric's lab."

"Thank you." She turned gracefully and left with a rhythmic swinging of her hips. If her next job interview was with a male she wouldn't be out of work long. And having had a bit of a scare Grace locked up and headed back to her condo. Outside the parking lot lights only accentuated the dark shadowy areas and as she walked to her condo Grace heard rustling to the side, the wind and leaves? Or a murderer stalking her? For the first time since she came to Oyster River, Grace was finding herself afraid.

Chapter 23

That Thursday morning dawned clear and a little warmer and Grace enjoyed the sea smell as she walked briskly past Eric's lab. Well, Eric's lab had become Marshall's lab, soon to be whose? When Eric died she left all the new director hunting to Adam. That had been a mistake, maybe she should try to provide some suitable candidates names? But who?

In her lab Grace just sat in front of her desk computer. This was getting her nowhere. She returned a phone call to Brazil. The gentlemen spoke English, but with a heavy accent that Grace could barely penetrate, and she may have helped him, she may have not. Anyway, it was a freebie. She had to concentrate on getting some money in. Grace must get into her work!

And she did, until finally feeling hungry, Grace looked about her lab. That east wall of empty tanks needed to be prepared for the affected lobsters they didn't have. It was 2:15 and she'd worked past lunch. The Brewsters! She was to be at their house at 3:00, Grace slipped on her jacket and headed outside. The harbor was almost still, with low green waves, while what little traffic the Main Road had was starting to build up. She decided to skip the car and head down to the docks. From the hillside she could see Kurt's sail boat home bobbed at anchor, but his yawl was out. Too bad, she was half hoping Kurt would be there and they could talk about the blue lobster project. Well she might see him when she got back.

A bit of wind blew from the land, blowing her short dark hair into her face. It was low tide, she could see lots of broken oyster shells at the high water line, must be a healthy community back in the depths. The little gray shingled guard booth was at the top of the Dock, before its gate that was always unlocked. ORR had talked about locking it after Marshall's death, but nobody had done anything. Inside the booth, she opened up a shallow wood cabinet that held racks of keys and she pulled out the set for 006, one of Oyster Rivers' yellow launch boats.

On a clip board, hanging from a nail there were sign-out sheets for ORR's motor boats, where everyone was supposed to log out, but usually didn't bother. Who had signed out the night Marshall had died? Grace looked at the lines above. The last two recent sign-outs were by obvious student groups, the rest were pre-Marshall's death. The boats had been going out, but everybody else was as lax as she had become. As an after thought she wrote the boat number, time, her name and destination on the sign-out sheet and picked up a pair of oar locks.

Not that anybody ever really bothered to check, Kurt was nominally in charge of the dock and research boats. He or his assistant kept the engines gassed and the hulls pumped out of rain fall, that was about it for supervision. Of course if Kurt went out the night Marshall was killed there wouldn't be any 'sign out' for his personal craft.

Low tide increased the angle of the ramp down to the floating docks as her footfalls thumped on metal grilling. She never got used to that bouncy feeling underfoot, it gave her a sense of unease. When she reached the wood floats, gold flecks sparkled in the green water below and the air had a diesel fuel and pleasant warm-mud smell. Grace unhooked the bow line of 006, or Betsy as she called her favorite launch. It was really a glorified rowboat, with a small out board engine attached and oars unshipped at the bottom of the boat. Grace got in and freed the stern line, then let the boat drift as she settled in on a hard plank seat by the engine. She checked the gas tank, full, Kurt was good about that. Grace gave a yank to the pull cord, nothing. She let it rewind and then really put her back into the pull.

The engine exploded to life with a cloud of blue smoke and rainbows of oil streaks on the water. Even at low tide she still had a foot and a half under the keel, as she turned the vibrating throttle handle to reverse, pulling her away from the dock. Once clear she shifted to forward, then opened up the engine to a low, steady push forward.

From years of practice Grace deftly cleared two other ORR boats and then Kurt's big sailboat. Opening the throttle more, she took a lazy arc out roughly following the harbor shore. To her right were thick, yellow-green marshes, where Oyster River emptied into the harbor from the Church lake dam. Beyond the marshes she could see traffic on the main road that ran in front of ORR. Her motoring disturbed an egret who unfolded his great, white wings and took flight. Gradually she swung southward, paralleling the houses and road that led to the little town of Oyster River Harbor.

Before the old harbor was a shore line of wooden houses, even a few pre-revolutionary ones like the Brewsters'. In that house, generations of the Joyce's family had lived and the thought that they would sell out because Marshall demanded it was ridiculous. Grace looked for a white shingled house, surrounded by clumps of flowers. With the exception of winter, Joyce always managed to have banks of lush yellow, purple, pink and white flowers in constant bloom.

Seeing the old windmill potting shed, Grace maneuvered alongside the Brewster's small dock. It was gray with wind and rotting at the edges, obviously needing some work, but then the Brewsters probably didn't use it much anymore. There was a small aluminum rowboat pulled up upside down on shore, but for fishing they took out their son-the-doctor's boat. As she tied up, Grace could see Joyce kneeling by one of the flower beds she was weeding. Finally looking up, Joyce waved and stiffly rose. As Grace was climbing up the slippery logs embedded in the grassy embankment, Joyce met her, bending down to scoop up a ball of black, white and orange fur. "Do you need a kitten, dear?"

"No, thank you."

"Be careful, there's five of them now, all running out

under your feet. The mother was pregnant when she appeared at our door in a rain storm, but I've already got three families willing to take her kittens. We'll have her neutered and keep her with the old gentlemen."

One of those 'old gentlemen,' or one of Joyce's tan pug dogs waddled after her.

As they started walking toward the house, Grace looked about. "It's beautiful here."

"Yes. Steward just laughed when your Dr. Marshall said he wanted us to move." She opened the Dutch door to the kitchen. "Steward! Grace is here."

Inside the kitchen, Grace smelled fresh brewed coffee and baking cookies as she followed Joyce past a wall hung with blue Danish Christmas plates. Joyce called out louder. "**Steward!**"

He was sitting reading a science journal in the living room by the bay window overlooking the Harbor. Joyce was almost shouting above him before he looked up. "**Steward! Grace is here!**"

Ever the gentlemen, he rose to greet Grace. With the exception of a few gray hairs at his temple Steward Brewster was bald, and like his wife, he was square faced, squared bodied. The fingers of his hands were thick, more like plumber's hands then what you would think of as a legendary scientist. He shook her hand warmly. "Good to see you again, dear."

Joyce left them saying. "I'll get the coffee."

Grace never liked the bitter taste of coffee, but she knew the Brewsters did, so she just settled comfortably in one of their over stuffed, pink floral patterned chairs.

"So how's the research?" Steward asked.

Grace found herself raising her voice at bit to compensate for the hearing problem Stewart claimed he didn't have. "Grants are a bit tight..." She searched for something interesting to tell him. "But I've got a French marine expedition that hopefully will be sending me some undersea, volcanic vent worms for DNA testing."

"Multi-celled organisms that never feel nor need the sun's light to survive? That can live off of sulfur compounds?" His face lit up. "That would be interesting! Can you keep me in the loop on those results?"

"Certainly. As soon as I get anything coded."

Stewart smiled widely. "Hear tell they're looking for a new Head of Research for Oyster River."

Grace nodded. "Yes."

"That Dr. Marshall didn't last long, but we were worried for you. Because of the trouble he gave you back in Pasadena."

Grace found herself staring at him in surprise. Had he known about that? In all the years she'd known and talked to the Brewsters, it was never mentioned. "I don't know what Eric said..."

"Eric didn't tell us. Remember, I was still accepted in the research community then, and we were a small group. Word preceded you, and, of course, without knowing you, we didn't know whose side was in the right. You claiming Marshall stole your research and him claiming you were a vindictive, ex-lover he dumped..."

"There was no affair!"

"Oh, we soon learned that." Stewart raised a dismissive hand. "You are not at all the trampy type, in fact you're too shy. Joyce is always trying to find someone for you..."

"If it's that hard, maybe she should give up?" Grace found speaking with Stewart was rather like talking with a beloved grandfather.

He studied the problem. "Well, for someone like you it is difficult. To find an unmarried man, comfortably near your level of intelligence. Then he has to be a man who is not threatened by a woman's acclaimed genius."

"Surprising I've had any relationships at all?" She said a bit tartly, mildly resenting any dissection of her personal life.

Stewart fixed her with a knowing look. "Dear, you don't meet men by hiding out in a laboratory all the time."

She continued. "My work is important to me. I don't have time to waste."

"You've just had bad luck. Joyce and I married young. Without her, I would have had a career in research, but I wouldn't have enjoyed it as much. Got my best ideas just bouncing them off her, even while she was trying to get some sleep."

"Not that I understood a bit of what he was talking about." Joyce was returning, carrying a tray with three steaming coffee cups and a plate of very dark, brown edged butter cookies. The cookies were in the shapes of little black eyed susans with chocolate shots for the dark center. "Left Steward to take them out of the oven for me. Shouldn't have."

He just smiled and picked up the most blackened one. "Can always eat the evidence!"

Joyce passed Grace a yellow pansy flowered pitcher of milk, saying gently, "So sorry to hear you weren't recognized by the Nobel committee again."

Stewart finished. "But you're very young, it's not everybody who becomes eligible at thirty and, since then, you've kept pushing out the limits. Forty-two is still a baby. You will be recognized and, hopefully, we'll be around to see it!"

That established, Grace took a few sips of her heavily creamed coffee before asking casually. "I can't understand why Dr. Marshall thought he could get you to sell this house?"

The Brewsters exchanged guarded looks, and then Joyce answered, "Yes, that foolish man did. He had the temerity to insist that we would sell to him."

Steward looked down at his almost finished coffee. "A most annoying man."

Joyce contemptuously continued. "He was going to help us get a mortgage on our next place. He suggested Hilton Head Island in South Carolina, although Abe at the bookstore said he wasn't offering enough to get us a house on the water. And us with mortgage! We inherited this house from my grand-aunt. It was built in the 1639 and it's never had a mortgage connected with it."

Steward laughed. "Marshall said he was doing us a favor. That down sizing would be easier for us when we lived in a condo with all the grounds taken care of."

"Those places only let you plant a tiny flower box by the door," Joyce added indignantly.

She wanted to keep them focused on Marshall. "Why did he think you would sell?"

Joyce spoke slowly. "There was that old scandal..."

Grace cut her off. "Which everyone knows about. It's alluded to on ORR's website. Marshall can't have believed that would bother you now?"

They again exchanged looks, probably deciding how much they wanted her to know. Finally, Joyce looked at her. "Then there is our youngest granddaughter, Faith."

Grace thought fast. "I wrote a letter of recommendation for her, for her graduate school, MIT?"

Joyce continued brightly. "Oh, yes. She's doing marvelously."

Stewart added. "But she was always planning to go for another degree. It's time she's working out problems on her own!"

Joyce looked directly at Grace. "Your Dr. Marshall knew of Faith and he knew Adam Greenfield had agreed to have her teach in January at Oyster River. Dr. Marshall said he had to 'approve' of Faith. He had her come all the way down from Boston last weekend, just to be judged by him." Joyce stopped and looked to Stewart. He became very involved with his next cookie choice.

Grace asked. "Did Charles Marshall threaten Faith? Or her career?"

Joyce looked directly at her, speaking very firmly. "It's over with, isn't it? That unpleasant man is dead, we still have our house and Faith will have her first teaching job. It's done."

Grace interrupted. "Adam would never have allowed Marshall to threaten Faith's job."

Joyce didn't seem so sure. "When Stewart told him that we didn't wish to sell, Dr. Marshall sent Adam here to try to convince us that selling would be best for us and the Institute. Adam even mentioned Faith, he looked so embarrassed and I was very ashamed for him. I don't know why he would have let Marshall use him, because Adam's always been so respectful of Stewart."

Grace could imagine what pressure Marshall put of the President of ORR. "Charles Marshall had a way of forcing people to do his bidding. But in time I think Adam would've stopped kowtowing."

Joyce was pouring her husband another cup of coffee. "When our granddaughter came down here last, she picked out one of the kittens to keep. So Dr. Marshall's demanding to see her worked out just fine. Now we can all forget about him." She looked to the windows. "We love having you here, but the tide will be turning and making it harder for you to go back across, so lets go outside. I want to cut you some flowers for you to take back home."

As Joyce cut a huge bouquet of blooms, a tan furred kitten playfully clawed at Grace's ankle. "Do be careful they don't get under your feet. Look at his pale blue eyes. We think the father is that unfriendly siamese next door, but only the one male looks siamese."

Grace picked up the kitten, it's tiny, sharp claws raked her hand, as she mused. "They've done a study concerning the fact that the male's genes seemingly dominate in their male off spring's looks."

"Oh, they've studied that have they?" Joyce asked.

"Yes. The hypothesis is if son looks like his father, the father is more likely to accept him as his own and protect the child and his mother. Natural selection at work via gene inheritance. "

Joyce stood up and moved to another banks of flowers. "Oh, dear, that sounds like 'breeding' thoughts, that we were so railed against in the Eugenics movement. The idea that you should care about what traits the parents will be passing on to their children. My, the pendulum does swing, doesn't it?"

Laden with three water filled coffee cans of mums and roses in the bottom of her boat, Grace opened the throttle and started motoring directly out into the Harbor. The wind and current pushed her slightly west and to starboard she could see the Octagon bobbing in the water. It looked like those yellow police site tapes were gone. Should she motor over and look at the death scene herself? No, she didn't feel up to looking at it again and the police must have found any clues.

Instead she reviewed her time with the Brewsters. They were certainly spry for eighty year olds, and they would never have been forced into selling, so no motive there. There might be some sort of weak motive for killing Marshall to protect their granddaughter, Faith. They both could certainly have piloted a motor boat, but all she saw in the yard was a small rowboat. And she couldn't see either of them with the energy to row over to the Octagon in the dark, much less attack Marshall. But they had the keys to their son's boat at the Marina.

Another line of research: Faith Brewster. She had been home that weekend and, in her twenties, she was strong enough to row a boat or sneak one out of ORR. If Marshall planned to use her to get her grandparents to move South and sell him their house, he would have turned on all his considerable, Nobel prize winning charm. He might have taken her out on to the Octagon or had her meet him there?

Did she go with him willingly, and then have to fight off rape? Did Faith accidentally kill him in self defense and then in panic motor away? Grace would have to put a new row on her murder suspect spreadsheet for 'Faith Brewster'.

Chapter 24

That evening when she picked Grace up at her condo, Freya was bubbling with happiness. "I contacted Evelyn Perkins."

As she settled into the passenger seat of Freya's old van, Grace looked at her. "Who is?"

"A well-to-do, old-family matron, who keeps up with everybody on the society pages, in the Northeast and Palm Beach."

"Why is that important?"

"You asked me to check out that new friend. Your Mr. David Edward Gardiner is not gay. He was married twice. First to the family maid, Lauren Murphy. They had daughter but divorced within a year, he got custody. Two years later, he married Sylvia Lasher of the Boston Lashers. They had twin boys who are now in college and it sounded like a very happy marriage until Sylvia died of cancer about a year ago." Finished Freya quite happily.

"He's not 'my David.'" Grace protested as Freya just kept driving, but like an idiot Grace continued. "Any proprietary girl friends?"

"Every available lady in the horsey set is hanging out for him–must make him gun shy. Has he called again?"

"No. And he probably won't, if I keep finding dead bodies."

"Maybe you should be calling him?"

"Is this Evelyn going to be here?"

"No."

"Good! Don't bring up his name or I'm leaving!"

With a wise smile on her face, Freya turned off the road on to a driveway that ran through a forest of slender, white birch trees. As the narrow, winding path approached Alma's house, the birches gave way to thickly planted greenish-black pines. They parked on a white gravel space, that opened up to surround a one story, Japanese style house and gardens with carefully placed stone lanterns. To the left a red wood foot bridge arched over a dark pond, while to their right 'causal' clumps of bamboo grew in front of worn water rock that formed miniature moss covered 'mountains'.

They entered the garden through a red, gracefully up swept Torii gate. Grace felt like she was walking through a calligraphied letter. Ahead was a black lacquered door, but to her right was inset a glassed atrium, with an internal garden of bonsai trees and a moss lined koi pond. Freya knocked and the black lacquered door was opened by a short, straight backed woman named Alma. She greeted them warmly, taking Grace's jacket and hanging it somewhere behind a door of black framed rice paper panels. Freya took off her light cape to reveal she was wearing a flamboyant yellow dragon embroidered kimono and as she swept into the main room the other five women seemed suitably impressed.

Grace noted the pale blue walls were hung with nubbed silk and they were decorated with sumi-e scrolls and colonial oil portraits. Alma's ancestors? The house wrapped around its atrium and she noted real flowers were arranged in the spare, oriental fashion about the rooms. Passing through the traditional living room and dining room, they walked out to a glass walled sun room over looking the arched bridge garden in the atrium.

On a oriental table in the sun room, Alma had set trays of bakery cookies. The others sat and talked as the hostess poured green tea in short, handle-less Chinese cups. Many of the other guests were giving Grace side long glances, making her feel like the prize pig at the county fair, but Freya had managed to seat Grace next to a small, silver haired lady, impeccably dressed in a navy pants suit with a bold scarlet-patterned silk scarf knotted loosely about her neck.

"Grace, this Linda Hartz. She been an art critic for years..."

"Retired now," smiled Linda.

"Grace was interested in knowing more about Miakos."

"Oh." Two bright hazel eyes studied her carefully. "You were the one who saw him jump?"

Grace nodded. "Yes."

"Was it an accident?"

"I don't think so."

Linda shook her head. "I can't understand that. I just can't ever see Miakos depriving the world of his magnificent presence."

"Was he depressed?"

She seemed to give the question some thought. "Not that I heard of. He was just divorced, but he was always finding some younger girl, marrying her and divorcing again."

"Maybe she got a large settlement?"

"Oh, no, dear. Since the '80's, he's been getting steel clad prenuptials."

"Who will inherit?" asked Grace curiously.

Linda had to think about that. "I have no idea. With all his women, I don't think he ever had children. The current divorce has gone through. I assume he had his lawyer set up a trust to perpetuate his life work, in some sort of museum, maybe...Miakos wasn't a great planner."

"Isn't his work in the museums?"

"His 'Grotesque Animalism' was in some prestigious shows, but not the permanent collections." Linda wrinkled her nose in distaste. "I never liked those urine sponges of his."

"Oh, yes."

"Neither did the Rockefeller girls."

"The Rockefellers?"

"It's a generic term for the people–mostly young women–who administer the large trusts, the ones that buy artists' work for the permanent museum collections. The 'girls' are mostly unknown, but they are the critics that really count. With such a dramatic death, I am sure they are scooping him up right now. Remember he's an elder statesman in the art world."

"The papers said he was only sixty-eight?"

"Oh, they go from progressive young turks to elder statesmen so fast today."

"Could he have been blackmailed? Say someone threatened to expose a love affair?"

Linda laughed at the thought. "If someone had tried, Miakos would have just called a press conference. He reveled in notoriety."

"Do you think he had money problems?"

"I don't know, really. He lived quietly in that shack of a studio. Give him a hunk bread and a jug of raw ouzo, and Miakos was happy. His last ex was a waitress before they married and, living with Miakos, she probably didn't have the time to develop really expensive tastes."

"He was having a show at the Gull's Eye Gallery. That's kind of a small venue, far from the City?"

"Oyster River was his home. He's been friends with the Ingersols for years so, of course, he had to show in their gallery at least once a year. With his reputation and the Gull's Eye's Internet exposure he could expect sales as good as he would have gotten in New York."

After a time the hostess left and came back carrying in a small, rectangular wooden box that was carved deeply and inlaid with mother of pearl in an Islamic floral style. Alma announced, "This year closes with the Fall equinox. Samhain draws nearer. For the coming Wiccan year, we must ask the spirits' direction for our highest destiny." She turned and stood before Freya.

Freya's lifted her voice. "We ask for guidance. For mercy. For the rich unfolding of the creative spirit within. May we know the prosperous path that the wise ones would choose for us." Her sonorous tones enveloped the room and several of the women folded their hands and bowed their heads.

Then one by one, the hostess passed among them holding out her box. Each woman reached in for a small roll of paper, tied with a thin, blue silk ribbon. With trembling fingers, a twenty year old opened her scroll, happily reading out loud. "'Unity of purpose'. Alex is going to propose."

Smilingly and nodding Freya pronounced. "I see a three. Three days, three weeks, or three months."

Unrolling hers, Linda laughed. "Patience. At seventy-one, what else can I have?"

When Alama stood before her, Freya adjusting the kimonos' voluminous sleeves and reached into the box, letting her fingers drift slowly among the rolls. Selecting a roll, she held it up, theatrically cocked her head to the side, and then shaking her head, she returned the roll unopened into the box. The hostess stood waiting patiently as if she expected this would take some time. Freya reached in again, closing her eyes in concentration as she lightly touched each of the rolls before finally withdrawing one. Everyone waited as she opened hers, and unrolling it carefully, she allowed a smile to spread across her face. "Yes," she announced grandly. "'Abundance'. My new book *More Hauntings of Oyster River Harbor* will be completed shortly and sell well."

"Very good," said a tall, yellow-haired woman.

The hostess smiled, and then walked to Grace, who had not expected to be included. As always, Grace preferred a watching, studying stance, but it seemed impolite to refuse. She reached down into the small casket and her fingers felt a number of paper roles still inside. Had more people been expected? Or were extra rolls put in to give fate more of a chance? Grace pulled one out, unrolled it and read out loud. "Enlightenment."

The others noted sagely as the hostess commented, "You will be drawn to the spiritual."

"No." The young girl seemed excited. "She will be

making more discoveries with her science!"

Grace smiled politely as never one to be out done, Freya had to push it. "She will discover who murdered Dr. Marshall and why Miakos died."

A sweet faced, heavy set blonde woman sighed. "Oh, that was so tragic, Miakos' drowning. Such a successful artist–for the world, such a loss."

A tiny, thin woman looked up. "Do you believe that the curse of the widow lured him to his death, Dr. Farrington?"

"No." Grace said.

Linda nodded her approval at Grace's negative answer, then said, "And Dr. Marshall, a Nobel Scientist, another great loss."

They all nodded and the young girl looked to Freya. "We should ask him who was his murderer."

Grace looked at her strangely. "He's dead."

"Freya could contact him–in a seance."

Several of the others excitedly agreed. "Yes, a seance!"

They looked to Freya as Grace tried not to glance down at her watch. She'd had enough of green tea and spirits for the night. But the hostess was leading them back to the dining room. The others seemed accustomed to this as they moved two more chairs to the dining table and started to sit down, saving the position at the head for Freya. Grace found herself sitting opposite to her friend, able to observe the whole table easily.

Alma carried in a large silver tray from her butler's pantry. On it were ten or more mismatched candle holders in pewter, glass, silver and brass. All were fitted with a single, white candle. She stopped before each person, who selected one and placed it on the table before her. Grace too selected a candle holder, hers was an uncoiling, brass dragon. Freya sat with closed eyes; her palms pressed down on the polished walnut table. The hostess took a firewand and lit each of the candles before she, too, sat down.

They all sat patiently, no one speaking. After a few minutes, Freya still with mediation closed eyes, reached out her hands and those sitting next to her took her hand, then reached out to the person next to them. Grace found herself holding the dry, but strong hand of Linda Hartz and the nervously wet hand of the twenty year old. When they joined hands, there was a faint twinge, like a tiny electrical charge. Silently, Linda guided Grace to lower their hands, so that even as they remained clasped, they were resting on the cool wood table.

Freya began to hum softly, then announced. "We think a white light about this circle. We ask for protection by our guiding spirits. Blessedness." She was silent for several long minutes, then in a deeper voice she asked. "Will the soul of Charles Marshall join us this night? We quest for truth."

Again a long silence, no one seemed to be impatient, most just sat holding hands, with closed eyes. Waiting, Grace found herself feeling awkward. She also seemed to sense an energy–a low current traveling from hand to hand. Was real or imagined? She would love to get an electroencephalogram measuring brain activity on each person during a circle like this. Could she get portable EEG units from the hospital or maybe the University lab?

Finally Freya spoke in her deepest voice. "There's a spirit here. A short woman. Her hair in a bun, flour on her hands...she cooks for a living..."

The curly-haired blonde responded quickly. "That's my grandmother. She was a cook at Low Heywood girls' school."

"I see the initial P–that's not her name...A place?"

"She was born in Pennsylvania and buried back there. Grandma's name was Eileen. I'm named after her."

"Your grandmother's worried about you, concerned

about you being alone, depressed. She says you'll meet someone shortly...on the new job you'll be getting." The blonde woman leaned back, with a happy smile on her face.

More silence.

A thin, brown haired woman spoke. "What about Dr. Marshall? Is he here?"

Eyes still closed, Freya took a deep breath, only to shake her head no. Again silence, and then. "Grace." When she spoke, Freya sounded surprised, "There is a presence here–for you. A young woman. You were beside her when she passed over. You gave her strength. She can't understand what happened. She doesn't know why? Why she is no longer. *Carlos no vino. Hace tanto frio...No entiendo.*

Grace recognized the words. Spanish. She silently translated them: *Carlos didn't come. It's so cold. I don't understand.*

Others at the table were looking to Grace and she had no idea why Freya was making all this up?

Chapter 25

More silence, then Freya opened her eyes and straightened up in her chair. "I'm sorry, we're finished. My shoulder is hurting, and I'm very tired."

Obviously disappointed, the hostess smiled. "We must do this again."

Polite leavings and then they were walking to Freya's car. Curious, Grace asked. "Why did you try to talk with Charles Marshall?"

"You do want to know who killed him don't you?"

"Certainly, but not through a seance. You make that up."

Eyes showing hurt, Freya stared at her. "I don't 'make' anything up..."

"I'm sorry. I know you don't lie!" Grace found herself fumbling, knowing she was hurting her friend. "But if your subconscious mind has no knowledge of the murderer of Marshall, it can't provide anything more than what your conscious mind already knows."

"The spirits aren't my subconscious mind playing tricks," Freya said angrily as they got into the car. "Your Popcorn Gene Switch theory, did you 'know it' consciously before your subconscious handed it to you? You said you first saw it in a dream."

"Yes. I had a dream, where I was teaching at a university forum. But in that case my subconscious mind synthesized my conscious mind's knowledge, re-configuring it."

"Only that?" There was a touch of frost in Freya's voice as she pulled out of the driveway.

Grace wished she'd never said anything. "You're correct. The conscious mind had the data, my unconscious drew a conclusion that the conscious mind could hammer into a theory, that could be tested. It's is a form of mental mathematics, where the sum of the parts are less than the sum of the whole."

"My psychic awareness is from the spirits beyond my perception." Freya's voice was uncompromising.

Grace found herself tightening her lips, this conversation was not going well.

Freya continued. "Sometimes, I know something that I should have had no way of knowing. Right now I know you are in danger, but not from the police, not from where you would expect..."

"The stuff about the blonde haired woman and her grandmother?"

Freya looked slightly ashamed. "Eileen's boyfriend broke off a two year engagement at the same time she lost her job. She's having a terrible time and needs a little something to hope for, but that doesn't negate the rest of it!"

"That message from some woman speaking Spanish, do I need encouragement too?"

Freya sighed and then spoke distantly. "No. I do know the police will not solve Marshall's death. You will." At a stop light, she seemed to shake herself slightly, and turned back to Grace. "I don't know how."

"But you couldn't contact the ghost..."

"The spirit."

"Of Charles Marshall."

"Grace, it's not like dialing in an area code and waiting for someone to answer. Marshall probably doesn't even know he's dead yet!" Freya was driving again, but seemed more preoccupied by their conversation. "When it's a fast, unexpected death, they don't know sometimes..."

Grace tried to take a less abrasive approach, "The 'Spanish spirit' of the woman calling out to me–drawing energy from me–why did you make that up?"

"I didn't make any of it up about you!" Again Freya seemed to slip into that far away look. "The girl–she was murdered–she is connected to all of you, in a web none of you can get free of."

"What?"

"I don't know." Freya shook her head as she made a left turn. "Write down what I said and it will make sense later. The weirder it is, the more sense it makes later." Freya concentrated on passing a car.

"Who is she?"

"Who?"

"The Spanish speaking woman. It was a woman, wasn't it?"

Freya seemed to look far off in to the distance. "Yes. A young woman."

"Who was she?" Grace asked.

"I don't know, but you should."

"I should?"

"She was very close to you, when she was dying, she reached out" Freya frowned with concentration. "Your spirit gave her the energy you had, but it wasn't enough to keep her here." Freya pulled up in front of Grace's condo and didn't say anything more as Grace got out.

Grace didn't believe in psychic energies and Tarot cards and spirits, but she had long ago accepted the fact that to Freya they were reality. Freya and Grace only disagreed where Grace considered it a religion and Freya considered her contacts with the spirits as scientific study. But as Grace faced the police the next day she realized Freya would be a lot easier to talk away the scientific basis of spiritualism if the 'spirits' weren't at times so perversely right.

Chapter 26

It was just after dawn, but she could hear angry words coming from the Jamisons' condo. Grace first heard them at the top of the landing as she headed downstairs. The strain of Sara's pregnancy or Bobby's job loss, or both? Grace moved to their door, then hesitated. It was really none of her business. More muffled angry words. Had Sara told Bobby it was going to be twins? If not, Grace would have to be careful.

She knocked lightly at the door and the raised voices silenced. Grace wondered if she should knock again, but Bobby opened the door. Brightly Grace pushed past him walking towards the living room. Bobby hadn't shaved, maybe for a day or so. Sara looked red in the face but with her pimply pregnancy mask it would be hard to tell if she had been crying.

"Hi." Grace started when nobody asked her to sit down. "It's early to be up."

Bobby looked ruefully away. "Specially when you don't have a job to go to."

Sara was spoiling for a fight. "Especially when we should be packing..."

The fighting was what Grace wanted to stop. "Well–that's what I was going to talk to you about. You know Kurt hurt his arm?"

Kind Sara was instantly concerned. "No. What happened?"

"A wheel kicked back or something, but he's having a terrible time trying to take the yawl out with one arm. Maybe if Bobby could help him?"

Bobby shook his head. "We've got to pack..."

Sara disagreed. "He's a friend who needs your help!" She looked to Grace. "He'll go now!"

Bobby did not look like he was going anywhere. "You're barfing all over, Ginjer's got a cold, I've got no job and we have to pack to move. I can't take time out to help Kurt!"

"I'm the one who's packing! You're just playing with Ginjer."

They were locked back in their private war, this wasn't what Grace wanted to happen, she cut in fast. "You may not have to move or Adam might find you another place and he's looking. Bobby, you'll just keep teaching. "

Bobby shook his head. "With Marshall dead, they've suspended the teaching schedule."

Grace shook her head. "That's changing. I--you and me will be teaching Eric's classes as before, which means you'll get half your salary. As for losing this condo to Diandra Hollings, with Marshall gone, she's probably not going to stay. I'm still speaking with Adam about the condo, but there's something else, a possible grant you could be hired under." She finished positively, "Kurt and I are trying to sell a marine study that would pay the other half of your salary for at least six months, maybe longer. Bobby, have you ever scuba dived?"

He shook his head. Sara looked stricken. "Scuba? Underwater? That's dangerous! The Sound is too cold to swim and it's almost winter." She looked to her husband. "That man went into the Harbor and drown!"

But Bobby had caught Grace's enthusiasm. "I've never scubaed. But I was on the swim team in High School, I've dived, I've snorkeled and I'm a fast learner!"

Grace spoke apologetically. "This whole grant hangs on Kurt being able to find a strain of blue infected lobsters."

Bobby was turning away. "Okay. If I'm helping Kurt in the morning and teaching in the afternoon, I gotta get dressed. Shaved."

A conflicted Sara looked to Grace. "That man in Harbor just drowned in that water."

"He couldn't swim, Bobby can."

"But.."

"They wear rubber suits--wet suits--to stay warm. You know Kurt wouldn't let anything happen to Bobby."

That last seemed to reassure her a little, so Sara reluctantly nodded. Grace gave her a confident smile and left, unfortunately not feeling as confident about Kurt being a sensible protector.

Back in her lab she finally managed a few productive hours, before a buzz from her laboratory doorbell. With Marshall about she had started locking herself in. As she walked to open it she realized that with Marshall gone, she no longer had to do that. She unlocked the door to see the Mac, tall in his tan police uniform. He started immediately. "Grace, you don't have to talk to me. Your lawyer wouldn't want you to!"

Grace swung the door open. "Come in. I'll talk to you about anything you want, but I don't know anything more about Marshall's death. "

He actually sighed. "It isn't about Marshall. Do you know a Gigi Ramirez ?"

"Who?"

"Gigi Ramirez ?"

"Mac, you know I'm terrible on names and faces."

"She's a new undergraduate student at Oyster River."

"What does she look like?" Grace wanted to get back to her work.

He hesitated as if deciding whether he should answer that or not. "Gigi Ramirez. That name doesn't sound familiar at all?"

"No."

"She apparently rented a house in town and signed up after the semester started."

"Rented a house? Were the dorm buildings full?"

Mac tried to look professional. "How about letting me ask the questions?"

This apparently was a police matter. "Okay. I don't know who you are talking about. She could be student here. You know I don't teach–well, that is changing–but unless a class is assigned to collect specimens for me, I don't socialize with the Oyster River student body. I don't have the time."

"And you're shy." He finished.

"I am not shy! That's your mother's incorrect hypothesis!"

"Okay. Were you out running by the library?"

"No."

He looked at her strangely. "You weren't?"

"No. Today I was..."

"This would have a while ago. We're not quite sure of the exact time, the body is too degraded. She was last seen alive on October 11th or 12th."

"The 12th was the day Miakos suicided?"

He was looking at his note book. "Bobby Jamison was her instructor and he last saw her in class on the 11th or the 12th. He wasn't all too sure, since new students drop out all the time and you guys don't take attendance, so he said it might've been later or earlier. Not much help."

"Is she dead? You're talking to Bobby as a policeman? Maybe he should get a lawyer?"

"Grace, stop trying to save the world, start thinking about yourself! Did you see her at all when you were running?"

"I don't think so. Certainly not dead..."

Mac shook his head. "Freya is all excited. Yelling that it must have been the day of Miakos death or Marshall's. You know the 'curse of the three'?"

"Why didn't they find her sooner?"

"Folks smelled it, but didn't investigate and didn't call us." He looked over his shoulder, as if expecting someone to follow him. "Please, Grace, try to remember. Did you run in the morning around that time?"

"It's been so crazy. This month, I have been running and I do the roads alongside the library a lot. Actually, I think I did, both the morning of the day Miakos jumped in to the harbor and the day before...why is it important?"

He looked away from her, instead he looked about her lab. "You were seen. Several times."

"Doing what?"

"Running near the library down the road to the propane tanks."

"So, I was there. Is that important?"

Mac was avoiding her eyes. "A driver for the propane company described you and says he waved to you."

"He probably did and I probably waved back. So?"

"Ms. Ramirez's body was found on the grounds of the Jones house."

"Jones House?"

"The white one on the fish pond near the bridge, opposite the Library park."

"This wasn't a natural death?"

"No. I'm studying for the sergeant's exam and I've got three dead people on my hands and my mother's getting all excited about some curse '*on the three brothers and their ship*'."

"How was this Gigi killed?" And would she be blamed?

He stood there for a moment, then said, "It's better you don't know." Mac looked to the door then back to her. "Look. I figured who you were from the driver's description, but he'd already guessed at your name. You're pretty well known around here. So as a police officer I came here, and I immediately questioned you. You told me you had been running around that time, but you weren't positive on the dates and you saw nothing unusual. You stated that you might have seen a woman named Gigi Ramirez on campus, since I told you she was a student at Oyster River, but that you did not recognize the name or know what she looks like. You're going to stick to that, right?"

He was rehearsing her. "It's the truth." she said.

"You will be questioned by State Police Detectives probably this afternoon. Stick to what you said and refuse to talk with them until your lawyer's present. You'll be okay."

"Bobby?"

"Don't worry about Bobby! They're not going after him." Having obviously deposed of a despised task, Mac turned and left.

She closed the door behind him, remembering the old axiom ' *to be forewarned, is to be forearmed*', but at the moment she felt totally defenseless. She'd have to call David's lawyer's nephew, what was his name? What was David's lawyer's name? Didn't she have his card?

She glanced around her desk, it had been in her jacket pocket, she probably had dumped it out on her desk at home. God, at this rate, she was never going to get any work done, but it would be worse if she wound up in jail. Her two assistants were coming in. "Inger, if anybody asks for me, I'll be at my condo." Grace set Inger to disinfecting the east wall of tanks, and Nick to going down to haul water at high tide to prepare a bank of specimen tanks for blue fungused lobsters, that they didn't have.

Back in her condo Grace began searching with an increasing anxiety, what was that lawyer's name? Alan Goldstein? She googled the name and found nothing. Then she looked in the phone book; lots of lawyers but none that she recognized. She could call David Gardiner and ask him, but she just didn't want sound like such a complete idiot. Grace keep pulling out drawers. Finally, in the kitchen junk drawer she found a simple, embossed card for Alan Silverstein, Esq. Grace dialed the number.

A woman answered melodiously. "Jones, Durham, and Silverstein."

"My name is Grace Farrington. I met Mr. Silverstein, recently, Alan Silverstein., and he mentioned a nephew of his who is a criminal attorney?"

"Mark Silverstein?"

"That sounds like it. Yes. Do you have a telephone number for him?"

"He's in this office, I'll transfer you." She sounded happy Mark had a client.

As Grace waited, her hands were sweating. She didn't do anything, why was she so afraid of the authorities?

"Mark Silverstein." A friendly sounding young male answered.

"My name is Grace Farrington. I met your uncle..."

"Uncle Alan. He mentioned your problem. I would be interested in talking to you, just to get all the background details. Maybe we can get together some day..."

"The police are coming."

"What? No, the question I should ask is why?"

"Probably to question me about a third dead body."

"How do you know this?"

She didn't want to get Mac in trouble. "A friend."

"How does did this 'friend' know about a dead body?"

"He works with the police."

"Doing what?"

"I rather not say." She was a mess and this wasn't helping anything.

There was a short silence, then the friendly young voice, got harder. "Ms. Farrington..."

She regretted his formal tone. "Grace. Please."

"Grace, as my uncle explained to you, hiding something from your lawyer is a lot like concealing your symptoms from your doctor. In the long run, you're the one who is going to suffer."

"A local policeman is named Mac Dell. Actually his name is Thor Dell. He prefers to be called "Mac". He's the son of my friend, Freya."

"Freya. That's how he wound up with a name like Thor."

"I've known him since he was a kid and I don't want to get him in trouble."

"He contacted you?"

"Mac said he was going to tell the detectives that he spoke to me."

"Okay. He's keeping it above board."

"He recognized me from the witness description..."

"There's a witness? Great." He didn't sound happy.

Grace felt so helpless. "All he witnessed was that I was running on a public road, alongside the property where they found the body. I often run there to exercise, it's a dead end street, no real traffic, so a lot of people run there."

"Did you see the body?"

"No."

"Good."

"Did you have any relationship with this body?"

"I don't even know who she is! Mac said her name was Gigi Rameriz and that she is a student here at ORR–Oyster River Research Institute."

"Is that large school?"

"No. Just a handful of students taking advanced courses in cell theory or marine biology, but I usually don't deal with them. And even if I did, I am terrible with names and faces and I don't care who is a student here..." Her voice was taking on an edge of hysteria. She stopped talking.

"Grace, where are you?"

"My condo."

"I'll need the address."

"They're probably coming here, shouldn't I go to you?"

"You'll have to talk to them some time. It is just important that you do it with me."

"There's nothing to say."

"Then you say that, but didn't you say she was supposed to be a student there?"

"I'm not good with names or faces. I'm not a people person, but she might have a book signed by me."

"How did that happen?" He always seemed to have a neutral, evaluating tone, as if trying to decide if she was telling the truth or not.

"Students are always bringing up one of my books for me to sign. I smile and ask their name and then write it to them."

"You signed a book for this Gigi?"

"I've signed four or five books this semester, it could have been for Godzilla, for all I know." This whole thing was getting her angry.

He sighed. " Don't say anything until I get there. "

"What if they come to the door?"

"Don't open it."

"Can't they break it down?"

"Not unless they have a warrant. I don't think they will."

"But if they do?"

"Lay down in your bed and say you were sleeping through the knocking. Just give me the address. I'll be there soon."

"Wait! What do you charge for a home visit?"

"Initial consultation is free. We'll work out the rest." He hung up.

Nervously Grace walked around her darkened condo. The curtains Kurt closed still shut the light and her view of the harbor, but she couldn't face opening them, so she just turned on the condo lights. All this time wasted, she should be in her lab working! Trying for control, Grace sat down and turned on her laptop and started running through her e-mail. A colleague in Brazil was trying to produce black orchids, but when he bred darker to darker, he got white flowers. Why? Grace typed him a short version of genetic switches interfering with each other, and then tried to think of a possible fix for him.

No buzz from the lobby door, just a brief knock on her front door. Grace went over and stood there, unsure of what to do, then she heard a voice. "Grace, it's Mark Silverstein." She opened the door.

Mark Silverstein was younger, shorter, and slimmer version of Alan with tanned skin and thick, neat, black hair. He had a quiet, unassuming smile, but a serious look about his brown eyes. They talked. If it came to a court case with Marshall, they discussed fees. Mark prepared her with several possible questions the police might ask her. It was three p.m., then four and Mark told her about his father and his uncle, both lawyers. He talked about his first job at sixteen, a beach guard. At five p.m., they started dinner, a chicken stir fry with her frozen vegetables and they were just sitting down to eat when the lobby door buzzer sounded.

Grace answered the intercom to Detective Noonan. She buzzed them up. Carrying their uneaten plates to her kitchenette sink, Mark just smiled. "Show time. Try not to volunteer anything."

This time it was Detective Noonan and Detective Urzi, without Mac. "Dr. Farrington?"

Mark reached out to shake his hand. "Mark Silverstein. Doctor Farrington's counsel."

Both detectives seemed to be unhappy about this, but Mark just turned and indicated Grace's couch and chairs. Noonan sat down, while Urzi just stood.

Noonan started off. "I understand Officer Dell has already questioned you?"

Grace thanked God Mark was there. "He didn't say much."

"A young woman's body has been found."

"What has that to do with me?" she asked levelly.

"You were on the library road, near where she was found."

"I run on that road all the time. So do a lot of other people, it's a public road." She realized she was sounding stressed.

"But you live here and you run all the way over there?"

"The Main Road here is narrow with traffic, while the one by the library is a dead end. I usually drive over, park and then run." They were silent, waiting for something else, so she nervously continued. "Often I stop at the deli and pick up a paper and danish before I go to my lab."

"You run at seven a.m.?"

"Before I go to my lab. It clears my mind."

"Did you know the victim?"

"I don't think so. I've talked to a woman cutting rose bushes there."

"What did she look like?" Noonan asked.

Grace shrugged. "Nice. In her fifties..."

The other detective stated, "This was a young woman, probably in her twenties, thirties at the most, apparently renting that house."

"As I've told you before, I'm not to good with names and faces. Mac..."

"Mac?"

Grace silently cursed herself for the slip. "Officer Dell, our local policeman, said her name was Gigi something or other and that she was a student here. I am sure she was, but I didn't work with her. That's all I know."

"But the day after you saw Miakos' suicide, probably the day you discovered Charles Marshall's murdered body, you were running alongside the lawn where this girl died and you say you know nothing about her?"

Grace stopped, not quite comprehending. "None of those deaths have anything to do with me."

The two policemen exchanged looks. "Then you are

saying that she was a student here, yet you don't know this woman?"

"We have students coming and going all the time. This Gigi could be eating breakfast in the cafeteria, alongside me; lining up to get a book signed by me; or taking my parking spot, but to be honest with you, I just don't remember her. Do you have a picture?"

Urzi looked to Noonan. Detective Noonan just shook his head. "That's not necessary at this time."

But as Grace thought about it. "If she was murdered–she was murdered wasn't she?" Mark, the lawyer, closed his eyes in sudden pain, but Grace continued. "If she died near the day Miakos committed suicide, perhaps he was involved? Maybe he tired to rape her? She fought back and he killed her, then realizing what he had done, he jumped into the harbor?"

Detective Noonan just said. "Uh huh. So you think that is what happened?"

She felt that was a trap. "I really have no idea."

The standing detectives spoke. "You were around three deaths. That's quite coincidence, isn't it?"

Grace chose not to answer.

Detective Urzi leaned forward. "You know, no one else seems to have seen Miakos's suicide. How can you explain that?"

"Actually several people saw Miakos' death! Speak to Abe at the book store. He'll tell you their names." Grace let a little frost go into her voice. "Perhaps by spending all your time questioning me, you're missing other possible witnesses who actually saw something?"

Both detectives exchanged looks and then looked from her to Mark.

Her lawyer took that as a cue. "Do you have any other questions for Dr. Farrington?"

Detective Noonan stood up. "If we do, we'll be in

touch."

Mark walked the detectives to the door. Grace just sat on the couch, until he came back. "Didn't do such a great job, did I?" She said.

"Well, I doubt whether you raised Officer Mac Dell's stock, but if you have told me everything, I think you're okay." She mildly resented the *'If you've told me everything.'* But he was continuing. "It sounds like they have nothing and are just stomping the bushes trying to flush a pheasant. Any pheasant." He picked up his jacket and sounded reassuring as he said, "Give me a call if they contact you again, but I think you're in the clear."

After he left, Grace had more time to think. Kurt found Marshall's body with her, but they weren't questioning him. Bobby knew Gigi, he was her instructor, yet the police weren't going after him. They kept questioning her. Grace sat quietly for awhile, trying to get up the energy to work on her e-mails. Instead she just found herself staring at those closed drapes.

Finally, she got up and made herself some raspberry tea. She looked to the clock, 7:35, soon it would be sunset. The drapes were still closed. Somehow, by opening them, she felt she would see that man jumping off the boat again, see the door of the Octagon wedged against Marshall's body.

She couldn't live this way. Determinedly, Grace carried her tea back across her living room and, setting the cup down on her desk, she walked to the wall and started pulling the drapery cords. She would live here and she would view her harbor.

Orangey sky with banks of dark clouds and water glinting with dancing golden reflections. Grace picked up the tea and let herself out on to the deck, finding soft sea breezes cooled her. So she ran along the road by the library, that didn't make her a killer. And, as she quietly drank her tea, she realized that another person regularly ran along that road by the library, Bobby Jamison. Bobby, whose wife said he hadn't slept at home that night of Marshall's death.

Chapter 27

Even working Saturday and Sunday Grace felt she was way behind, yet Monday she found herself pulling up her 'Suspects' spreadsheet again. She added a heading for "Gigi", with columns under her name for 'Motive, Means, Opportunity, Pro, 'Cons' and 'Total', then Grace went down the list. From the way the police were questioning her suicide seemed out of the question.

In Gigi's death she had no motives for Kurt, Katherine, Diandra or Adam. For the 'Opportunity' column, she had to put a possible for Bobby. He ran in that area and, after his fight with Sara, he left the house and didn't come home that night. Maybe a Motive: he worked with the students, but why would he possibly want to kill Gigi? Some men, when their wife was pregnant, slept around. But Bobby? No!

Again 'Random Madman' seemed to be the best shot, Grace gave him/her a 98%, but Random Madman was the one the police were least likely to be able to track down. Frustrated she returned to the pacifier of her research work. Which didn't go well that day.

The next day the appointment at *Affiliated* also couldn't have gone worse. As usual, she had forgotten the time and the day until Kurt burst into her lab. "Hurry up, lady. We're due at *Affiliated* in twenty minutes!"

She looked for her hand bag and realized it was home. She had planned to go back to the condo and refresh herself before the appointment. "I have to change!"

"No time! We're going to be late, lady!"

Outside she saw he had parked his motorcycle in the handicapped spot at the curb.

"Where's your truck?"

"Cain't afford the transmission repairs." He was rapidly looking around. "Where's your hatchback?"

"Lent it to Sara."

He shook his head in disgust. "Jes get on."

Thank god she usually wore pants. She climbed on the big Harley behind him and ran her arms around his waist as he strapped his visored helmet on. She didn't have a helmet and figured that might be against the law. Her hands were resting lightly on his waist as he kicked the stand free and gunned the engine. When he started off, she found herself sliding off the back of the bike. He had to stop at the main road, so she pushed forward closer to him and grabbed hold of his trunk desperately, with spread, clutching fingers.

On the back roads, Kurt raced to make up for lost time, on no-pass roads he passed over the solid yellow line and kept going. As Grace had to mimic his weight shifts, she was terrified that if she leaned too much in one direction she would overturn them both. Even with a helmet she doubted she could survive a fall at these speeds–at least she thought they were going fast, until Kurt hit I-95. There he had three lanes to dodge and weave making his own road between cars, and pulling away from trucks going seventy miles an hour. When they pulled into *Affiliated*'s parking area, she was wind-burned, sweat-wet and shaking from sheer terror.

Kurt laughed. "I'm gonna have bruises from your grasping fingers for weeks!"

Grace tried to brush back her hair, no comb, no lipstick, nothing. She was still trembling, as she tried to quiet her mind when they walked into the imposing five story lobby of chrome and glass, complete with a hanging three story, gray shard mobile. Like he owned the place, Kurt marched up to the desk. "Dr. MacKay and Dr. Farrington. I believe we're expected."

They were. A respectful Brian Kancir came down to the lobby and ushered them into the elevator for the third floor conference room. Three men were already there, obviously in some kind of financial discussions, with spreadsheets and charts before them. These papers were carefully concealed in folders as Grace and Kurt entered and sat down.

The meeting was short and sweet and unproductive. Brian had printed out her e-mailed proposal and had it bound in blue covers, which he passed out to everyone there. Kurt and Grace were introduced to a white haired CFO, a young engineer type and a man at the head of table, thirty–to--forty, with red hair.

The young engineer started the inquisition. "Why should we be interested in what you've found?"

Kurt was all business. "It's a lobster fungus or growth that excretes a substance that has remarkable skin softening qualities."

The engineer asked. "Do you have any samples?"

"Not at this time. The original samples were used up, before we realized the extent of the discovery. Our proposal includes money to recover more samples."

The engineer looked positively pleased. "Then you can't guarantee that you will produce anything?"

Grace finally spoke. "That I'm afraid is precisely true."

But Kurt followed up. "Still the preliminary samples showed marvelous results that were nearly miraculous."

With a slightly superior smile, the young engineer type closed his blue folder, signaling that as far as he was concerned the meeting was finished. The older, white haired CFO across from him was analyzing Kurt's budget figures, pursing his lips but he didn't seem unduly put off. "These figures would be reasonable, if you could present us with your fungi specimen to be tested, but our money could be wasted on a fruitless treasure quest?"

Kurt nodded in agreement. "That's entirely possible."

"And," the CFO glanced to his red-haired boss. "You stated that this discovery might smooth and soften skin, but you didn't say how much it could bring in for *Affiliated*?"

Kurt just smiled. "With the baby boomers aging, I

think you would know better than we would what *Affiliated* could charge for a miraculous cream that would make the ladies look younger."

The red-haired man at the top of the table smiled and pressed his fingers together.

"Dr. Farrington, your reputation is well known. Do you think this excretion could be eventually marketed as a beauty pharmaceutical?"

She wasn't going to lie, but the old '*I must get this grant*' kicked in. "I touched it once, lightly, and it took two days before that soft, slipperiness would leave my fingers. It seemed to soften and tighten. Whether it's reproducible in the lab, whether its not toxic to humans in the long term, or whether its marketable for *Affiliated*, I can't tell you. We really can't prove anything more unless we undertake this study and find some testable samples, but I have a personal intuition that we may have discovered something amazing here."

Mr. Red-hair nodded, then asked. "I understand that Dr. Charles Marshall had just joined Oyster River Harbor Research?"

"Yes. He had." Kurt coolly acknowledged.

"And he died?" Sounded like the boss wanted to hear the whole storey.

But Kurt only said, "Very unfortunate. A great lost to science and Oyster River."

The white haired man asked Grace. "But what happened? The papers mentioned some sort of attack?"

Again, Kurt took point. "Actually the police haven't said anything much to us at all, and if you will excuse us gentlemen, Dr. Farrington and I both have to get back to our work. Did you have any more questions on the project?"

Brian Kancir seemed a little surprised by Kurt's abruptness, but the red-headed man just nodded and rose politely as Brian escorted them out.

Outside by his bike, Kurt reached for his helmet, but Grace intercepted his hand. "This time, I'll get the helmet."

"Need my visor."

"Not if you go a **lot** slower!"

He relinquished the helmet and smiled. "Of course, pretty lady."

"And before I get on this thing, you have to swear not to pass anything with me riding shot gun." Grace fumbled with the buckle on the helmet. Kurt pushed her fingers away, and he tightened the strap under her chin as she muttered to him. "That was a great waste time."

"Don't know. You know who Gaydosh is?""

"Who?"

"The red-haired guy you were introduced to, sitting at the top of the table."

"No." She replied.

"Big time inventor, big time risk taker, started three of his companies from scratch. *Affiliated* bought all of them for millions. Then they made him CEO before he was thirty-seven."

"You've been studying?"

"Aaup. Googled him."

Grace shook her head. "Well, after this pathetic showing, I personally don't think Gaydosh or Brian Kancir will ever be knocking on our doors again."

But, that evening, when she got home there was e-mail asking her and Kurt for their social security numbers and the routing number of the bank accounts they wanted their grant electronically deposited in. For *Affiliated's* house organ, there was also a request for them to arrange an appointment for the Company photographer to come and take pictures of their labs. They wanted pictures of their new scientists in front of tanks full of lobsters that didn't exist yet.

Funny, even when things are going well they can be frightening.

Chapter 28

Monday's weekly dinner with Freya didn't go well either. Neither seances or murdered victims were mentioned, yet Grace felt a cooling of their long friendship.

More headaches as Bobby showed up at Grace's apartment that night. "You're teaching tomorrow afternoon's class."

"On what?" She couldn't do this!

"At this point, Eric would be discussing how Dr. Grace Farrington's Popcorn Gene theory's explains the affects of 'gene coded on and off switches', which determine directional development."

"He did?"

"Yhep." Bobby handed her a sheaf of papers. "This is the syllabus for the whole course, we are at week six. The PowerPoint demo for your presentation is on this flash drive, study it." He walked over and inserted the drive into her laptop. Bringing up the program, he put the slide demo on auto play. "Follow that sheet of points."

Grace looked helplessly at the slides. "What should I wear?"

Bobby considered her for a moment, before laconically answering, "Clothes?"

"Should I put on some sort of lab coat? A dress?"

"The students have seen you walking about, they know what you wear. I've already gone over your background and papers, but most of them knew who you were before they came here. You're one of the reasons students come here to study." Seeing her face, he went from firm to coaxing. "They're already impressed with your work."

She didn't want to do this. "Maybe we should wait for me to speak until the end of course, when they can't get their money back."

"What's with you?" Bobby was unrelenting as he sat

down. "I have scheduled you for three lectures. Only three! Tomorrow is the first. Now, Eric would stroll in dressed in casual clothes and he'd sit down, right in the middle of the students. Do maybe twenty minutes of lecturing and then ask them for their ideas."

Grace instantly pictured Eric carefully listening to each student, like he had listened to her years ago. She flushed with warmth at the memory of their first meeting, how important, how privileged she felt, just because the famed Dr. Eric Larsen was talking with her. Like he accepted her, not as a uneducated undergraduate, but as an important member of the scientific community. This class of students would expect that from her. "I'm not Eric."

"Yhep." Bobby nodded his head in complete agreement. "I'm going to have you standing up front, on the raised dais, behind the podium, so you'll have something to hold on to. If you stretch it, the PowerPoint show should go twenty-five minutes. Do you want to advance the slides yourself or have me do it?"

She wanted to get on a boat to Antarctica, but Grace reminded herself that this class would keep Bobby working and his family fed. "I'll advance the slides."

"Good. When the slide show finishes, you'll give a short question and answer period."

"What if nobody asks anything?"

"Then I'll come up with questions–easy ones!"

"Bobby, the police questioned me about a student, Gigi Rameriz."

"Yeah. Me too. More bodies piling up around here." He was closing down the slide demo.

"Did you remember her?"

"Gorgeous and she expected you to know it. Showed up third week of class, knew her stuff and then she was gone. With the great Marshall croaking, I didn't give her disappearance a thought. We always lose a few–drop outs that is."

"That night Marshall died, where did you go?" She tried to ask casually.

"What?" He seemed genuinely puzzled.

"Sara told me you two had a fight and you didn't come home the night Marshall died?"

His face darkened and he just glared at her. "You're interrogating me?" Furious Bobby stood up. "So you think I killed Marshall? Well, Dr. Farrington, before you turn me into the police, I might suggest you think about who will be teaching your classes!" He left angrily slamming her condo door.

The next afternoon, Grace had rehearsed several apologies, but when she saw Bobby, they didn't seem to be needed. True to his black Irish heritage, after a quick thunder storm of anger, Bobby's sunny nature returned. Neither of them mentioned the night Marshall died.

And that afternoon, it nearly went as he said. Grace decided to put on a long, white lab coat over her blouse and pants, then felt silly as she walked up before the class. Bobby had set the podium with her notes, a carafe of ice water and a glass. He pulled the slide demo up and to Grace's surprise the smart board hookup worked this time. Then the students and Bobby were sitting quietly before her, looking at her, waiting.

Just to put it all off for another moment, Grace poured herself a glass of water, took a deep sip, then determinedly set the glass down and started talking. Familiar material made her less nervous, but on the second slide, as she raised her arm to point to the mitochondrial DNA, the back of her hand brushed the water glass, knocking it over. Water cascaded down over the podium; it splashed icily over her pants, notes and shoes; as the glass smashed down on the floor. Bobby just closed his eyes in pain and no one said anything.

Chapter 29

Ruefully, Grace looked down at the dripping mess, then she flicking away ice cubes from her notes with her hand, as she kicked the broken glass aside, tartly commenting. "My family is an outstanding example of clumsy, behavioral genetic inheritance."

The students actually laughed at her poor joke and the next slide illustrated a typical 'switch on' gene reaction. Immersing herself in work Grace always found comfort and in no time at all, she was easily slipped into the question and answer session. In fact, it was Bobby who the ended the class, looking pointedly at his watch. "Dr. Farrington, we've run twenty minutes over."

Grace prepared to leave but found she had a line of students, so she sat at the desk, signed books and answered more questions. It hadn't gone badly and three of the students had come up with scenarios dissecting genetic inheritance basics from some remarkably original slants. They were all wrong, but they had her looking at familiar material through their unprejudiced eyes. There might actually be something that could be learned from the raw visions of students, Eric may have been right.

Standing on the dock the next day, Grace turned her jacket collar up, as the wind from the harbor had a cutting edge as Kurt and Bobby were motoring in the lobster yawl. Still in his black rubber wet suit, Bobby hopped off the boat to tie up. On the dock he stumbled, going down on one knee, but he quickly hauled himself up to tie off the lines. Holding her breath, Grace felt like the mother of a new Little Leaguer, watching her too small son drop the game losing ball. On board Kurt was gathering a few buckets, but seeing her questioning look, he just sadly shook his head. No blue lobsters today.

She walked over to where Bobby was tying up the stern. "How's it going?"

He smiled tightly. "Crewing for Kurt, I've sprained muscles I didn't know I had."

"The diving lessons, how are they coming?"

"Tomorrow I'm descended into Davy Jones' locker." He tried to speak lightly, but he looked pale and beaten.

She looked him directly. "Can you do it?"

"I have to!" His face filled with determination that it lapsed in a spreading smile. "Seems like I passed my DNA on to two! Sara's pregnant with twins! Both boys!"

Grace had to act properly surprised. "Twins! Oh, wow."

"Yhep. That's why she's been having so many problems." He looked out over the Harbor. "For my kids I can dive in a little cold water."

The next morning, Grace got up stiff and feeling out of condition. She hadn't run since she heard of that girl's death, but Grace had the irrational fear that leaving ORR she might find another dead body. Ridiculous. She forced herself to drive off of the campus and did a short run by the library, then drove to the Firehouse Deli to pick up her danish. Paying at the counter, she saw two newspapers with Samantha Carson's stories. The one in *The Sound Times* looked like just the facts of Gigi's death, tied to a rehash of Miakos' suicide and the murder of Marshall. Grace picked up a copy to read later.

It was the other tabloid's headline that was screaming out to her.

Chapter 30

Bylined Kit Samuels, Samantha's nom de plume, was the **CURSE OF THE *SIREN* STRIKES AGAIN!** The tabloid had a full front page, monochrome drawing of the ORR Administration building. On top of it was a woman in billowing skirts on its high widow's walk, screaming into a raging storm. In the right upper corner were oval insets with line-drawn portraits of three bearded seaman, while on the lower left side were three more ovals featuring photographs of the faces of Miakos, Marshall and a laughing young girl.

Inside the headlines shrieked **WIDOW'S CURSE CLAIMS THREE MORE!** There was a two page, color photo spread of the Octagon, wreathed with yellow crime tape, surrounded by police craft with an inset of an unrolling scroll, retelling the 'ancient curse' in ye oldie type and another box photo of Marshall's bleeding body. This was the worse kind of yellow journalism! With ORR getting publicity like this, they'd all be a laughing stock, getting no respectable grants, no intelligent students and no rich patrons. They would be overrun by gawking tourists, perhaps she'd still have to move out of Oyster River anyway.

Still standing at the counter, Grace skimmed the account; her friends weren't helping. In the story Dr. Kurt Mackay recited the legend of the *Siren's* unnatural wreck and the untimeliness of the June Northeasterner. He pointed out that the State University archeologists were diving in just that area, perhaps disturbing the wreck? Samantha had gotten a full account of finding Charles Marshall's body from him. Grace noted gratefully that Kurt had left her out of his graphic recital that began with "*I'm not a superstitions man, but living my life on the sea, yer sense when the winds are wrong*".

Freya, billed as a '*professional hauntacologist*', gave a more lurid spin to the back story of the Widow and her curse 'of the three faithless men'; more harebrained copy as Sam struggled to tie the three new deaths to the ancient curse. Grace rapidly read on, the witness of Miakos' jump in to the waters was only named as an '*eminent woman scientist*' at Oyster River Harbor Research.

Sick to her stomach, she stood reading by the checkout counter, finally looking up to find the Indian clerk glaring at her. Grace bought the tabloid and took it out to her car to finish. Sitting there, she tightened her lips as the story continued with the discovery of Gigi Ramirez's body. Thankfully there was nothing about the police questioning Grace in the story, but Gigi's death really had nothing to do with the 'Curse of the Three'. Technically, she died on land, only near the harbor, but the newspaper woman had deftly ignored that.

There were pictures of Gigi that Grace studied, trying to recognize her as some student's face, but couldn't. There were no pictures of the body, which had probably deteriorated pretty badly before it was found, but there were photos of Gigi's that family and friends must have supplied. A young, slender, twentyish girl with dark hair and eyes and a proud, almost arrogant smile. Gigi with her white Pomeranian, Gigi blowing candles out on her birthday cake and the one that Grace found the most disturbing was Gigi on a ski slope, laughing. This girl was just beginning life–she shouldn't have been killed.

And Gigi's death shouldn't be considered part of the Widow's curse. The *Siren's* curse should have been three philandering men, dying in the harbor. The authorities had only found two men, Marshall and Miakos or would they net yet another body?

More pages, more pictures. A living Miakos's naked torso being body painted by some famous neo-Expressionist in the '80s, a shot of his paintings and a picture of him in his casket. Shot of a younger, blacked-haired Dr. Charles Marshall accepting his Nobel, distant angle of the Octagon in the harbor and a readable photo of the sign at the entrance to Oyster River Research. All sensationalism and superstitious claptrap. It made everyone at ORR look like possible homicidal maniacs, but it probably wasn't actionable in a court of law. Could she ask Mark Silverstein? No, he was doing enough handling her criminal problems. Tossing the paper on to the passenger seat, Grace didn't feel up to starting work in her lab.

Instead, she drove back to the Library, parked and walked up towards Abe's bookshop. She needed to know more about this girl who Sam claimed died as part of the 'Curse of the Three'. She passed Lord & Toms. High pricey, classic women's wear. If she was going to that fancy awards dinner with Kurt, she would need something to wear. Lord & Tom's didn't really do evening gowns, and she didn't feel like wasting her time today.

Grace found Abe sitting and reading, with no one else in his shop. She had to stand there for awhile and finally give a slight, theatrical cough before he looked up and smiled. "Grace. Police now questioning you about three bodies?"

How could he sit here, oblivious to everything and everyone and still learn it all? "Yes." She said ruefully. "How do you know?"

"Mac Dell was in here picking up a study guide for his sergeant's exam."

"What do you know of Gigi Ramirez?"

"She's dead."

"Other than that?"

"Not much. She was only here couple of weeks or so, renting Bonnie and Nat Jones' place."

Grace added. "She signed up late to take undergraduate courses at ORR, but I never met her."

"Aaup." Abe didn't seem to doubt that at all.

"I hadn't seen a rental sign on that house?"

Abe nodded. "Nat Jones was temporally transferred to

Beijing and Bonnie wanted to live in China with him. Arlene Labella is the real estate agent, she had it rented before it even got listed. Bonnie would've had a fit if she'd known what she was getting for a tenant."

"Why?"

"Whal, you know that property. Low stone fence, tangle of bittersweet briars, and then an acre or so of mowed lawn around the pond?"

"Yes."

"Joe the mailman was delivering a package he couldn't fit in the mailbox. Walkin' up that graveled driveway, he see's a girl face down on the grass sun bathing on a towel. Jes a red bikini bottom on. Hearing him, she casually sits up, holding that towel across her chest."

"She was topless?"

"Aaup."

"The Town line starts right there."

"She jes starts talking to him pretty as you please. Real California girl." Abe gave a dismissive smile.

"Only this is New England in the Fall. You think she's from California?"

"Nope. Arlene said from her accent, she sounded more Southwestern, with an undertone of Texas drawl and Mexican. Although Gigi's more of a French name."

"Do you know what that rental cost?"

"Nope. Could ask Arlene since its gonna be on the market again."

"Would you? Don't say it's me asking."

He nodded. "It's gonna be a pretty penny. That house has been in the decorating magazines."

"How could an unemployed, student afford a full house?"

"Don't know." Abe mused. "Indulgent parents? Inheritance?"

"Most graduate students don't have money for lunch."

" Meybe Arlene knows. Got a special order she'll be coming in for soon. Give you a call?"

Returning to her lab, Grace tried to calm down, but it really bothered her to be behind in her work. Everything was going badly. She took a deep breath and reached for her assistants sign in sheets. Inger, as ever, was punctual and finished her projects, on the other hand Nick--always a bit flakier-- had just put his hours in. Doing what? He put down 'cleaning up'? Must have been Inger's idea, since Grace hadn't been leaving them work other than activating that East bank of lobster tanks. Those tanks were cleaned and bubbling with sea water, but empty of blue lobsters they didn't have. Her data printouts were filed and the place looked neater, Grace must have a week's worth of aide assignments written up for both of them before she left today.

Finishing that and firmly settling down, Grace started to prioritize her tsunami of phone and e-mail messages. She wouldn't bother answering any old contacts looking for gossip about the murders. There was one from David Gardiner, asking her out to dinner. She hated wasting time, but she had really enjoyed the man's company. And for use of his lawyer, Grace felt she owed him something. She called and left a message for him, saying she'd be available next week. When she got back to paying attention to genetic questions, there was a lot to go through. First priority was any person or institute that she was being paid to consult for.

Still by noon she stood on the docks again, watching for Kurt and Bobby's return. Bobby was diving with Kurt in the morning and teaching her classes in the afternoon. As they unloaded, like a fool she asked. "Any blue tails?"

Coming up to her, Bobby shook his head regretfully.

Grace looked at him. He looked thinner, paler, well, naturally, his summer tan was fading. "How's it going?"

"Sara? She's doing better. Barfing less."

"I mean your diving?"

His smile seemed genuine. "It's not that bad. Just swimming with a scuba regulator stretching your mouth, sort of like braces in High School." He was trying to joke, but seeing her face he stopped. "You know, I think when summer comes, I'm really going to like diving. What you see under there is great. We've got these big underwater spotlights, and Kurt has taken me to the *Siren's* wreck–God, that is something! We just swam in between the masts of a two hundred year old ship. Some guys used to feed their families from that ship, by hunting whales for four to five years from port."

"What do you think of the curse?"

"The curse is that it s cold! God, even in the wet suits it is cold as a witches' tit down there–but don't tell Sara I said that! It's a job–one I'm thankful for!"

"If we don't find blue tailed lobsters, we can't ask for extension." Grace sadly pronounced.

"Lady, you can always ask!" Kurt was carrying two metal tanks over. "Of course we can! Bobby, get these tanks repaired for me, will ya."

Bobby nodded as he took them and moved off.

Grace said nothing, as Kurt moved closer. "Hey, how about you joining me aboard and warming me up a bit?"

She ignored that. "Those 'wild life' pictures you were taking?"

He looked puzzled, and then must have remembered his stake out of the boat house. "Tried sittin' out there in the main channel a few nights. There's big windows, with lights behind them, but at dusk Katherine Marshall keeps pulling the curtains across. Cain't see anything."

"Why is she still here?"

"Talked to Adam about that. Seems the police haven't released Marshall's body, it was definitely a murder. So the authorities have requested she stay accessible, but since fish and guests stink after three days, Adam wants Katherine out.

Still our beloved, yellow striped President ain't gonna even suggest it. After all, we paid the Marshalls to come here, and then we murdered her husband."

"So we don't know how long she's staying?"

"Nor do we know about Ms. Diandra Hollings. Katherine told Adam that Diandra's salary and room allowance were to be cut off immediately. Kind hearted Adam arranged for ORR to pay her a two months severance and she'll have till the end of the month at the motel."

"Motel? We're paying for the Shoreline?"

"Aaup. It's coming out of ORR's endowment funds, Marshall wormed that arrangement out of Adam. When she leaves the motel, sounds like Diandra's got nowhere else to go."

Grace nodded. "Gail's been sending out her resumes. No responses yet."

Kurt smiled. "With her qualifications, Diandra Hollings's not gonna get a job, unless she's sending out lipstick autographed DVDs of her rear end sashaying."

Grace looked in the direction of the Point. "So you didn't see any strange men in the guest apartment with Katherine?"

"No stranger. But two nights ago, I got a great picture of one of her visitors, arriving just before dark."

Grace turned back to him. "Someone you recognized?"

Dramatically Kurt nodded, then continued. "Oyster River Research's President, Adam Greenfield."

Chapter 31

It was totally dark. She looked at the clock. 2 A.M. Grace had woken up to the phone's ringing. Some fool got the wrong number. Strange, how you always felt you were required to answer the phone just because it rang. Still half asleep, Grace picked it up.

"Grace?" Male voice. Eager.

"Who is this?"

"Me."

Oh, great. "Do you know what time it is?"

The happy voice wilted a little at her exasperation. "Grace. It's me, Abe. And I was reading and I didn't realize how late it is."

She closed her eyes, cuddling the phone against her ear. "That's okay. I'm up late too."

He continued on. "I've been studying the silk road–you know, the trade route Marco Polo took from Venice to China? Did you know that Mongolian Queens once controlled it?"

"No."

"According to this author they did."

She laid her head back on the pillow. "That's fascinating, I'm sure. But you weren't calling me for that, were you?"

"Oh, no. I just got a phone call from Nat Jones."

"Who?"

"He and Bonnie are in China. They were renting their house to the student who was killed."

Grace eyes widened. "Gigi?"

"Aaup."

"Did they ever meet her?"

"Nope. It was done through the real estate agent."

"Then they don't know how she afforded the house?"

"She didn't." Abe let the line go dead, while Grace waited for the other shoe to drop. Finally Abe continued, "The first check that Nat got was signed by Adam Greenfield."

President of Oyster River Research? "Was it from an ORR account?"

"Nope. Nat says he thought it was funny that it was one of Adam's personal checks."

"What?"

"Aaup. Mr. Married, all manner of sobriety, President ORR. Past President of the Beth El Synagogue. And he had a little gal pal on the side. Rachel will kill him!"

No, Grace could not see Adam and a ripening young undergraduate. He'd have to be out of his mind. He had kids older than Gigi! But a middle aged man, feeling mortality drawing closer–desperately wanting to be young again, could he have fallen into an affair? Did Gigi threaten to expose him? He had a lot to lose. Still, Grace just couldn't see methodical, conservative Adam murdering a girl, then just leaving her body on the front lawn. Or did his wife find out and kill Gigi? "Adam and Rachel have been married for years?"

Abe supported. "They married as kids in college."

"Do you think Rachel could kill her husband's lover?"

"Nope. Rachel's a lawyer–she'd have hauled them into court and sued the stuffing out of both of them."

"But Adam's with this young girl?"

Abe thought about it. " Never heard anything like that about him. Man's a womanizer, word usually gets around."

But a very conservative, uptight married man, buffed by middle-age hormones, meeting a young, promiscuous girl. Did he decide it was his last chance to have a fling? Did that fling go horribly wrong? "Thanks, Abe." Grace hung the phone. Adam having an affair with Gigi? Adam's probability percentage column total just zoomed up. And she would have to add a row for 'Rachel Greenfield' on her Suspect spreadsheet.

Chapter 32

Friday Grace decided to push things. She called for an appointment to speak with Adam Greenfield, to find out just what relationship he had with Gigi Ramirez . Answering his line, Gail said the earliest appointment Grace could see Adam was Wednesday, unless they had another crisis that had him running over.

Grace took out her Suspect spread sheet to update it. Under the Gigi's columns, Grace noted that Adam might have had a strong motive: To cover up his relationship with Gigi. He had Means: He was in the area, had his own truck and boat and working in construction Adam was stronger then most men. Opportunity: Did he finish dinner with his wife and say "Excuse me, dear, I've got go murder someone?" She couldn't think of a realistic Pro. Con: Grace couldn't see Adam having an affair, much less killing a blackmailing mistress. Also a Con: When did he have the time? Whatever the motive or means, she could not believe Rachel will lower herself to kill her husband's girlfriend. She gave them both a weak 25 % for motive and means.

But as she always did when dissatisfied with her hypothesis, Grace studied the entire spread sheet, forcing herself to ignore past assumptions. Now as she looked over the columns, another possibility emerged, in one of her 'Farrington Fusions' she recognized a pattern that was there and should have been seen before! A friend who betrayed her!

Furious Grace pulled on a jacket and hurried down to the ORR docks. She could see that Kurt's yawl was tied up and by the lights in the *Lovely Lady's* port holes, she knew that he was in there. In fact, when she climbed aboard his sailboat, he was just coming out.

He smiled to see her. "Grace..."

Furious, she stepped in front of him. "**You set me up!**"

"Lady?"

"Your arm wasn't hurt!"

"Wasn't hurt that badly," He amended, looking guilty.

"You got me to help you pull in lobster pots, and then ferried us to the Octagon Houseboat. You knew Charles Marshall was there, dead!"

"Grace,..."

"Explain yourself!"

He looked ashamed. "Night before I was out in the Harbor after dark. Recognized one of ORR's boats--know the purr of those engines like they were my own children. Whal, voices carry over water, so I heard someone talking. It sounded like Marshall..."

"He was talking to someone?"

"Aaup. There were two of them, the other person had a voice too soft to make out. Since Marshall seemed hell bent on getting rid of me, I figured it might not be a bad idea to keep an eye on his doings."

"Marshall was with who?"

"Too dark to see."

"Didn't they see you?"

"Probably not. There were heavy clouds that night and a quarter moon jes peeped out a little now and then."

"They would have seen your running lights at anchor."

"Whal, I didn't actually have running lights."

"In the channel?"

"Yeah."

"What were you doing out there?"

"Some personal diving."

"With your lights off?"

"Aaup."

Grace suddenly knew. "The ship wreck. The *Siren*. The one the marine archeologists are searching for. Were you taking something off it?"

"Actually, I was returning something. The ship's bell."

"Oh, lord, you've been ripping off an historical wreck. One that the University is now investigating?"

He shrugged. "A little salvage. Law of the sea."

"Isn't there some Federal Law about how many miles off shore you must be to rip off potential archeological sites?" Under her glare, he shrugged again, so she continued. "How late was it when you saw Marshall alive?"

"Eight thirty, nine? Wasn't lookin' at my watch."

"So. You saw a boat coming from our dock with two people. You can guess it's up to no good and you see it's headed for the Octagon. Right?"

"Aaup. Figured Marshall planned a roll on the carpet."

"What?" Grace asked.

"Course that Berber carpeting leaves a burn, but we've all used the Octagon to impress our lays. "

She kept glaring at him. "No–not all of us!"

"Aaup. Well that weak moon peeped out and I saw two shapes reaching the Octagon. The one I figured to be Marshall was tall and clumsy. Whal, the man didn't look much good at it, but the smaller figure, a woman most likely, moved fast. She poled them in, climbed aboard and tied them up. He handed her what clinked like bottles, then she reached out a hand to steady him up on to the Octagon's deck."

"Could you identify her?"

"Dark shape, feminine laughter, shorter than him and 'bout your height. That's all."

"Then what? You get closer?"

"Nope. I had the Coast Guard vessel timed to be swinging back, didn't want to be caught out in the Channel, with no running lights and no explanation. I hauled anchor as quietly as I could, while I saw lights going on inside the Octagon, then somebody was pulling down all the shades. The next time a real dark cloud blotted out the moon, I motored out of there."

"Then what?"

He couldn't meet her eyes. "Grace, it was late. Been diving in the cold water and I was hungry. Motored to the Neptune, so I could tie up and get myself a bowl of chowder in the bar."

"You're telling me you were eating while a murder is going on?"

"Hell, I didn't know someone was getting killed. I met some friends and had a few drinks."

"When did you leave?"

"I was there until they closed."

"Then you came back to the ORR dock?"

"Sort of." He looked away. She glared at him and he shrugged. "Since I was on the harbor again, I figured I'd drop in on the Octagon. Maybe catch someone in flagrante delictos."

"And?"

"The lights were out and there was no boat tied up to the Octagon. I tied up mine, climbing on the deck, planned to go inside, see if they left any evidence. Tried to open door, but found it was blocked, finally managed to shove it open."

"Was he alive?"

"Naw, I felt his neck. He was stiff, going cold and I was there, alone, with bad blood between us. I shut off my the running lights and motored back."

"Then what?"

"Couldn't call the cops, without them knowing I was there. Even if somebody else found the body, clues would point to me, with people at the Neptune knowing my boat was out on the harbor that night."

"So you decided Grace would make a great patsy," She finished bitterly.

Shamefaced he said, "Most of that morning, I was standing out there on the dock, trying to figure out what to do. Then you come marching down. You're a pristine scientific lady, with clean reputation, while I'm an outlaw biker, KKK member. I go out there myself and report finding a body, the police got their killer before lunch."

"But how could you involve me, when you knew Marshall had stolen my research?" Grace stopped as the realization hit. "But you didn't know..."

"You never said anything about Marshall all the years I've known ya! All I heard from Adam was that Marshall was bragging that he was your beloved mentor."

"He stole my first research theories, claimed them as his own, and won a Nobel prize."

"Didn't you fight him?"

"There was a Board of Inquiry."

Kurt looked tired. "But you were only a graduate student..."

"And he accused me of having an affair with him! Being bitter when he ended it!"

There was silence as Kurt's face drained of color. "So they have bad blood and maybe spurned love as motive for you killing him. That's why they've been going after ya. Grace, I'm so sorry. I'll go to the police, explain how I tricked you."

"No. Then they've got you and those detectives will probably figure I talked you into helping me kill him. We've got to figure this out ourselves. The giggling lady passenger, do you think she killed him?"

"Don't see how. Marshall was a big man and pretty trim for his age. Saw him running with Diandra the first morning he was here. A smaller person, trying to kill him could've only hit him from behind and that person would have had to know, if they couldn't kill him on the first blow, Marshall would've gotten them. The fact that he blocked the door meant he was alive for a bit."

She sighed. "You should tell the police what you saw on the water, before someone from the Neptune talks."

"Cain't."

"Why not? You were diving at night, studying nocturnal sea creatures. Don't say anything about the bell and the *Siren's* ship wreck. You saw Marshall, went to the Neptune, then later stopped at the Octagon. The door was blocked, and you went away until daylight."

He was looking directly at her. "Grace, if I describe that female figure with Marshall, in the Police's eyes, I could be describing you. Lady, I've done you enough harm already."

She realized he was right. "If you are questioned don't lie, but maybe if we just stay quiet, misdirecting the police is only a small felony."

Kurt smiled widely. "Hell, I do two of those before breakfast!"

He started to turn away, and Grace put her hand on his arm. "When you finally returned to Oyster River's dock that night, was the launch still missing?"

He thought about it, his eyes staring far away, as if he was seeing and searching the whole dock that dark night. "No. Both were tied back up."

"Both?"

"I was on the Harbor before Marshall motored out, but there was also a boat missing when I left the dock. I checked the clipboard before I went out, no sign outs. Figured it was one of the graduate students taking a joy ride."

She frowned. "They aren't supposed to do that."

"Grace, that's why they don't sign out."

"If the female figure with Marshall was Diandra, what if his wife took the other boat out?"

"Katherine Marshall know anything about boats?"

"Not that I know of, but I don't know anything much about her." admitted Grace.

"The Hollings gal seems comfortable walking down a plank and she's a strong runner. Suppose Marshall was with another woman, girl friend #2. Diandra goes into a jealous rage and killed Marshall and his new lady friend?" He suggested.

"At his age, Marshal couldn't have the libido to be doing two girl friends and a wife."

He gave a leer. "We men can surprise ya."

"Okay. Marshall is out with Bimbo 2, headed for the Octagon. In a blood rage, Diandra has taken out the first boat and is lurking in the Harbor. She follows them to the Octagon. Knocks on the door. Says hello, then bludgeons Marshall and his girl friend. I don't think Lizzie Borden could have managed that–but what happened to this mystery girl friend #2's body?" mused Grace.

"That's easy. Diandra fed her to the sharks. The tide would've been going out, lots a feeding crabs out there before ya get to the Sound."

"Why didn't Diandra get rid of Marshall the same way?" she asked.

Kurt shrugged. "He was too heavy for her to haul off the Octagon?"

Grace tried to visualize it all. "He seemed to have lived to reach the door?"

"Diandra hammering them. Thinks they're both dead. Drags girlfriend # 2 off the Octagon's deck..."

"You see any dark stains on the decking outside the door?" Grace asked.

"Nope. Maybe she didn't bleed?"

"How convenient."

Kurt shook his head. "While killer girl friend #1 is pushing girl friend #2 into the ocean, Marshall wakes up. He manages to reach the door blocking it as he passes out."

Grace shook her head. "Think about it. Marshall came here and in less than a week he found another girl friend? One that he trusted enough to have sex with on Institute property? Isn't that a little hard, with a wife and a jealous assistant monitoring him?"

"That Gigi girl who was killed by the library. Maybe

she was Marshall's second girl friend?"

Grace tried that out. "Marshall and Gigi go out to the Octagon. A jealous Diandra has guessed he's going to be on the Octagon, and she has been lurking out on the harbor. Diandra kills Marshall and his new girl friend, Gigi. Does Diandra look strong enough to carry a grown woman's body off the Octagon? Stow it in a rocking boat? Motor across the Harbor, beach the boat. Carry the body up on shore, past the library security lights, across the road, to then plop it behind the Jones' stone wall in the bittersweet?"

Kurt rubbed his jaw. "Don't sound too practical."

"I'd say so."

"Grace, maybe we could get a better handle on this murder if we enacted it? You know. You and me, sneaking out after dark tonight on to the Octagon."

She could see where this was going, "Screwing on the floor in the center of the computer stations? All for scientific experimentation, right?"

He grinned widely. "Aaup."

"No way!" Grace turned and walked away.

But as her anger cooled, she had to live with some nastier thoughts. Kurt was intelligent man, a studious man. His 'rednecked' persona was to just endlessly rile the politically correct types, but he could use a gun, a knife. For his slight build, he was an exceptionally strong man. A man who could swim across the harbor for fun, much less from the houseboat to land for an alibi.

Marshall towered over Kurt, but if Kurt could rip an octopus off a dying diver's face plate, he certainly could have overcome Marshall. And Miakos, who just jumped in the water and killed himself? Could a man like Kurt, by clever needling, have convinced Miakos it was better to die than live? Why would Kurt want to kill Miakos? Were they fighting over the same woman, Tina? That was ridiculous; for self preservation Kurt steered clear of married women with excitable husbands, *'who wouldn't agree to a threesome in bed.'*

Better to concentrate on the motivations she understood. Marshall wanted the 'hillbilly' off ORR staff and would have had the stature to do it. Dr. Charles Marshall would end Kurt's job, and with Kurt's reputation and limited academic credits, there might not have been another position for him, or he would have had to settle for a position where he would be demoted to 'graduate assistant' status. A man as proud as Kurt could not have stood that, but would he have resorted to cold blooded murder?

Chapter 33

Early Wednesday, Grace left her lab and headed to the Administration building for her appointment with Oyster River's President. Adam sat behind the desk of curly maple. For a brief flash, Grace felt like a high schooler called into the principle's office to discuss her bad behavior. At least he offered her a seat.

"Grace, I understand your first teaching class went very well. I always knew you could do it! Now, we've got to think about the Summer sessions."

"I'm not teaching." She said firmly.

"I've been keeping the Jamisons in the Institute condo." He pressured.

Grace was not there to haggle, she was damn tired of having her valuable time wasted. Without a preliminaries, she demanded. "Why were you paying Gigi Ramirez 's rent?"

"What?" Adam looked shocked, almost frightened.

"Why did you pay a murdered girl's rent?"

He licked his lips, started to say something, then. "Well, it doesn't matter now. Yes. I was paying her rent, sort of."

"Sort of?"

"Oyster River was."

Grace couldn't believe that. "ORR was paying for your love nest?"

"No! It was Dr. Marshall's money. A...it was a settling bonus. Money for Dr. Marshall and his wife to resettle themselves in our town."

"A bonus? But you didn't use an ORR check?"

"That would have been inappropriate."

"So how did it work?"

"I–the Institute--paid Dr. Marshall with a check, that he cashed it and passed the cash back to me–none of which I kept. You do understand that?"

"Of course." She said sarcastically.

"I put that money it in my personal account and wrote a check for the rental of the house for his use."

"His use?" She asked acidly.

"The use of a student, whose education he was generously sponsoring...privately." Under her cold eyes, he lamely finished. "To help Gigi in pursuit of her educational goals."

"Do the police know this?"

He paled. "They haven't said anything about the check at all."

"Probably didn't ask anyone the right questions," Grace commented tightly. Or more likely they were holding the questions back until they got more on him.

Adam tried to put a good face on it. "If they bring it up, I'll just tell everything as it was. Do you think they'll believe me?"

"The question is will your wife believe you?"

Adam seemed to get even paler. "Do you intend to tell the police about this?"

"I'm trying to stay as far away from the police as I can." Grace sat back in the carved wooden chair. "Katherine Marshall was used to her husband playing around, but what if Diandra found out that Marshall had another girl friend? What if she took one of the boats out and killed him on the Octagon?"

"No. No. It wasn't Ms. Hollings–I know. She was not on the houseboat."

"How do you know?"

"There was an impeccable witness with her, when Dr. Marshall was killed."

"Who?"

"I'd rather not say..."

"Adam! The police are questioning me for murder and maybe you next! I think this is a time that we definitely should be talking to each other!"

He looked down at his big hands, then finally looked her directly in the eyes. "This is a volunteer job, mostly an honorary title, President of Oyster River Harbor Research. I just took it for..."

"Adam, there's been two–no, three deaths. At least two of them we know were murders."

"Okay." He thought a bit, then. "This was told to me in confidence."

"Fine."

"Katherine Marshall is–was--tremendously jealous of her husband, to the point of almost irrationality."

"Since he openly had two mistresses, it doesn't seem to me that her suspicions were all that unjustified," Grace sweetly supplied.

"During the time Dr. Marshall was killed, Katherine was with Diandra Hollings."

"Wait a minute. How exactly can anyone know the time that he was killed? The Octagon is freezing in this weather without the electric heaters turned on. Even if Marshall had just eaten, and they were timing by the digestion of his food, they still could only have a rough estimate of the time of his death? Unless they have a witness we don't know about, the police could have only pinned his death time to a two hour interval, and even that would have been pushing it."

Adam looked down at his hands again.

Grace pushed. "How do you know the time he died?"

He just sat there looking for a way out and obviously didn't see one. Finally Adam spoke again. "Katherine told me that at six p.m., Dr. Marshall apparently showered and changed at his home. At six thirty, he told his wife he was going for his weekly meeting with me..."

"Did he notify you in advance that you were going to be his alibi?"

He looked embarrassed. "We were supposed to have

weekly meetings at seven, but it was understood that he might not show up."

"You put up with this?"

"He was such a great catch for Oyster River, a Nobel winner."

"So you covered for him?"

"I was out at other meetings. If Katherine had called my house, my wife would have said I was meeting with Dr. Marshall. If Katherine asked me later, he told me to say we had met at the Empire diner in Stamford."

Grace tried not let her distaste show. "And Katherine is the crazy one?"

Adam missed that. "Well, his wife apparently went through his papers and found Diandra's address at the motel." Adam looked shocked at this violation of Marshall's privacy. "At about eight she went right down and banged on the door, demanding to be let in."

The Shoreline motel had an office, in the center of two, one story, pink-painted wings, with rooms opening out on to the parking lot opposite the beach. If Katherine was banging on Diandra's motel room door, everybody would hear it. Grace remembered Katherine hammering on her door that late night, drunkenly demanding to know where her husband was. "Did Diandra answer the door?"

"She had to. Katherine was screaming and everyone could hear her, the police would have been called soon."

"So Katherine walked in, checked the hotel room, and saw her husband wasn't there?"

Adam winced. "I know the other side from Ms. Hollings. I've become the DMZ between them. Diandra denied that Dr. Marshall was there, then she denied he was still coming. Katherine refused to believe her."

Grace remember the stink of Katherine's whiskey breath and her refusal to listen to reason.

Adam continued. "Diandra said, *'Fine, if you want to*

wait for him, wait'. She figured Katherine would leave, but she didn't. Katherine just plunked herself down on the only chair and sat there, for four hours."

"Four hours?" Grace couldn't believe that.

"Well, she just sat there. Diandra was pretending to read a research paper, across the room on the bed. It was warm and after a time Katherine started nod, then snore."

"Why didn't Diandra throw her out?"

"She wasn't strong enough to physically throw out a woman of Katherine's weight. And Diandra didn't want to call the police and face the embarrassment of publicly being called a tramp."

"She could have walked out."

"If she just left Katherine alone in the motel room, Diandra was afraid she might wake up and trash her things."

"Did they try to phone Marshall?"

Adam was exasperated. "I don't know. Ask Diandra or Katherine. The police told me they thought Dr. Marshall's died around 9 p.m. If Katherine was sitting there in the motel room, Diandra has an alibi from a woman who hates her guts."

That night when Grace updated her murder's spread sheet, she had to drop Diandra's 'Opportunity' column from 80 % to 5 % . She got the 5%, because how unlikely as it was, Diandra could have sneaked out and killed Marshall, while Katherine was sleeping it off. Katherine's Opportunity column went from a 20 % to 0, because Diandra was her alibi.

Unless Grace could believe either of them foolishly hired a professional killer, she was back to Unknown Random Killer or Bobby Jamison or Kurt MacKay. Or, if she looked at it from the police's perspective, herself.

Chapter 34

"Grace?"

She went from closely focusing on her computer screen to the suit jacketed man standing in her lab. "Oh, David." She'd forgotten she'd agreed to go out to dinner with him. Grace looked back at the computerized slides again. "I'll be right with you. I just want to check this..." Why was there a color change? Something was going on with the cell wall, but it shouldn't.

Grace typed notes into her computer and started bringing up different slides on the multiple screens before her. Studying. Comparing. She would have to send Duwon at Woods Hole her comments on these slides. Grace brought up another slide of that same cell culture, now when there should have been a color change, there wasn't. After multiple-notes later, Grace finally turned away from her screen to realize David Gardiner was sitting there on one of her lab chairs with a patient, bemused look on his face.

She moved to shut down her screens and started apologizing. "Oh, how long have I kept you waiting? I get lost in data sometimes."

"Actually I was enjoying watching you work. You have the laptop open to the same pictures that you've put up on those screens up there?"

"They're all budding cells from a black seaweed."

"And that screen?"

"Again the same species from Woods Hole, a cell that is in mitosis."

He sounded supremely interested. "The one your laptop looks different?"

She was surprised he noticed that. "E-mail photos from a colleague of mine at Cal Tech. My popcorn gene switch holds they should all be developing the same way–they aren't."

He cooked his head to the side. "Can't you just consider them the exceptions that proves your rule?"

"No. What I have to do is try and figure out if my 'rule' needs changing or redoing."

"Do all scientist try to disprove their own theories?"

"If they want to be right–yes."

"But Charles Marshall?" He was studying her with his head cocked to the side.

She looked down at her papers. "Was known for defending his work by tearing down the reputations of anyone who had the temerity to question the great man's pronouncements."

Obviously seeing his question disturbed her, he changed the subject. "Hungry?"

"That's right. You have reservations at the Pier for 6:30."

He smiled gently. "It's a bit past that."

She looked at the clock on the corner of her screen. 8:10 "We've lost the reservations and I'm hungry. We could we skip the Pier and maybe get into The Burger and Beer? It'll be faster."

He looked horrified. "No, thank you! I think the Pier will be able to find us a table and provide appetizers immediately. Do you want to go back to your condo and change?"

Grace was unbuttoning her lab coat, and she looked down at her plain blue blouse and pants. "This isn't good enough?"

He studied her head to toe. "Well...your shoes are different."

She looked down at her feet. "Different?"

"The style is the same, but I think the left one is black and the other is...navy?"

Oh, God, he was right. "It was dark in the bedroom this morning. Maybe I should change, but that'll take more time..."

"You certainly don't have to change. If you're hungry, I think we should just go to dinner."

"I'm starving." As she hung up her lab coat, he was holding out her car jacket, what a lovely, old fashioned curtsy. Soon he was handing his car to the valet at the Pier, a big, three story high, modern, sweeping wood building on the beach. Inside, the foyer had a brown ceramic tiled floor, with tall potted plants, and a high arched bridge over an artificial salt water pond.

As they crossed the bridge, Grace looked down at the lobsters with their banded claws. David waited patiently, as she scanned each lobster for a sign of the blue fungus, but no luck. On the other side of the bridge, several foursomes were waiting for tables; it didn't look promising for eating soon. The men were dressed in dinner jackets, the women in satin blouses and velvet skirts. That was why David had mentioned going back to her condo, she was not properly dressed for this.

The maitre d' smiled at David. "Good evening, Mr. Gardiner."

David turned to her. "Any place you'd prefer?"

It all so looked so crowded. "Anything, as soon as you can." The whole rear of the building was a huge bank of story and half windows that overlooked ocean's waves.

The maitre d' seemed apologetic. "The only table open right now would be the bar?"

David looked to her and Grace nodded. "That would be fine."

They started following the maitre d'.

A large man sitting down, hailed them. "David! Good to see you."

David nodded politely, but kept walking. As they headed for the twelve foot high windows overlooking the surf, another man seemed to recognize David. "Mr. Gardiner." Two youngish, highly dressed women with the party looked Grace over from head to toe, obviously, not impressed by what they saw. Grace started to stop, but David just smiled politely and cupped his hand under Grace's elbow, gently pushing her forward. "You'll have to excuse us."

In the bar area a waiter hastily took off two extra place settings as the maitre d' pulled out a chair for Grace. Their table was right on the black nighted water, with the building's outdoors lights reflected on the incoming translucent green waves, breaking on the small beach underneath the pilings. She noted those waves were rolling high, a storm coming in.

Feeling terrible, Grace started to arrange her heavy, blue linen napkin on her lap. "I am so sorry."

"About what?" A concerned David looked up from the specials sheet.

"I should've gone back to my condo and changed."

"Why?"

"Your friends are all dressed up. I've embarrassed you in front of them."

He briefly looked back at the main dining room. "They're business acquaintances, not friends. If we had hung around their table any longer, Max probably would have pulled out a financial proposal for my perusal."

"But I should've have changed, you suggested it."

"I suggested you might wish to change, because my late wife, Sylvia, would not leave the house unless she was dressed perfectly. Once we had a fire once in our Bangkok hotel. The alarms were going off, smoke filled the hallways and I rushed back to find her in the bathroom, combing her hair."

Grace smiled. "It was important to her."

"Normally Sylvia was a very sensible woman. If she was working at the health care carnival, she'd be in jeans, as she nailed up the booths, but her hair always looked perfect."

The waiter came for their order. The Pier was famous for it's Royal Surf and Turf, crabmeat stuffed lobster tail and

Kobe steaks with caviar sauce. David Gardiner could obviously afford it, but what was he expecting out of this meal? Sex? Prestige? Some sort of research commitment? Would he be disappointed if all he got tonight the pleasure of her company? Grace decided on the modestly priced Scallops Alfredo.

David was asking her, "What wine would you like?"

"Just unsweetened ice tea."

"With lemon?" The waiter asked.

"Yes."

"I'll have that too." David said as he looked to Grace. "You like shrimp?"

"Yes."

He turned to the waiter. "We're **very** hungry. Bring us two double shrimp cocktails and some of your fine rolls as soon as possible. "

The waiter nodded and hurried off, David turned to her and continued. "But when Sylvia went out in the evening, her outfits had to be perfect. She had me buy tons of Polaroid film just so I could photograph her from all sides, so that she could study the effect before we went out."

"A perfectionist."

"Fortunately, they came out with digital cameras. Saved me a fortune in film."

"I really don't have the time to..."

"To waste on something you think unimportant?" He smiled that slight smile of his. "But you still look lovely."

"In a polyester shirt and knit pants? I don't think that's what your friends would say."

"We do not dress to their standards, they dress to ours. When we were walking in, I saw several heads turn to look at you."

"Recognizing me in newspaper photos of a possible mass murderess?"

"Those newspapers credited you with being a

renowned scientist. I'm sure there are several people who recognized you as such, and if the amazing, brilliant, Dr. Farrington wears two different shoes on an evening out, you may set a fashion trend."

He was gently teasing, but Grace felt herself blushing. The waiter had hurried and was now was returning with two humongous goblets of scarlet cocktail sauce, with massive snowy shrimp hanging off them. Another waiter immediately followed the first, with a blue linen covered basket of freshly baked rolls. As she chewed a flaky, buttermilk biscuit, Grace found herself contentedly looking out at the ocean and darkness beyond. It was a comfortable silence, David was truly a relaxing man to be with. She wanted to know more about him. "Your late wife. Nailing boards, was she a carpenter?"

He seemed surprised. "No, she was my wife. Her grandmother insisted Sylvia graduate nursing school before we could marry, so that if anything ever happened, she'd be able to support herself. We had to wait a whole year." He shook his head. "That was ludicrous! Even if I turned out to be a total cad, who wouldn't support his family, Sylvia's side was almost as well off as mine. She had two trust funds before she was eight years old."

"Then she never had a job?"

Again he seemed to be surprised at the question. "Sylvia was my wife. She raised our two sons, pretty much raised my daughter from my first marriage. Of course, I regularly discussed our business affairs with her, she had a very good grasp of investment basics. A woman should know the finances, in case anything happens to her husband." He was selecting another roll. "Sylvia was on the board of just every charitable activity around: orphaned children, homeless veterans, way-ward horses. I'm sure they would have been very happy if we just wrote a check, but Sylvia was raised to feel that one has rent to pay for living in this world. She was an immensely dedicated, organized person, a type that most volunteer organizations really need."

Grace studied him quietly. "You still miss her."

He looked back her and didn't answer for a moment, saying finally. "Yes...a great deal. When I see a promising foal or hear a clever bit of jazz, I want so to share it with her again." He signaled a waiter to bring a refill for his ice tea. "I don't think about that as much as I used to. It's been...over a year now." He continued. "And you, Grace, why have you never married?"

"I am married."

That seemed to stop him. He looked up from his croissant. "I was told you weren't?"

"I'm married to my work." She was choosing her words carefully about something that seemed to mean much to him. "There is never enough time to do everything in this world, you have to decide what's important to you. Your wife was correct, we are all given certain talents, and put on this earth to use them, it's almost a debt that must be paid."

He nodded in agreement as their waiter was bringing the salads. As they finished dinner, that quiet enjoyment of his company seeped away in her usual anxiety in social situations. While he paid the bill Grace wondered what did he expect? To sleep with her? To have her work for his conglomerate? He certainly didn't need her puny social connections.

More practically, what did she want of him? Not to go to bed, not so fast, but he might expect that. They weren't kids. Did he have protection? Should she just say no just because it was the first date? But if she turned him down, would he ever ask her out on another date? Was this dinner a date or was he just feeling out a prominent scientist, before joining the Board at ORR? Should she invite him in to her condo? Some men felt that going to a women's apartment was kind of commitment. Would he?

Oh, God, she was so hopeless at this. She was still

debating as David turned off the Main Road to ORR. Grace found herself faintly perspiring from nervousness. She did like him and she did want to continue the relationship. What did the condo look like? Had she cleaned up the breakfast dishes? Her bed really wasn't made. Okay, Kurt would never care if the bed was made. Grace suspected David wouldn't either. But by asking him up, what was she offering?

As they drove toward her condo building, Grace relaxed. He was enough of a gentleman, with a reputation to protect, that she could invite him up to her condo. Where it went from that, well, maybe, for once, she could live without planning everything out. "Would you like to come up for coffee?" She thought about it, then awkwardly amended. "I mean tea–you like tea--I have tea."

Chapter 35

He glanced down at his watch. "Unfortunately, we got a much later start than I had planned and I have an important meeting tomorrow. Perhaps some other time?"

Humiliated, Grace pushed open the door and hurried out of his car. "Yes. Yes. Some other time." She didn't look back as Grace hurried upstairs. Obviously, she had made no impression and that was the end of Mr. David Gardiner!

Next day's work started off even worse. Three phone messages from Mark Silverstein. "Grace. Please call me–no, I think you have to come to my office today. A few minutes only, but it **must** be today."

She tried to ignore her lawyer's messages and get to work, but she couldn't. Grace called his office and made an appointment. Soon she was finding a large, white, converted Queen Anne house, with a discrete gold foil lettered sign 'Jones, Durham and Silverstein, Attorneys at Law'. In just twenty-five minutes, she was sitting in Mark's office, if anything so small could be dignified as an office, just a partitioning off of what once must have been a small breakfast room with a chair for her, a small desk and chair for him and no room for filing cabinets.

Her new criminal lawyer was all smiles. "I hadn't appreciated what as eminent client I had. I've been reading about you, the awards you've gotten and some of your writings."

"You're interested in the genetics?"

"I'm interested in you."

Is this what she interrupted her work for? "I'm really too busy to socialize."

His face got serious, and he began fiddled with his pen. "This is not social. As your Attorney of Record, the police have contacted me."

Grace felt herself getting cold, as if all life's warmth

was draining from her. "And?"

"They are requesting your fingerprints."

"Why?"

"Well, they found several fingerprints on the houseboat..."

"But I admitted..."

He swiftly corrected. "You stated–you don't admit–you state!"

"I stated I was on board." She copied carefully. "And they can't date finger prints?"

Mark rubbed his finger across his jaw, resting it on his lips. "Well, fingerprints in Marshall's blood would be presumably dateable."

"Mine weren't! His body blocked the door–I couldn't have gotten inside! But if his blood splashed over my older fingerprints, would that look as if I were there?"

Mark raised a quieting hand. "Perhaps they are trying to match prints and eliminate people who should've been there."

She stared at him, demanding to know. " Do you think I killed him? Would you still defend me?"

"A lawyer's mission is to defend innocent people and to defend guilty people. My job is to give you the best defense under the law. Now if you are innocent, I defend you one way. If you are guilty, anything you tell me is protected, but I can do the best job possible for you if I can anticipate what might be coming up?"

She wanted to just get up and leave, but something had to be done. "I didn't kill him."

"Actually, I don't think you did." He said in a calm, reassuring voice.

"But the police do?"

"I don't think they know who did what. In fact, I believe Kurt MacKay and Robert Jamison have also been called in for their prints."

"Do you think they have the killer's prints?"

"I doubt it. Not if they are calling in everybody."

"Can you ask them?"

"Unless you are going to court, I can't demand to see what they've got, but I've heard they've had divers off the Octagon for several days. If the state is going for all that expense, that probably means they don't, or at least didn't, have the murder weapon. Sea sprayed door handles are not the easiest thing to lift prints off of. No, I think this fingerprinting is to just try and put a little pressure on to see if anyone panics."

"Do I have to give them my fingerprints?"

"If they arrested and booked you, you would have to give them your prints. You could refuse until then." He looked hard at her. "But if what you have told me is totally honest, I think you should just cooperate. You're to go to the precinct where they questioned you before. No appointment is needed, do you want me to go with you?"

That would lose both of them hours of work. "No. I'll be fine." She said without really believing it.

"Now, if they want any other tests: blood, hair, mouth swab, say no. That they must clear that with me first. If they just ask you any friendly, casual questions, you are to tell them in a friendly, causal manner you can not answer anything unless your attorney is present. Understand?" The serious tone of his voice frightened her.

She felt to compelled to say something. "I didn't kill Charles Marshall. I didn't like him and I considered running from him. I wasn't inside the houseboat after he... I did try to push the door in. There will be my prints on that door. And probably old prints inside, I've worked on the Octagon for years and nobody much cleans it up, unless one us women is there working on it. There's probably coffee cups in the waste basket there from last Spring..."

Mark smiled tightly, obviously trying to calm her.

"Yes. Yes, but..."

She continued. "Kurt and Bobby, they didn't know Marshall well enough to want to kill him. But if I ever do wind up in court, I don't want my defense to be based on the fact that either of them might have done it." She looked at him wanting a confirming response.

He evaded it. "I believe you're being fingerprinted to eliminate any smudges you might have left, so the true murderer's prints can be detected. Probably it is the same thing with your colleagues."

"Your billing hours for all this, studying me, calling police, that must be adding up. I'll need to work out a payment schedule."

An almost kid like smile spread across Mark's face. "Our receptionist came into the firm's morning discussion, saying Dr. Grace Farrington had just called and would be coming in to see me in half an hour. The firm's senior members were suitably impressed. Both of them have seen you interviewed on one of the Science Channel series. Uncle Alan pointed out that David Gardiner had referred you to me. Mr. Gardiner is one of the firm's "A" clients and the firm likes keeping the 'A's happy. Now, I'm sure the firm would like me to be bringing in lots money, but having a prestigious client is the next best thing. Don't worry about my fees."

The warmth of his appreciation wore off as she parked her car at the police station. She hoped she might run into Mac or Ben, or any other officer she might know. She didn't. There was definitely no fawning deference to the eminent Dr. Farrington here. A cold desk sergeant told her to wait over on the hard, wooden bench. Sitting there was like being in trouble in high school.

It was past lunch time and she was hungry but afraid to hunt through the police station for a candy machine. The clock ticked time away as she was just kept sitting there; maybe this was a preview of her up coming life in jail? After what seemed like hours, a stocky, uniformed man came out and picked up the clip board from the Sergeant. He had her follow him into the back room. She expected to dip her fingers into another squishy, green, ink pad, but this time they had a glass tablet connected to a computer.

Grace was reaching to press her prints in the blocks outlined on the glass, when he rudely grabbed her index finger and roughly forced it down, rolling it across the block. He did that with each finger, on both her hands. The prints were appearing on a computer screen. She was actually very curious about the program, but before she could start questioning him, he was sitting back down in front of his screen and with a curt nod he dismissed her. Well, if he could turn his back on her, he wasn't treating her like a prospective murderess.

Chapter 36

Still upset from the police station, she settled back into her lab work or tried to. Her unanswered e-mail list seemed endless and next week it would be November. How much lost time had all this cost her? Her head was bent, as she heard the lab door opening, oh, shit, she hadn't locked it with a mass murderer running around. She might be the next victim of the Widow's curse!

Somebody coming in. A man with buckets. Kurt! Grace jumped up and met him joyously. "You found blue tailed lobsters! I've had Nick working on the tanks and Inger's running salinity checks to make sure it matches the sound at twenty feet. I'll turn on the cooling..."

Kurt shook his head, sadly saying, "Nope. These are disgustingly healthy. Bobby's still back at the boat, re-loading scuba tanks. Figure we can get one more dive in before dark, but he says if you take these to Sara, you guys can have her lobster bisque tonight."

Or lobster bake at her house for David? Or for Kurt? Suddenly Grace's mental alarm bell rang. Kurt was being extra nice, which meant Kurt MacKay wanted something. "What's the catch with the catch?"

He looked innocent. "I jes know how you like lobster."

"And?"

Kurt was smart man. He reached into his jacket pocket and pulled out a folded sheaf of papers. "You remember that formal do you agreed to go to with me?"

"Yes. In the City."

"Well, it's at the Japanese Embassy."

"That should be nice."

"Aaup. But there is a little security clearance problem."

"Japanese or U.S.?"

He was giving her a big, friendly smile. "Both."

"Both? For just a minor awards dinner?" She took the paper--papers–from his hand.

He looked embarrassed. "Well, there'll be a member of the Japanese Imperial Family handing out the awards there. We're not getting one."

She started unfolding the sheets of printed questionnaires, line after line to be filled out by her. "Great. At least the ones for the Japanese are in English."

"I asked for those special. You just got to fill in some blanks, make a copy of your driver's licence and passport. "

"Both?"

"Jes give'em to me. I'll copy them for you."

She raised a skeptical eyebrow. "Then what? I find out some under-aged bimbo is buying whiskey, with proof in the name of Grace Farrington?"

He smiled slyly. "Hadn't thought of that."

She glanced at papers. "They want my colleges, addresses and phone numbers? My high school and my elementary school principal's name?"

"They said they would come to your laboratory for the interview." Kurt added helpfully.

"Interview?!" She looked back at the questionnaires. "Do I own a gun? Do they want the serial numbers? Kurt, my last fellowship for National Globe Magazine took less documentation! With this kind of background checking, how in hell did they pass you, with your KKK and biker associations?"

Kurt looked sheepish. "Had a bit of trouble with that and had to call my Japanese researcher friend, Skipper. He had enough pull to get me passed. Maybe I should call him about you?"

This was too much! "I'm in the midst of teaching a whole semester of graduate classes and I haven't done a syllabus yet. We have entered a binding agreement with *Affiliated,* taking their money, spending that money on a study of diseased lobsters, that we can't find. That sounds like we might be looking at fraud prosecutions! The police are fingerprinting us for a murder, maybe two, and for a plate of rubber chicken, you want to drag your friend Skipper's reputation into this kettle of souring clam chowder?"

He raised a hand to calm her. "Stop worrying about the classes. Bobby did all of Eric's and he's told me he's got that covered. All you got to do is show up one or two times, like Eric did, and turn on the charm for the students."

"I'm not Eric, I can't do charming! Look, Kurt, I just can't handle this Embassy dinner on top of everything else! Another time, I could have, but not now!" With finality, she handed back the security papers.

She expected an argument, for him to try to cut a deal, but he only nodded. "It's a bad time for you, shouldn't be pushing ya. Keep the lobsters anyhow." He turned, his shoulders a bit slumped.

Grace thought it might be a ploy, but he just kept walking, not looking back. When he reached the door, she called out. "This means a lot to you doesn't it?"

He turned slowly. "Yeah. I've been writing and e-mailing Skipper for years. He's always studying minnows and is considered quite an authority on them. He knows your work well, thinks highly of it and wanted to talk with you about it at dinner." He stopped. She said nothing, so finally Kurt continued. "Yeah. I bragged a lot about my work, my connections and my relationship with you."

"Relationship?"

"Jes as a fellow scientist." He looked away. "If Skipper does ever come out here, he'll see I live in an beat-up old sail boat, that my research diesel blows a fog bank of blue smoke, and that I fight for lab space with undergraduates. Whal, playing the eccentric scientist can only get ya so far."

She walked over to him, touching the fabric of his jacket arm. "Your work is damn good!"

"I don't have any awards... haven't published much."
He lowered his head.

How could he run himself down so? "You've singled
handedly found a new shell disease, diagnosed it and set up a
treatment plan that may have saved entire season's oyster
crop."

"That's something." He admitted.

"And when you discovered that your sponsor was a
major polluter, you went after them."

"Yeah, those son-of-bitches were willing to give me a
research contract worth a million and half, if I kept my mouth
shut."

"But you didn't."

"Aaup and lost my biggest grant. Still, those bastards
would have poisoned every creature in the Sound and not
thought a thing of it." He looked out the windows toward the
Harbor. "But, I could've had a really cool yawl..."

"If you had another chance, would you still turn them
in?"

He twisted his lips bitterly. "Aaup."

"Then your friend Skipper should be proud to know
you." She stopped for a moment, then squared her shoulders.
"Kurt, you've got to publish more, you can do it! You will do
it and I'll see to it! When this next Director of Research comes
in–he's got to push for the recognition your work deserves!"

Kurt smiled lopsidedly. "But Skipper's only over here
fer a week, and he's got loads of meetings to catch up on." He
thought for a minute. "If I can coax him over to Oyster River,
would you spend a little time talking with him?"

More work time lost, but, "I could talk with him, if he
comes here."

"Only I asked him months ago; he wanted to come
here, but said his schedule is pretty tight, he's headed for
Washington after this." He looked back at her, not pleading,
just stating. "But if I walk into that dinner with a classy lady

like you on my arm, a respected lady scientist, one whose work Skipper is interested in... " He stopped, his face unreadable. "You don't owe me, but..."

But she did. Grace owed him for years of chaotic, but solid friendship, that at weak points in her life had strengthened her resolve to fight. She took the papers back and penciled nine numbers across the top page of the United States Homeland Security sheet. "That's my social security number. Give it to the American State Department. Have them check my security clearance with the Pentagon, and then have them clear me with the Japanese Embassy."

He seemed surprised. "How high a level you got?"

"If I told you, I'd have to kill you." She turned back toward her desk, calling over her shoulder. "It will be high enough to clear me for a dinner, with a member of the Imperial family, who is sitting way across the room."

He started following her. "Is this a lapsed clearance?"

"No. It's active."

"Active? I know an ex-Air force guy doing research for a defense company, his company has to pay every year to keep up his clearance. They're bitching because his clearance is so high, the higher the clearance, the higher the price. Who paying for yours? Oyster River Research?"

"No."

"You don't pay that yourself?"

"No."

He thought about that. "The U.S. tax payer–through the military?"

"Kurt, I don't want to get into this."

He studied her carefully. "Saw you get on a boat once–Navy cutter. Followed ya a bit, seeing ya headed for Crabapple Island, couldn't get nearer cause that island is off limits for civilians. That's where they test all the stuff, like anthrax, that you don't want spreading on to the land. That was about the time when they were trying to trace that smallpox weapon source, so I figured you were working for those guys?"

"Kurt, you've got your escort to the dinner. Now shut up."

He gave a friendly leer. "Yes, Mam. Gotta think of a way to thank ya properly."

Chapter 37

Knowing him, she smiled tolerantly. "Shouldn't you be hunting some blue tailed lobsters?"

"Aaup. I'm going." Kurt stopped before door. "For the dinner, what color formal gown are ya wearing?"

"Why?"

"Maybe I should get yer a corsage?"

Oh, shit. "I've haven't made up my mind which one to wear yet. I won't need flowers."

But she damn well would need a dress. After he left, Grace regretfully shut down her computer and set out her instructions for her assistants. Freya had needed to switch their next Monday dinner to today and since Grace was pleasantly surprised to find they were still talking, she immediately agreed. Maybe Grace could pick up a dress before she went to Freya's? But first she had to haul these lobsters over to Sara's cooking pot.

In no time she was parking in the small forty car lot, in the center of Oyster River Harbor town. The mall would have had a better selection, but she really didn't have the time. Lord & Toms carried country lady classics tending toward casual but probably no gowns. She crossed the street past the Cheese Shop and Freya's, to a white, two story house set back twenty feet or so, now converted to a dress shop, *The Country Dame*.

A wooden porch led to a black varnished door, with multi-paned windows. Inside were round tables displaying folded, heavy silk scarves, in all the colors of mums in bloom and racks of coordinating blouses and woolen pants. At a central desk, a young clerk talked into her cell phone, as she unconsciously picked at the ring piercing her lower lip.

On her own, Grace found a rack of evening gowns against the back wall, in some nice colors: indigo blue to go with her eyes, black jet beading for her hair and a apricot. She decided against the shorter, cocktail dresses, she needed something more formal. She picked out a floor length gold net over gold satin in her size that wasn't half bad. Should be good enough for staring across the room at the Imperial family. Grace looked to the sales girl.

The Sales girl's attention had crawled deeper into her phone, and she was now industriously texting. Grace saw a curtain in the back, that must be the dressing room. Should she just try it on? Grace flipped the price tag over, six hundred and thirty six dollars for one night? With greater respect, Grace replaced the gold gown back on its pole altar. She glanced at a few of the other prices, nope, not getting a gown here! She walked out, wondering how the sales girl, who seemed completely oblivious to her, always seemed to keep her back to Grace, no matter where she was in the store?

When she came outside, Freya's shop was to her right, but Grace needed to do something about this dress thing. She turned left on the worn cement sidewalk. More stores, a private house, then the Sailor's Church, a white clapboard structure with a tall, central bell tower. To the side was a step down entrance to the basement, where they had the 'Church Redemption' shop.

Maybe they've something used? When she opened the door, a bell on a curl of brass bounced and jangled. A white haired lady was sorting clothes donations from a box that originally held Dewars Whiskey; looking up, the saleswoman smiled at her brightly. "The leaves are starting to turn."

"But it's warm–Indian summer." Grace surveyed tables covered with sets of champagne flutes, only slightly chipped, boxes of costume jewelry, and brightly colored toys. On the sides were shelves of books and aluminum cooking ware.

The saleslady continued as she worked. "Nicest time of the year. We have a sale on books and records."

"Does anyone still play vinyl records?"

"We can sell you a phonograph. It's right over there."

"Actually, what I was looking for is a formal gown."

"Oh, we have lots of wedding things. Shame to wear them just once." Rapidly, the elderly lady moved two boxes, got out from behind her counter, and lead Grace over to the clothing racks at the back of the basement.

To Grace's relief, someone (probably this volunteer) had hung everything by size with homemade, cardboard number collars marking off the sections. The volunteer left her at the rack to walk back and continue her pricing. On the pole there was even less of a selection than at the last shop. A kind of limp, tired lot: prom dresses; lacy wedding gowns; and some mother-of-brides. Not much for a thin, tall woman, no fall colors, but Grace narrowed it down to a pale blue with neon blue-shot beads, a strawberry ice cream pink A-line with huge flowers, and a citrousy chiffon.

The cheery voice behind the desk called out. "You can try them on behind that blanket curtain. Let me get the back lights on for you, we leave those lights off to save on electricity."

Grace turned the tags over, twenty to thirty dollars, these dresses definitely started looking better. Behind the green army blanket, she tried all three of them on in front of the frameless mirror hung against the wall. Her favorite, the blue needed a new zipper and had a stain. Could she get that fixed in time? Probably not. The citrousy chiffon made her look pregnant, quite a feat on someone as thin as herself. The pink, with it's huge upholstery looking flower print–well, it fit and it wasn't stained. Maybe she could get the bow off. The deciding factor: it was only twenty bucks.

Grace carried it to the counter. It looked like it had been ironed, all of these things here did. She looked over and saw an ironing board in the corner. When the saleswoman wasn't greeting, sorting, pricing, sweeping and selling, she was probably ironing all the donations.

"Oh, you found something. Good! Such pretty

flowers."

Grace handed it to her and the saleslady wrapped the gown in tissue paper, and then slipped it in to a Bloomingdales's shopping bag.

"Now, if you have anything you want to pass on–recycling is all the thing now, so we give credit for donations."

Grace shook her head and handed the saleswoman a twenty dollar bill.

The woman headed over to the green cigar box she used as a cash register. "Now lets see. It's marked twenty..."

"Do you need tax?"

"No, and that rack is half price today, so it's just ten."

Grace took her change and wondered if the sweet saleswoman had sized up her clothing and decided the church shop should dispose a little charity on someone dressed so poorly.

Outside she breathed crisp, fall air and was glad to be away from the smell of old clothes and musty books. As she stood there Grace noticed a two foot wide by three foot long brass plaque on the front of the church; curious, she realized in all these years here she had never read it. In 1896, it was dedicated to the sailors and ships that left Oyster River Harbor never to return, idly she scanned down the list. Towards the bottom was the *Siren,* Grace looked over the long list of lost sailors and Capt. Benjamin Smith, Lemuel Smith and Wardell Smith led the list. Those men had existed, lost their lives at sea and had been mourned, so that silly witch's curse hadn't been a total fiction.

Back up the street to another set back and the stairs to Freya's New Age Shop. As outside the sun had sunk below the tree tops, Freya had her soft lights on and that huge, pink salt crystal by the door glowed warmly, from the light platform underneath it. Freya was just finishing the sale of some agate worry beads. After the customer left, she turned to Grace. "Well, just made the total profit for today–all of fifty cents."

Grace nodded. "Maybe someone will rush in and buy the pink crystal for a few thousand?" She noted that Freya had a white wrapped bandage on her hand. "You cut yourself?"

Freya nodded. "Splitting live oak branches is harder than it looks in *Viking Ship Building* illustrations."

"Do you guys actually intend to go out rowing on the water with that furring?"

"Faering."

"When you finish building it?"

"Yes." Said Freya proudly. "We have a few volunteers helping us already. Wednesday evenings and Saturday afternoons down in the old Boatwright Barn."

"There's no trespassing signs at the entrance."

"We've got permission from the Museum." Freya was throwing down a challenge. "We could use your help, not that you will ever get out of your lab." Freya looked Grace's hand. "What's in the bag?"

"Dress for a formal dinner."

Freya looked delighted. "David Gardiner has..."

"No, its over with Mr. Gardiner. Kurt MacKay's got a scientific friend visiting, and he's dragging me along for my reputation."

Annoyed Freya grumbled. "You have to buy a dress for that bigoted fool?"

"It's formal affair at the Japanese Embassy in the City, a member of the Royal family will be there."

An appreciative smile spread over Freya's face. "You'll be dining with the Imperial family?"

"I'm going to be sitting at the geek table way across the room."

"You've got to get a book on etiquette. Japanese etiquette."

"Why?"

"You have to know how to address him or her. You're Royal Highness? Your Majesties? Your Emperorship?"

"Since it is a minor awards dinner, they probably roped in some distant relative to sit there in a kimono and eat chicken."

"It's at a New York Embassy!"

"Okay. Eat prime rib. I probably have to address him as the first cousin, twice removed from the Emperor's brother-in-law."

"You've been to the White House," Freya protested. "Saw the President."

"At the White House, the closest I got to the President was a 'nod by' on the reception line."

Excitedly Freya reached for the bag. "Let's see the dress." Rather than have the bag ripped, Grace surrendered it, but Freya's smile faded as she pulled out the limp organdy. "It's pink. Bright pink."

"Yes."

"That isn't your color. And those huge flowers..." Freya looked her up and down. "This is a summer dress..."

"It's the right price." Grace said firmly.

An unhappy Freya looked to her. "What–they paid you fifty bucks to take it?"

"You want me to try it on?" Grace asked, she needed to get this over with so they could have dinner.

Freya stuffed it back in to the paper bag. "Have you ever been over to *The Blue Peacock*?"

"Is that a new restaurant?"

"No. It's that fancy woman's shop, across the road, alongside Abe's book store. You've seen it! Come on." Freya grabbed her cape from the back room.

"Wait a second–it's not five. You can't close up your shop yet."

Drawing herself up to her full six foot height, Freya

closed her eyes and pressed two fingers against her forehead. "No, I do not intuit any more customers today." With that pronouncement, Freya went to the door and turned the sign around, so now 'closed' showed outside.

When Freya started marching relentlessly ahead, Grace found it just easier to follow. Down past the Cheese shop, across the street to the beginning of the parking lot. There was a tall, narrow, two story house painted forest green, with tan, gingerbread trim; an oval sign hung out over the sidewalk proclaiming '*The Blue Peacock*' with the words were configured into a stylized Peacock's tail. Grace followed Freya up pitted granite steps, between two high, bow windows that were decorated with elaborate carved Victorian chairs, draped with silk blouses and long, pearl necklaces.

Grace put a staying hand on Freya's arm as she reached for the door. "They don't show prices. That means it's too expensive to even look in there!"

"We're trying to pick out what would be the best style for you. Rose has a tremendous eye, we'll get her to pick out something flattering, then go to some bargain basement at the mall and try to reproduce it."

"That's wasting the saleswoman's time."

Freya made an elaborate show of looking through the windows. "I don't see any other customer in there. Besides, Rose is down at my shop every lunch hour, drooling over that great, pink crystal of mine, she rubs her hands on it for energy, says it's warmth helps her arthritis. We both know she hasn't got the money to pay for it, but I never complain about her rubbing healing off my crystal. She's not going to say anything about us trying on her dresses."

Inside, Grace found herself wanting to hide her offending recycled shopping bag, while the tall, aristocratic, silver haired woman looked at Grace as if she was a bag lady coming in to use the rest room.

Still, Freya was all charm. "Rose, this is my friend,

Grace, you know, Dr. Farrington? She needs a gown for an awards dinner." They had walked into a room furnished with a heavy Empire horse-hair couches and light, elegant Adam chairs. Against the back wall, two beige levered doors evidently discretely concealed try on rooms, on either side of a seven foot tall, beveled mirror in an rectangular, cherry frame. Along the other walls, three antique wooden wardrobes were opened and lined with light moss colored velvet to display drawers of jewelry, racks of bright blouses and long skirts.

Rose and Freya were moving to a large wrought iron rack at the left and Grace just passively followed as Freya bubbled. "It's a formal reception for a member of the Japanese Imperial family."

Madam Rose didn't seem to think that was in any way out of the ordinary. She just studied Grace from head to toe and then pulled off three floor length gowns. A white Grecian, a scarlet empire and topaz blue wool crepe. "Try these on."

"Are they the right size?" Grace foolishly asked.

They were. Grace started to look at the first price tag, but Freya just brushed it out of her fingers. "We're just looking. Grace, try them on, I want to see each one of them, before we leave!"

Grace went back to the first dressing room and found a gilded Louis XVI chair, gilded framed, full length oval, mirror and gilded, baroque dress hooks. She looked at the three gowns and really liked the blue, putting it on first, letting the soft wool crepe flow down her figure. Across the front, there was a simple, sumi-e like design, that must have been hand painted: silver brush stokes of wind bending bamboo grew from the hem to the bodice. Nothing like this could ever be reproducible in the Mall's bargain basement. This dress thinned her waist, with the folds at the top subtlety added to her bust, while the waist line dropped in irregular, over lapping panels making her look graceful. Even the topaz blue really brought out her eyes, it just felt right.

When Grace walked out of the fitting room, Freya was over with Rose by the window, as always, trying to sell her merchandise. "Now Rose, if you had that pink crystal set right here, you could sit by it, while you're crocheting. The pink matches your aura and will resinate with your energy level, increasing the good vibrations of your showroom."

Rose didn't look sold. "It's a bit expensive..."

"Not if it increases your health, wealth and happiness." Freya pointed out.

Grace coughed to get their attention. Two sets of calculating eyes studied her as if under a microscope, as Rose nodded, saying, "Needs to be taken in a touch at the bust, I could take a dart there."

Freya cocked her head critically. "The color's a bit light for fall."

Rose corrected. "Makes her own skin stand out more, gives warmth. You know, Freya, one of those wide, green jade bracelets you sell, that would be beautiful for this, just one set on her right arm."

Freya nodded. "She could borrow it. Grace, walk a bit in it." She looked to Rose. "Is it too tight on the hips?"

Rose shook her head. "No, look at the drape, it falls perfectly."

Freya shook her head, grandly announcing to Grace, "Still, I want to see the others."

Grace stepped back in the changing booth and looked in the mirror. Any dress here would be expensive, but she tried to look dispassionately at the blue gown, the way it just wrapped around her figure like it was made just for her. If she bought it, she could wear it for David, she could almost see his eyes light up in appreciation. And, if she ever did get the Nobel nod, she'd need a gown for the Swedish Royal family. It could be considered a career investment.

Grace maneuvered the price tag, so she could see it.

Oh, my God, with what the gown cost, she could keep one assistant employed for months. Sadly Grace half swirled before the mirror one least time, letting the gown's loveliness fall about her hips. She stared one more moment in the glass's reflection at a woman almost beautiful, then very, very carefully pulled it off.

She looked at the price tags on the other two gowns. Each were less than the blue, but still too much for her to pay, it was ridiculous to even try them on.

From beyond the louvered door, Freya was commanding. "Grace, I want to see those other dresses."

Rather than waste time arguing, Grace just slipped on the white and walked out. Rose and Freya was deep in discussion of "rose auras" and "energy levels". They briefly looked up at Grace, then Freya said. "Try the other one."

The scarlet fit too tightly on the hips, but to get it over with, Grace walked out and paraded past them and just kept walking in a loop back to the dressing room. Taking it off, she made sure that all the dresses were carefully rehung on their hangers before carrying them out.

Rose met her, taking the three dresses from her arms. "I'll take care of those. Now, Freya mentioned you have a authentic Chinese blouse that needs a skirt. Look at those over there."

Freya was already looking through the rack. "This brown velvet's not bad..."

Embarrassed, Grace just wanted to get out of there, saying softly to Freya. "We need to get going." After all her years of work and research and discoveries what did she have? Not enough to splurge and buy a dress in *The Blue Peacock*.

As Freya was looking at a glass case of necklaces, she called out to Rose. "You know, some of my gold wire wrapped fossil necklaces should be here. How about taking some on consignment?"

Slipping a large silver box in to a silver shopping bag,

Rose returned from the backroom. "That might work, the delicate ones. I'll be by tomorrow to select some as a trial and maybe some of your matching handcrafted rings for the junior debs. Yes." Rose put the fancy silver bag next to Grace's reused church bag. "I do hope your dinner is a success. We do alter for free, and I could tighten that bodice just a touch. But you might be better off with one of those special jell padded bras."

Grace stammered, "I–I-I'm not buying one of your dresses. They're lovely, but...not right now. I'll have to think about it."

"I'm sorry," Rose said firmly. "We don't accept returns."

Chapter 38

Grace was floored. "I never said I would buy anything!"

Rose looked at her. "You didn't. Freya's bought the dress."

Grace looked to her friend. "Freya! Which dress?"

"The blue, it looked the best on you." Freya looked to Rose for confirmation.

Rose smiled knowledgeably. "Oh, yes. Most flattering."

Grace noted an art deco blue peacock decorated both fancy silver bag and box. Beautiful, but not for them. "Freya, you don't have the money either!"

Freya grandly swept up both shopping bags, starting out the door and Grace found herself just following helplessly. "One does not need money, when one has a three foot high, pink energy crystal." She looked back to Rose. "Both our shops are past closing. I'll have Mac carry it over tomorrow at lunch. Rose, I think it may help that pain in your shoulder, too."

Rose just smiled, as she closed the door behind them, locking it firmly.

Outside, Grace just looked at Freya. "I can not accept this!"

Freya only replied, "Who used her grant money to pay for Mac's junior college?"

"This dress cost too much."

"You are talking retail, remember Rose and I pay wholesale prices for our stock. Rose desperately wanted that pink crystal, but she could never spend that kind of money. I want you in this dress that I never could afford, but we've managed to reach a transaction that everyone but the tax man would be happy with. Your contribution is to just wear the dress." She held out the silver shopping bag.

Long term friendship with Freya meant the jockeying

of two strong wills. Over the years, there were a few times, very few, that they had deadlocked. Without ever putting in words, both of them had long ago decided, when they were at total odds, the person who felt strongest should be the person who prevailed. This time it was Freya. Losing graciously Grace reached out and took the shopping bag and simply said, "Thank you."

"Now we eat out?" Asked a triumphant Freya.

"First I want to stop at Abe's."

Abe--as usual--was reading. Freya got a cup of Abe's free coffee before she browsed. A couple were standing at his counter, but Abe read on.

Grace called out. "Abe, you have customers."

He looked up. First at the couple with their books to be purchased, then back, regretfully, at the book in his hand and he sighed. Then put his down and reached for their books. "Ah. Crock pot recipes. Can't go wrong with that in the fall. Will that be cash or credit?"

Grace waited patiently for his customers to leave and then started, "Abe, when I was at Miakos' show almost all his paintings were sold out."

"Elise was in here the other day, now they're all sold out. She wants that concrete period piece he had traded me for some Art Deco porno. Shame he couldn't have had all that money while he was alive."

"Who is Miakos' heir?"

Abe blinked and pushed his black frames higher on his nose. "That'd be interesting. He was just divorced from Tina. She's gone back to waitressing at the Alpine and she still has that newspaper delivery route."

"Newspaper delivery?"

"Aaup. Still does it on her bicycle. Miakos said she did it to keep in shape. Up at dawn and pedaling, keeping the inches off her hips."

"Then she'll inherit?"

"Whal, they just divorced." He stopped to think about it. "Course most people even with a bitter divorce take awhile to change their wills, if Miakos ever made a will in the first place. I don't know just who would know, but I'll look into it for you. If there is a will it will have to be probated. Don should know." He trailed off.

"Tina waitresses at the Alpine?"

"It's a biker bar, up off Laddin's Rock Lane. Looks like a Swiss ski lodge, set in bunch of pine trees, with picnic tables and swings for the kids."

"At a biker bar?"

"Bikers getting older." He looked up at her hard. "But a rough place at night! Don't go there alone, ask Kurt MacKay to go with you, he probably knows Tina. She's got red hair."

Grace said. "I owe you."

"Come in some Saturday and do a signing of your books for me," Abe said. All the time they were talking, he had been making sidelong glances at his neglected book. Seeing Grace satisfied, he picked up his book, moved from behind the counter and sat in one of the over stuffed couches by the coffee urn.

There was something else she needed. "Do you have any business etiquette books?"

He pointed to a set of shelves, jammed under the window as he dove back into *Tales of the Silk Road*.

Grace found an etiquette book, a thick, hard cover called *Proper Traveling*. The section on Japanese royal titles covered half a chapter: Heika used for sovereign royalty; Tennŏ means "His Majesty the Emperor". Nope. They wouldn't be sending the Emperor for a minor awards ceremony. Denka, non-sovereign royalty. Kakka is 'Your Excellency', that includes ministers, ambassadors. That would probably be all that she needed–Kakka but she still tried mentally pronouncing Denka–she always found Japanese a vocally strident, aggressive sounding language like German.

For Grace it was better to read than speak.

Grace kept reading. 'When addressing others, one should be aware of their status, the difference in your status to them and one's degree of familiarity.' She really should read this whole thing, Grace looked for the book's price, fifty-six dollars? For a one minute introduction on the reception line? If she was presented to anyone important, she'd just do the universally understood gesture, she'd smile and look clueless. Putting the book back Grace looked to Abe. "Are you closing? Do you want us to lock the door?"

Abe never looked up. "Nope. Might get a customer."

Grace nodded and left him immersed on the Silk Road, knowing that with Abe reading, someone could come in, steal a book, steal the cash register and carry out the couch Abe was sitting on, without Abe ever being the wiser.

Chapter 39

On Wednesday the phone in her laboratory rang.

"Grace, it's David Gardiner."

The gentleman who just dropped her home after dinner because he was in such a hurry? "How did your meeting go?" She asked coolly.

"Meeting?"

"After dinner at the Pier, you had to hurry off to a meeting?"

He had to think about it. "Oh, yes. I hadn't packed yet. I got a little sleep before the limo picked me up at 5:30 in morning, unfortunately, there was some sort of storm, somewheres, so my plane to Rome had a three hour delay."

"Then you missed your meeting?"

"They couldn't hold it without me, but they refused our terms. Not worth the trip, just one of those wasted days," He said disgustedly.

Flying to Rome? Well at least he had an excuse for brushing her off.

David was continuing. "I was wondering...I love the possibilities of a symphonic orchestra, and there are so few opportunities to hear really good ones these days. The Boston Pops will be playing in New Haven this Saturday. It's short notice, I know, but would you like to go?"

She would love to, but. "That would have been nice, but I'm going to an awards dinner in the City this Saturday."

"Oh. If you need an escort, I come with a tuxedo?"

She smiled at the thought of his business card, '*have tuxedo, will travel*'. "Thank you, but I'm already the escort of another gentleman."

There was pause, and his voice had an almost imperceptible cooling. "Well, perhaps some other time."

Grace had the distinct feeling that if he hung up now, she would never hear from him again. "You know, David, I heard that a really good Hibachi restaurant just opened up, *Fuji Mountain*, maybe we could do that some time? I really like Japanese."

"Haven't had Hibachi. Must try it. When would you be free?"

When was she ever really free? Her work was never done, but if she wanted to spend time with him she had to make some sort of commitment. "Tomorrow night 6:30?"

"Excellent. Where will I pick you up?"

"My lab?"

"I'll be there."

For a moment she imagined him coming in the door as she swirled before him in the *Blue Peacock* gown. No really appropriate for what was supposed to be a non-threatening dinner between to friends–well, acquaintances. She'd wear her Chinese silk dragon blouse, but she needed to get a long skirt or at least fancier pants. After she finished today she'd head for the mall, maybe buy some sling back shoes; no high heels because David was just her height. More hours wasted from work, but it was time she went on a real date again.

Since she had already broken from her work related line of thought, Grace pulled up her Suspect spreadsheet and studied it carefully. She was getting nowhere on Marshall's murder. And now she had to add that her assistant, Bobby Jamison, knew Gigi Rameriz, since he was her Instructor. Did Gigi know Bobby was to be meeting with Marshall? Could she have been a witness against him, so Bobby killed her? She couldn't believe that. Maybe there was another angle she could look at? Could Miakos have killed Gigi? She was found days after Miakos died, but the newspapers said the police weren't exactly sure of when she died. What if Miakos killed Gigi, and then realizing what he had done he jumped in the harbor?

The more Grace thought about it, the more she realized she needed another date--right now--an escort for a place where you didn't dare park a black Mercedes. She kept checking from her laboratory window until she heard Kurt's lobster yawl chugging in, then grabbing her jacket she headed out to the docks.

When she reached the boats, Bobby walked past her with his shoulders in a tired hunch and his hands stuffed for warmth in his windbreaker. Seeing her, he only nodded slightly and walked on.

Kurt was kneeling on the boat's deck untangling some wet netting. His own face a tangle of weary lines.

"Kurt?"

"No blue lobsters." He said without bothering to look up.

"I figured as much. Kurt, want to go to a bar with me?"

From the bobbing yawl's deck he had to look up at her, suspiciously asking, "Is this a trick question?"

"Nope. There's a place on Laddin's Rock Lane, in the pine woods. Looks like a ski house from Switzerland with a lot of motorcycles out in front."

"The Alpine."

" Does the Alpine serve food?"

"Not so much that you might want ta' eat any of it." He thought about it and had to give credit due. "Whal, they do a have a real hearty chili."

Grace said, "We can take my car."

Kurt wearily shook his head. "Grace, you don't go to a biker bar in a station wagon! You got a leather jacket?"

"There's a dress code?"

"We're going on my bike, if I slide on gravel on a turn with the motorcycle, it's lot better to be peeling leather off a jacket then yer skin." He looked to his boat. "I got an old one that should fit ya."

She vividly remembered the last time she rode his bike. "How about an extra helmet?"

He retrieved a jacket for her and an extra helmet off his sailboat and coming back on to the dock, he smilingly hooked his arm inside hers. "Lady, you drinking booze during workin' hours? Jes why yer're taking this sudden slide into wild abandon?"

"Do you know a Tina who waitresses at the Alpine? "

"Describe her rack and ass."

"She's Miakos' widow." That didn't seem to ring a bell. "She has red hair?"

"Might know her."

"We can question her..."

Grace started, only to be cut off as he exploded. "Question?! At the Alpine? Hell, lady, you keep your mouth shut when you aren't sipping a drink or tongue kissing me. I'll do the talking. Jes go in and order yer drink."

"Apricot sour."

He closed his eyes in pain. "I'll order the drinks. Ya got yer choice of Budweiser or Beck's."

"If it's beer only, maybe a Corona with a lime slice?"

He looked stern. "Alpine don't do Mexican. Only good old U.S. of A."

"Becks is brewed in Germany."

"Whal, U.S.A. and Aryan."

Grace understood the Aryan German bit when she saw the remnants of third Reich uniforms decorating the walls and some of the shaved-headed patrons. Inside, the Alpine was wood-walled, smokey, and punctuated constantly by raucous laughter. Grace started to slip into a seat at one of the round tables by the door, but Kurt put his fingers around her arm and guided her past the bar to a dark, high walled booth at the back of the room.

As they walked over several patrons looked up and smiled at Kurt. He settled her in a booth then headed back across the room, stopping to smile-up a big breasted, blonde waitress. At the bar he joked with the bartender, then talked awhile to a red-haired waitress, before finally turned to two hulking guys leaning on the dark wood bar. Amazed Grace studied Kurt, who stood up proudly, like an equal to these mountain sized outlaws. She was watching him when she realized two more hulking men were now over shadowing her booth.

The first guy was heavy-set, shaved headed, with a thready van dyke. His tight-eyed friend was tall, scrawny and wearing what looked like a bicycle chain around his neck.

"So Kurt's got a new broad," Heavy-set said to scrawny.

"Kinda flat chested for Kurt," Scrawny returned.

Should she smile, curtsy or run? Somehow Grace doubted that the traveling etiquette book would have had the answer. "You know Kurt?" No, she wasn't supposed to question.

Van dyke answered. "Maybe."

Grace had to say something, because they were looking at her like she was on the menu. "Kurt tells me the chili here is real good."

"Got fresh whitetail in it today." Van dyke said in a flat voice.

White tail? Deer meat she guessed. Road kill? Kurt was coming back to the table. Grace instantly felt comforted when he put down two sweating brown bottles of beer and slid in the booth seat, putting his arm around her shoulders possessively drawing her close.

Kurt looked up at the massively-set guy. "Wayne, see ya got yer bike chromed."

Wayne's face lit up and like any proud papa, he reached for his wallet and started pulling out pictures. "Got photos before and after. Look at the rust on that fender! Had that all redone, chromed the handlebars, carburetor, exhaust–everything!"

"A masterpiece," Kurt pronounced as he passed the

photos to her and Grace tried to smile appreciatively.

Tight-eyes still kept staring at Grace. "Nice lady you got there."

"Ted, this is Grace." Kurt looked proudly at her, and then held up two fingers to emphasize her achievements. "Police questioning her for not one, but two separate murders!"

Grace tried to smile modestly, as both bikers seemed properly impressed, with Wayne muttering admiringly. "You can pick 'um, Kurt!"

Somebody had called a game and Kurt's friends drifted off as they started throwing darts across the room to a target on the wall by the door.

"Are we going to throw?" Grace asked softly.

Ken rubbed her shoulder. "I am, when was the last time ya threw?"

She thought about it. "College?"

"Yer not throwing, Lady, those are weighted, steel tipped darts with sharpened points. Ya miss and one of those tough guys at the tables under that target's gonna be real pissed."

"It's dangerous to sit over there by the door."

"That's why were sitting back here." He called out. "Sam, chalk my name on the board!"

"How many guys get hit?"

Kurt drank his beer, as he watched for his turn. "Not many. The guys here hit where they're aiming. Cause if we get a newbie in here, who thinks he's hot-shit, we let him see some poor throwing. Get some real money bet, and then we throw in Tanya."

"Your girl friend, who throws knives at carnivals?" Several other men were looking at Grace with hungry eyes. "You know these people–am I safe?"

Kurt shrugged. "Unless Tanya comes in and finds me with another woman. Then we're both in trouble, cause I wouldn't be betting on you in a cat fight."

"What about Tina, Miakos ex-wife?"

"She's the redhead, carrying the tray with the four beers. She'll be on break soon and will join us."

"Kurt, you're well known here?"

"Told ya I'd been here before."

Grace smiled tightly. "You didn't tell me you're the leader of the pack."

"Nobody leads here. Too many would challenge, jes out of contrariness."

"You never took me here."

He studied her seriously. "Didn't seem to be yer kinda place."

Grace picked up her bottle and looked around. "Might like it."

"Come with me when ever you want." He held up his empty beer for the bartender to see. Then he lowered his voice speaking real seriously. "Jes you **don't ever** come here by yerself!"

When the chalked names above Kurt's got crossed off, he headed off to throw. Grace was impressed with his marksmanship. Eventually he came back with another beer, just as Tina, carrying their two bowls of chilli, joined them. She was an athletic red-head, late twenties, with three piercing in one ear, four in the other, who slipped into the booth tight alongside Kurt. "Hear you're interested in my late husband? Naturally the bum suicided the day after our divorce was final."

Grace consoled her with, "You might still inherit something."

"Nobody found a will. Course Miakos would never have thought about anyone other than himself." While they dug into the chilli, she ate some of the peanuts on the table. "Won't get nothing from his estate, but I'm responsible for fifty percent of his debts. Always spending on his 'art'. This 'last phase' he had to have authentic concrete chunks from the Berlin wall and gold wire–you know what real gold wire costs? He was even talking about buying tiger urine from some zoo."

"Have you checked with a lawyer? Maybe his current sales might pay off all the marital debts?"

Tina's bitterness made her look brittle. "Honey, there aren't enough paintings in the world to pay off our debts. And you need money to pay a lawyer to file bankruptcy."

"But Miakos' paintings sold for hundreds of thousands of dollars?"

"When he sold something, which he hasn't been much for the last few years. None in the years since I married him. Hell, he wasn't even painting anything... mostly just sitting there playing those damn computer games."

Grace had to bring it up. "You had a newspaper route?"

"If I didn't, we wouldn't have had any food."

"But you still loved him?"

Tina stopped, looking into the distance. "We nearly didn't go through with the divorce. We got together to the sign the papers and he was real eager for me." Tina reached out and Kurt passed her his beer, and she took a sip. "We did the dirty. Like old times." Tina took another drink from Kurt's beer, pressed her lips together, remembering. "I was lovin' him again, and then he started talking about this little tramp in Oyster River. Miakos heard how she was sunbathing topless in front of half the town, so he went to her, describing himself as the 'great' artist and said he wanted paint her–that's how he always starts. Well, she looked him, called him a dirty old man and told him to get the hell off her front lawn. So he screwed me to cry on my shoulder."

They were silent for a time, then Grace said, "At the Gull's Eye gallery, Miakos had sold three paintings before he died."

Tina didn't look impressed. "Money wouldn't have gone far. Wife number two and number four were threatening jail, if he didn't come up with the alimony. We had three mortgages on the studio and of course those sweet gallery friends of his were raking in fifty percent and framing fees."

Grace thought about it. "You should see a lawyer–those sold paintings were marital assets!"

"If there is anything, freaking Lawyers will steal the rest of it." She looked deep into the foam in Kurt's bottle. "Hit the studio last night and scooped up what was left of the gold wire." Tina looked up to see the bartender signaling her and shouted. "Keep your pants on. I'm coming!" Then Tina looked directly at Grace. "You were the one him saw him jump?"

"Yes."

"Then he wasn't pushed? Like some guys he borrowed money from didn't take him out?"

"There was no one else in the boat." Grace said reluctantly.

Tina drank more of Kurt's beer, looking older with the lines of pain etched in her face. "Mikey was always afraid of the water. I can't see him killing himself..." She put the beer down, got up, and quickly walked back to the bar.

In time, Kurt walked over to the bar for another beer, and then walked about the room talking to someone at just about every table. Grace was just finishing her beer when he rejoined her. She looked at the full one in his hand. "I think I'd like another one."

He studied her. "Nope. You can have some of mine, but you got to be sober enough to hold on to me on the ride back."

That was true. Outside the wind was a wet cold, with sharp stars peeking through the pines. She felt happy and free as she climbed on to the bike behind Kurt and on a slight beer buzz she relaxed behind him more, cuddling her head into his soft leather jacket as she held tightly to his waist. He took a decent pace, not seeming to hurry back to ORR, in fact she was a bit let down when he finally reached her condo.

As she handed him his extra helmet back, Grace asked. "Do you want to come in?"

"Love to, but got an appointment."

Appointment? Or another date?

With a smile and smell of beer and gasoline he was off, leaving her frustrated.

And alone again.

Chapter 40

Grace awoke with a slight headache and again didn't feel like running. She poured out some frosted flakes and took this over to the dining table set just before the sliding glass door to the balcony. Pretty much every morning was now starting with her opening up her Murder Suspect spread sheet on her laptop.

Under suspects she added a row for "Tina". In the Motive column for Miakos's murder Grace typed anger at the divorce? Possible inheritance? What was her hypothesis for Miakos' actions? Maybe the divorce had just been set up to garner publicity for his art show? But the show still wasn't selling well and Miakos was deeply in debt to the wrong people? So he needed a bigger stunt.

He rents a boat and makes a show of jumping, but underwater Tina would be swimming with scuba gear. He's to jump, and she's to buddy breathe with him, as they both swim back to the shore. There would be a big search and then 'miraculously' Miakos would show up to mucho publicity! His paintings would sell big time.

Con: Miakos drowned. Tina missed the connection? Or maybe a Pro: a jealous Tina deliberately refused to save him because she had found out he was going after Gigi?

Means: did Tina scuba dive? She knew Kurt and he was always offering to school his lady friends in whatever. Maybe Kurt was the one that was supposed to be diving, the one that Miakos expected to save him? That might be the kind of over-the-top, crazy stunt Kurt MacKay would find amusing. Then something went bad? Kurt picked him up, but Miakos drowned on the swim to shore? That water would have been cold for a diver in a wet suit much less one who had stripped naked like Miakos.

The morning Miakos jumped, Grace had hurried from her apartment to the dock. Kurt would have had to swim out from the Harbor, strip off the wet suit and be dressed and breathing normally when she got there. If Tina was going to kill her husband for money, she should have done it before the divorce. No, none of those hypotheses were working. Kurt was not out swimming in the Harbor and Miakos was known as a non-swimmer.

And as Kurt had said, he didn't really know the red-headed waitress very well. Kurt might sin by omission, but Grace had never known him to tell an outright lie. She left Tina's row in the spread sheet, but with a dismal over all percentage of 15. Tina was the wife and they had problems, she was athletic enough to be a swimmer, but a faked suicide was not much of a theory to follow up on.

It was a relief to close that spread sheet and open "Genetic Evolution of the Human Eye". A colleague in Missouri might be losing his shot at tenure because of his opposition to a strident Creationalist fraction. They claimed that such a complicated mechanism as the human eye could never have involved independently. Primitive eyes had light sensitivity, nerve connections but how did an iris form before a ball of fluid protected by a transparent lense? Intrigued Grace was trying to recreate a plausible genetic trail for the evolution of the human's eye. It was a lot harder than she first imagined.

Much later when she got into her lab, Inger told Grace that her lawyer had left a message. She got back to him immediately. "Mark, this Grace Farrington. Is there a problem?"

Mark hesitated before he answered. "Don't get upset." Her stomach clenched as he continued firmly. "The District Attorney has notified me that you are a person of interest in Charles Marshall's death."

"They're saying I killed him?"

"Not exactly. Not yet anyways, but its even more important that you do not answer any questions unless I'm with you."

She tried to calm herself down and think rationally. First she had to narrow the scope of her problem to something that was manageable. "If they are saying I am 'of interest' in Marshall's murder, then they've decided I had nothing to do with Miakos or Gigi Ramirez 's deaths?"

Again Mark took a long time before answering. "We should be speaking in person."

"Please! I'd like to narrow the scope of my problems down."

He didn't sound happy. "Well, you can't. The paper work only mentions Charles Marshall, but if they were going after you for three deaths, they would be wise to only openly pursue just one."

"Why me?"

He hesitated, then said slowly, "At your initial interview, you were less than forthcoming about your past relationship with Marshall."

"That was years ago and there was no relationship!" But by not admitted the scandal in a timely manner it was her fault she was chief suspect.

"With the constant T-V and newspaper coverage, the police are under great public pressure. Obviously they can't prove anything on anyone else they've questioned, and now they have no one else to go after."

It was her turn to be silent.

"Grace? Are you still there?" asked Mark.

"Yes, thank you. I guess that's all."

"Unfortunately it isn't. I wouldn't allow permission, so they are going to a judge for warrants to search your laboratory and your apartment building."

'"The whole building?"

"Under these they could. But I think they will only be interested in your apartment and common areas such basement laundry, your foyer mailbox and any storage."

"Oh."

"Strangely they didn't ask to search your car." He said almost to himself. "That's either carelessness, they've already done it, or they're sure they won't find anything." He seemed to focus back on her. "Do you want me to oppose this further? We might still be able to block it?"

"I–I don't know. You can't stop a warrant."

"This is not a swoop in, knock down the doors type, they're being very open about it, and telling me. If they had some spectacular evidence that they could've presented to Judge Arnau they would have done a 'no knock'."

"They can search all they want, because they're not going to find anything."

"They're probably going to take your laptop and computers."

They couldn't! "**No!** I can't work!"

"Will you let them look at your computers?"

She just sat there for a moment. "Must I? Should I?"

"Well, I assume you're a smart enough woman to have gotten rid of anything incriminating before this."

"There's nothing incriminating! They can look at my computers. They can copy what ever they want on to theirs, but my work is confidential and some of it classified."

"It will remain so." soothed Mark.

"But I need my computers to work." Oh, God. This was terrible. "Could you e-mail the judge and tell him that?"

"I am going to be in Judge Arnau's court in one hour discussing these warrants." He stopped and then said, "Grace, is there anything else I should know? That I should protect?"

"I did not kill Charles Marshall or Gigi Ramirez or Miakos or Cock Robin." Her voice was going in the hysterical range.

"I believe you."

"Do I have to be there? When they search?" She felt revulsion. "I mean some strangers pawing through my bra drawer."

"It's probably better if you aren't, just leave the keys with someone you trust. Unfortunately, after the judge, I have to go into the City. Do not go back to your apartment and straighten things up. They probably have someone watching to see what you'll do. What are you going to do?"

"I'm going over to Freya's and cry on her shoulder."

"That sounds good and it should keep them busy following you." Again a pause, then Mark said carefully. "My Uncle Alan mentioned you've had dinner with David Gardiner?"

"Yes, I'm going out with him tomorrow." Why was he asking? "Is that some kind of a problem?"

"No! No way. Ethically neither myself or Uncle Alan can talk about your case to Mr. Gardiner, but if you are going to cry on anyone shoulder, cry on a guy who has a standing table at the Republican fund raisers and golfs at the same country clubs as most of our judges." As he hung up he added. "And don't read too much into this search business, Grace. Again, the police are under a great deal of public pressure in this case. I think this is just busy work by them."

After he hung up, Grace looked about her desktop. It was a mess with stacks of readouts, speaking requests, student aide time cards, she started neatening things up but her lawyer had said don't do that. And why should she make it easier for the police? What about the Murder Suspects spreadsheet on her laptop?

She had the laptop with her now, but what about the things she had on Bobby and Kurt? If she erased them, the authorities might be able to recover the document. To totally delete it she would have to physically destroy the drive and that would make her look all the guiltier. Grace keyed up the spreadsheet. Studied it.

Kurt's Pro's were pretty wild guesses, except the fact that he found Marshall's body the night before when he was alone. More damning was her tracking of Bobby's Motives,

Means and Opportunity. If the police saw this...she copied the spreadsheet on to a flash drive, then deleted it from the laptop, emptying the re-cycle bin a few times to bury it further. If the police wanted her Suspect Spreadsheet let them work for it!

Inger was feeding the minnow tanks. She must have heard some of the conversation as she came over looking concerned even though Grace forced a smile. "Could you work overtime today?"

"Got to call my boyfriend but sure."

"The police are coming to search here and my apartment." Grace separated out her car keys. "You have your set of the lab keys, here's my apartment keys, this one's for the mail box and that's one for my storage bin in the basement. The bin's got my apartment number on it. If they let you, could you stay with the police, and kind of..." She couldn't continue.

"See they don't plant anything?" Inger asked sympathetically.

"Yes, but they might not let you watch. And then there's the lab..." It seemed hopeless.

"Nick will be here soon, and he can watch the lab. You gave me the keys and made me responsible for your apartment so I will stick with the keys."

Feeling like she was about to cry, Grace nodded and hurried out. She didn't want to drive directly to Freya's, not without calming down first. Before this mess Grace would have gone to the library, and found peace walking along her harbor road. Now she didn't want to see the yellow police tape hung over the bittersweet at the pond house. She was about to pull out of ORR, which way to turn? Finally, she just pulled across the road through the fish hatchery up to the Congregational church. Grace got out of the car and walked to a bench over looking the lake.

Mallard ducks quacked and swam away, while the white swans stayed at a good distance but kept a close watch for bread being thrown. Orange leaves floated on the brown water and it was so peaceful and free here, Zen like. She was innocent but innocent people go to jail sometimes and wind up on death row. God, she was panicking, she couldn't think straight. Finally, she forced herself to sit quietly, watching the leaves fall from the trees. The bright maple leaves blew diagonally, gently floating down, hitting the water in a growing frame of tiny, dark brown rings.

After a time her mind quieted. Well, if she was arrested, convicted and condemned to death, she'd have years of appeals. She could sit in a the prison library and carry on her research and it might not be so bad after all. No social obligations to cut into her time, Grace wouldn't have to worry if David was going to kiss her, or if she should go to bed with Kurt. She laughed out loud. It had a touch of hysteria, but it loosened her up, as the nearest ducks took flight in a blur of wings and splashing water droplets.

Okay, if the police were stupidly pursuing only her, she had to find who was responsible. Kurt? No, if he had done it, they never would have found the body. Bobby in a fit of anger? Possible, but perversely Bobby probably would have felt justified and would have admitted it. Adam Greenfield? Keeping an unpaid, part time job as an Institute President was not a realistic motive to kill Charles Marshall. Rachel Greenfield might talk someone to death, but she was entirely too civilized a person to bludgeon Gigi or Marshall. Katherine Marshall had Diandra as a alibi. But Katherine was sleeping during the time she 'alibied' Diandra.

Katherine went to her motel room, so Diandra knew Charles was off with another woman. The wife goes into a drunken slumber allowing Diandra to sneak out, and drive to the ORR dock. Had Diandra and Marshall been screwing on the Octagon already, so she could figure he'd take his next girlfriend there? Did she take the first boat out and sneak on to the Octagon, hiding when Marshall arrived there, then kill them both?

The hypothesis had too many holes, Grace had to find another one. It couldn't have been Gigi who was murdered on the Octagon because Diandra alone could never have killed her, carried Gigi's body to the boat, then up on to the beach and across the road into the tangle of bittersweet vines. Maybe Marshall had a third girl friend?

Diandra finds them making it on the Octagon floor. Hits Charles with what? Unnamed Bimbo #3 tries to make an escape, reaching the door and outer deck. Diandra manages to hit her on the head with whatever, and Bimbo #3 goes into the water. Were there any missing women reports that the police weren't checking? Grace wondered if she could persuade Mac that there might be a fourth body feeding the fishes and that he should start looking through the police computers for missing women reports?

Why didn't Diandra also dump Marshall in the water? While she kills Bimbo 3, Charles was only stunned and he manages to block the door before Diandra can return and drag him into the water. He is dying from an inter-cranial hemorrhage and Diandra guesses this and leaves. No, First Diandra ties Marshall's love boat to hers and motors both back to the ORR's dock. Then she sneaks back to her hotel room, managing to clean off any blood and be sitting calmly reading on her bed when Katherine wakes up?

The Cons disputing this one would go down the entire column. Like where did Diandra find a weapon, on the Octagon or did she bring something with her? Perhaps a small anchor from one of the launches? That would have meant premeditation and it doesn't go along with the fact that Katherine just showed up unexpectedly. And why bother to take the first boat back to the dock? To delay questions, to cover up the murders, but if Katherine hadn't woke up, Diandra had a perfect alibi?

Grace tried to tweak the scenario: Katherine shows up

and falls asleep, causing Diandra to suspect Marshall is on the Octagon with another woman. She takes the second boat out and hearing them having sex, Diandra becomes enraged.

She waits outside with the boat anchor, when the first one comes out she hits him or her and the body falls in to the water. The second lover comes out and she hits that one on the head, pushing a second body into the ocean. There might not be blood on the outside of the Octagon if it was done fast enough. Needing time for the bodies to float away, Diandra might have tied the first boat on to hers and then motored it away to divert attention from the Octagon.

But what if Marshall was in the water, but just stunned? After Diandra left, did he swim and pull himself up onto the Octagon's deck? Half unconscious did he manage to crawl back inside, trying to block the door from his killer as he died? Could Mac get the police to test his clothing for seawater residue? Why hasn't Bimbo #3 been reported missing?

And what if #3 wasn't a Bimbo, but a Bambi? An innocent Marshall was going to 'show' the Octagon too? What if girl friend number three was Faith Brewster, Stewart and Joyce's granddaughter? Faith was young, smart and pretty so Marshall would've undoubtedly been after her. If Marshall had called Faith in again to discuss her teaching next semester, she might not have told Steward and Joyce. Her grandparents would think she was in Boston, her Boston friends would think she was with her grandparents.

That was a hypothesis she could test. Grace took out her cell phone and dialed Gail.

A professional voice answered. "Oyster River Research Institute."

"Gail, this Grace. I've got to reach Faith Brewster. Do you have her number in Boston?"

"Yes. But you can't reach her."

"Why?"

"I spoke with her yesterday because I needed some more details for the class she's teaching Spring semester. Faith told me she was going to Quebec with friends for a few days."

"Then you did speak to her? I mean do you know Faith's voice?"

"Aaup." Gail mimicked the nasal New Englander clip of the Brewsters. "If she calls do you want me to pass along a message?"

"No thanks." Grace ended the call. Well, fortunately Faith didn't die on the Octagon and odds were that Gigi didn't either. Yet Marshall did and Diandra was still a possibility. Could she have hired someone to kill her unfaithful paramour? If Grace could just get the police to question her closely, put on some pressure...that wasn't going to happen while they were tossing Grace's apartment.

But something might happen if Grace could get Freya to help her!

As Grace walked to the church parking lot she noted a second car parked down below at the fish hatchery. She couldn't see who was in it, because he or she was reading a newspaper. When she passed the car she noted it was a man's large hands holding the paper. Driving out to the main road, Grace could see several police cars at ORR, white with blue streaks–State Police–at least three of them parked there. Getting ready to search her lab and her apartment building.

Her cell rang and it was an anxious Gail whispering. "Grace, the police are here."

"I know."

"They wanted directions to your lab? I gave them, but..."

"That's fine. Inger is taking care of it, don't worry."

At Freya's store, Grace rushed down the stairs and didn't waste time. "I need your help. I need to make Diandra start talking."

"How?" Asked a startled Freya.

"I want you to run a seance at the Roost."

Freya's face was conflicted. "You don't believe in spirit contact..."

"But Diandra might! Especially if I tell you what to say." Pleaded Grace.

Freya looked grim and angry. "I won't do that! Grace..."

Grace cut her off. "There is probably going to be an undercover state detective in here any minute. The Troopers have a warrant and are searching my apartment and lab right now."

Freya looked out the door as a business suited man started down the steps and her anger melted to concern. "When are we doing this?"

"30 after dark, tonight–no, I'll need time to prepare. Friday?"

Freya sighed. "Yes."

Grace nodded. "If I can get Diandra signed on I'll call you."

The business suited man came in and developed a sudden interest in the beaded necklace displays by the door. Grace handed Freya some lavender incense and ten dollars and the shop keeper rang the sticks up and returned her change. As Grace left she smiled politely at the plain clothes man shadowing the door, while Freya just glared at him.

Boldly Grace drove back into ORR and parked in front of what she would always call Eric's Lab. In front of her own laboratory there were dark jacketed state police, in gray cowboy like hats, carrying computers out, but nobody was really looking at her as she climbed the three steps to Eric's lab building.

Pass the foyer, inside the Lab A suite, the huge front room was filled with stacks of cardboard boxes, probably most not even opened from Marshall's move here. Head bent,

Diandra was sitting at the desk absorbed in inventory sheets and she didn't seem to realize anyone had come in until Grace spoke. "You got my letter of reference?"

Diandra looked up, saying gratefully. "Yes. That secretary friend of yours passed it on. That was kind of you."

"I've mentioned your name to a few labs I have contact with," Grace lied. "No opening yet, but I might find someone to look at your resume."

"Thank you." Diandra smiled genuinely.

Grace looked about at the boxes stacked everywhere. "Quite a job here."

"Yes. All of Dr. Marshall's professional life is here. I can't believe he's dead, such a vital man. I can't believe I'll never be able to talk with him again." She finished sadly.

Grace spoke carefully. "A friend of mine does seances. We may be trying to contact Dr. Marshall."

Diandra looked shocked. "You're a scientist, how can you believe in that garbage?"

"I don't know. Freya's comes up with some amazing things. I've been fascinated by her circles, wondering if there really isn't something to them?"

Diandra studied her. "That's your secret, isn't it? Dr. Marshall said you would follow a line of research that others would find ridiculous, but that you kept hammering at it until you found something."

"Or if nothing turns up, I widen my net." Grace looked at the walls of boxes. "For the seance my medium requested that I get something connected with Dr. Marshall, something she could contact him with."

Diandra looked about the desk. "Here's a pen he used." And she dug through some papers. "This is his signature."

"Can I borrow them?"

"Well they all belong to the grieving widow," she said sarcastically. "Not that Katherine cares a bit. If Charles had lived, she would have been out on her fanny."

"He was divorcing her?" That was interesting news, and Grace also noted that for Diandra 'Dr. Marshall' had become "Charles'.

Chapter 41

"Katherine didn't know it, but he had a lawyer. He told me." Diandra put the pen and paper into a yellow envelope and handed them to Grace. "You can keep those."

"Thank you." Grace turned away as if leaving, and then turned back trying to make it look like an after thought. "Would you like to come?"

"What?"

"To my seance."

"Why? Charles isn't gonna speak. I don't believe in ghosts."

"But if you came the medium would have a positive connection with Charles Marshall through you. She might be encouraged to dig deeper."

"A seance to contact the dead? I don't think so." She appeared to dismiss it as beyond consideration.

Her last chance to save herself and Grace was striking out. "Please, I want to give this experiment the best shot I can." No response from Dirandra, so Grace pressed. "And I have been putting your resumes out there."

Diandra looked conflicted. "When is it?"

"Friday. Just after dark, at the Roost."

"Then I can't make it, I was going out to dinner with Dr. MacKay."

Kurt moving in on the grieving girlfriend? Of course. "That would work out! We need another person to fill out the circle. One of the things I'll be studying is the slight electrical discharge that seems to occur when a group joins hands, and I'm sure Dr. MacKay would be very interested in observing any demonstration of biosynthesis."

"Natural body electrical fields forming a circuit?"

"I think so, but I would like to observe it more."

Diandra obviously didn't expect to speak to Marshall, but she needed Grace's help. "All right, if Kurt will agree."

"Good." Grace nodded. "I'll see you there. And maybe by then I'll have heard about a position for you."

Back at her lab the police were gone, but so were all the lab's network of computers and her laptop. Looking worried, Inger handed her keys back and a receipt that promised--by Judge's order–that the computers would be returned Friday afternoon. Mark Silverstein's talk with the judge accomplished something at least. Well she still had phone messages to answer and study protocols to set up. Working always calmed her, but it was certainly a lot harder without her computers. Still by evening, Grace was a bit more optimistic. They would have their seance on Friday, but tonight she could have a mini-escape from the morass her life had become, she would enjoy a dinner with David Gardiner.

Where was this relationship going? Was he expecting to sleep with her tonight? Did she want to sleep with him? She didn't know, but Grace looked forward to just being with him. After 6:00, Grace put down her DNA journals and then she freshened up in the ladies' room. She'd brought down her pale-golden Chinese blouse and black linen pants, changing well before David arrived promptly at 6:30.

He looked admiringly at her. "That blouse is magnificent."

"I bought it in Beijing when I was there for last year's genome conference. They are making some fantastic scientific progress."

He smiled. "China is a fascinating place, changing from overstuffed bicycles to cars, going from the late nineteenth century to the twenty first in mere months."

"Medieval still in back country," she added as they started walking out of her lab.

"Did you get to the back country?" David asked excitedly, then he hesitated and switched topics. "Are the police still questioning you about Marshall's death? I do know lawyers a lot more practiced then Alan's nephew, perhaps I could..."

It was an opening and she needed all the help she could get, but David had been born with the gift of wealthy parents. That gift must have come paired with the curse of always wondering if someone was befriending him just for his money, and Grace couldn't use David any more than she had. "Things are going fine with Mark."

As they walked outside she could see his black car was parked in front of her lab, but someone else was walking up besides David's car, someone hauling three huge buckets. Kurt.

"Hey, lady. Glad I caught you."

David looked at him. "We were just leaving for dinner."

"That's sounds good–I'm hungry meself." But Kurt had a bit a triumphant smile on his face. "Been diving after Bobby's classes. Was gonna call it off early tonight, cause the Sound's really getting choppy and the viewing jes a foot or so even with our lights, but Bobby kept insisting we dive while there was still some air in our tanks."

Grace was looking down in to the buckets with their writhing contents. Something solid and black, with flashes of orange and what was that? The evening light was fading as the parking lamps winked on and gave a greenish tinge to everything. Still as Grace squatted down by a bucket in the reflecting water she could still see a large lobster with a bit of bright blue on the back of his abdomen. "You've got one!"

"Blue tails–I've got four!" pronounced a victorious Kurt.

She stood up and hurried around to look in each bucket. "This one's too undersized, both of them. They should be thrown back."

"You reporting me to the lobster board?" Exploded Kurt. "Besides we ain't eatin' them–we're jes studying 'em."

Excited Grace nodded. "We'll get them in to my tanks.

I haven't got the water refrigeration on..."

"Start it going, but lobsters are hearty, they make it." Kurt replied.

Grace was still talking. "First, we'll borrow the camera from Fritz's lab and get some good digital pictures." She pointed into the bucket. "This one we'll name 'One Antenna'..."

"Grace!" Kurt protested, "No names! They're not pets. They're research subjects!"

"Fine. We'll tag them with four digit numbers. Maybe we should do a six digit with the first two digits indicating location found? I'll need to run a DNA on all them. What's the best way to take blood from a living lobster?"

Kurt was shaking his head. "My tests come first! I've got Bobby bringing over some normal lobsters and we'll put them in the tanks with these to see if they catch the blue whatever. Your assistants have got to keep behavioral logs, hourly during the day, recording how our subjects are moving and eating." Kurt turned to David with just a touch of a triumphant smile. "Sorry to ruin your dinner."

Grace looked up with apologies. "This will take some time, maybe all night."

David blandly returned Kurt's smile. "No problem. I find watching scientists at work fascinating and since we're all hungry, I'll order pizzas for the lab. Grace and I will have pepperoni and mushroom, what do you want on yours?" He asked Kurt, as he helpfully picked up one of Kurt's buckets. "It just so happens I have an excellent digital camera in the car, so I can be of help."

Kurt scowled, but Grace beamed at David. "That's wonderful! We'll photograph them before we transfer them to the tanks."

As they entered her lab, she turned on the lights back on. "If these samples live past a day, I'll e-mail Brian Kancir at *Affiliated* with a progress report." She had her fingers in the bucket, reaching out to the largest lobster who snapped at her with his claw. "They seem to be attacking each other. We didn't have anything in the budget for special claw holders did we?"

"They sell restraints for lobsters?" David asked.

Giving him a sour look of contempt, Kurt shook his head. "Go to Staples for a box of wide, short rubber bands." Kurt set down the other two buckets before the banks of bubbling tanks.

Things were looking up, but Grace decided to wait until David wasn't around before she filled Kurt in on their seance Friday.

Chapter 42

Friday evening it was even colder, The Captain's Roost, with its central tower and mansard roof topped by a widow's walk, dominated the landscape. Grace searched for the keys Gail had given her as wind gusts swirled pale leaves over the shadowed lawn. Yes, perfect place for a ghost story. Even not believing in resident spirits, Grace found herself nervously looking about as she unlocked the back door into the dark, rear kitchen. Freya had met her carrying a bulging suitcase, that Grace eyed as they walked through the kitchen into the main room. She had to ask. "Are you planning on moving in?"

Freya ignored the comment and looked critically about the cadaverous hall. "No. No, this is not what we need. It's too big."

That was another complication. "We could go to my lab? The cafeteria has tables, it might be empty, but the research library will be in use now."

"What's upstairs?" Freya looked at the ceiling.

"On the second story, the former bedrooms are now offices and storage. And there's the old Library."

"Library?"

"Not really technical books, those are in the new Admin building. This is stuff from the original owners, science books gathered over the years and some truly beautiful early sea creature folios from the 1800's. They were going to throw them away, but Stewart Brewster persuaded them not to. The Board of Directors uses the old Library for its meetings."

"Then it must have a table and chairs." Freya nodded excitedly. "Yes, I remember, you had a book signing there once. Aren't there book cases along the wall, a huge fireplace, and windows over looking the Harbor?"

"This hall has most of that," Grace pointed out.

"No." Freya looked all around again. "This is too

open." Freya hauled up her suitcase and was walking out toward the front of the house that faced the main road. The unremodeled foyer was impressive, a two story space in the front tower, with an intricate inlay of exotic woods on the floor. It had a huge compass rose in the center that spiraled out and a double edged border, with alternating blocks and stars ambled around the edges of the room.

At the back of the foyer a narrow, spiral staircase rose that Grace knew had been built by ships carpenters in the 1800's. As they climbed it, Grace marveled at the consume skill of some wood wright hundreds of years ago. Slender, smoothly curving stairs and banisters, with delicate touches of carved holly leaves and vines, useful, spare, strong and maybe beautiful–the ultimate New England craftsman's art.

When they got upstairs the library was to the right, its arched entrance flanked by two, eight foot ivory elephant tusks gifted by one of the African hunter patrons. The wide entrance had two recessed pocket doors, which Freya sailed in ahead of Grace.

After some fumbling, Freya finally found the light switch and a weak yellow light flooded, as they surveyed the room critically. To their left two seven foot tall built in bookcases flanked an almost walk-in, white marble fireplace, while on the right side were tall, small pained windows overlooking the Harbor. Set about the room was massive Empire furniture and a huge 1820's floor globe, befitted a world traveling Sea Captain's home.

Freya studied the walls. "Wall scones, old hurricane lamps, but dry, we should have gotten kerosene for them. Never mind, I've got candles in my bag, when we start you'll turn out the lights." She also had two massive candelabras, a fire lighter wand, a huge pile of black velvet cloth, sandlewood incense and a silver hand bell. Freya looked at the heavy mahogany table in the center of the room. "How many people are we having?"

"Just us. Diandra. Kurt and Bobby. Five."

"Tables's too big. We have to hold hands during the seance."

"Do we have to?"

"The energy should flow."

Great. They could haul a card table up from downstairs but that would kill some of the ambiance. Grace noted some darker lines in the perfectly matched polished tabletop and she sank down with her knee on the floor. "Freya, light one of your candles and bring it over here."

Freya held the flame low and on the underside of the table, Grace could see metal locks. "There's two boards that can come out." She pushed hard against the first stiff metal lock but it was frozen in place. Grace tried to put more of force against it. Finally it rotated. She started on the others and said when she stood up, "They're unlocked. You pull at one end of the table and I'll get the other."

Pulling at the heavy mahogany table leaves that had been in place for ages was a tough task, but finally they had separation. Freya easily hefted out one of the boards as Grace struggled to lift the other. "There's a room off the library over here." They stashed the boards and then pushed the rest of the table back together on its runners. Grace remembered this room was wired for recording the Board of Director meetings, but she didn't know how it worked or where it was set up. Damn. She should have asked Gail.

Freya surveyed the table and nodded professionally. "Still large for four but we can manage." She tossed her bundle of black velvet cloth over the table, like a dark night sky, and it overflowed to the floor. While Freya lighted the incense, Grace set out the two silver candelabras, placing five of Freya's white candles in each.

As Grace lit the candles Freya drifted to the fireplace, staring in to space to prepare herself.

Grace went over, speaking softly. "We just need to put

a little pressure on. See if Diandra cracks. Just do what you always do..."

Freya frowned down at her. "What do I always 'do'?"

"Go into a trance." Seeing the angry flush on Freya's face, Grade amended. "An altered physic state..."

"A state you don't believe in."

"Meditation states have been verified by CAT scan imaging, advanced Yogi practitioners can willingly access mental levels others of us seldom reach."

"So if your machines show a spiking print out the psychic world exists?"

"No. It shows that something we don't quite understand is happening in the human brain and body. That we have much more to study and learn."

"Grace, to please a friend would you fake the results of your research? In good cause?"

Obvious Grace knew where this was going. "No."

"But since my psychic powers are just illusionary, it's okay for me to isn't it?"

It wasn't and Grace was ashamed for asking her. "Do you want to call this off?"

"Yes!" Freya looked away and finished wearily. "But I don't want to see you go to jail."

They could hear doors opening down stairs. Freya continued. "I will sit and meditate at the table. That's not just for show. Guide your friends in and seat them, then pull the pocket doors shut."

Grace looked at the tall opening concealing two heavy doors. "They're nearly two hundred years old. I don't know if they've warped."

Freya shook off discord with a wave of her hand. "Just try. Then turn off the lights and you'll sit down opposite to me."

Grace saw Kurt was now walking up stairs with Diandra and Bobby followed with Sara. Why didn't she think to put out hors d'oeuvres? But should a very pregnant woman, with a history of premature labor and miscarriage be at a seance trying to contact a murdered man? What was the matter with Bobby? "Sara, I didn't know you were coming?"

"Gail said she'd babysit, because I've always wanted to see a seance."

Great, maybe they should be selling tickets. Bobby was moving another chair over to the table while Kurt had chivalrously held out Diandra's chair, deftly maneuvered her alongside Freya, who sat with eyes closed and head bend.

Grace's pulled at the first pocket door. Stiff resistance at first, than a smooth, squeaky pulling. She moved to the second door and started to pull it closed, but stopped when she heard something. Not the nervous, uneasy shuffling around the table behind her, but sounds ahead of her. A steady tread. Soft footfalls climbing up the circular staircase, coming closer, Grace found herself reacting with irrational fear.

It wasn't cleaners, not today, the building should have been locked and empty. For a moment Grace got the wild, unreasoning intuition there might really be ghosts. That long dead Jersillda was coming back, climbing these stairs to protest the desecration of the Captain's house.

Grace stood frozen at the door as a dark figure ascended stairs before her. A short, very solid haunt with modernly styled hair and dress. Katherine Marshall was marching up the staircase. As she walked toward the library, her eyes were cold and hostile, and Grace realized she was blocking Katherine's entrance.

Forced to stop, Katherine spoke coolly. "I understand you are trying to contact my husband?"

"It's an experiment." Grace nearly stammered.

"Is it?"

Grace didn't move. Katherine moved uncomfortably closer asking. "And you didn't invite me?" Grace could smell liquor on her breath.

"I didn't think you would want to come," Grace finished lamely. As she found herself moving out of Katherine's way, she wondered just how the widow found out? Diandra wouldn't have told her. Was Grace's lab bugged? Did Marshall bug his own lab? "It might bring painful memories back for you?"

"A chance to talk to my husband again? Of course I want to come!" Katherine firmly walked forward and stood surveying the table. This wasn't going as Grace had planned. Marshall's widow was walking towards Grace's chair, the only empty seat left around the table but Bobby immediately stood up and pulled over one of the heavy carved East Indian chairs into space between his and Grace's chair. He stood, politely holding it out for Katherine. Like Queen Victoria, Katherine didn't even bother to look to see if Bobby was pushing the chair under her, she just imperiously sat.

"Always room for one more," Freya murmured then she opened her eyes and raised her head. "We will begin when Grace joins us."

With difficulty, Grace hauled the second door shut and then walked to shut off the lights. She found a plate with two toggling buttons, those must be the original switches from when the Roost was electrified in the 1930's. With them all waiting, Grace pushed out the electric lights button, now in the darkness the candle flames seemed to grown, their light leaping and dancing on the walls. Feeling again that this was a very bad idea, Grace settled down in the last seat at the seance table.

Flickering candle light gave movement to the shadows, as Grace settled in, Freya looked her directly in the eyes but did not smile. "We will join hands and remain holding hands during the seance." She commanded before lowering her head again.

Katherine's hand was smooth and warm. Kurt's big paw was calloused and reassuring as he gave Grace's hand a little squeeze. But this time when the circle was joined, Grace did not feel that slight electrical surge she had felt during Alma's circle, later Freya would tell her one of the participants was deliberately or unconsciously obstructing the energy's flow.

This group obviously did not know the proper seance protocols, because Katherine began loudly asking. "Is she going to just sit there?"

Freya raised her head and opened her eyes again. In a dreamy voice she said, "Are there those who have questions?"

"Yes. I'd like to speak to my husband," Katherine announced firmly. "There seems to some question about his wishes?"

Diandra looked directly at Katherine. "He wanted his work respected. A library set up in his name, where young researchers could go study."

"What? Young girl researchers? The late Dr. Charles Marshall's Chair of Infant Sexology?"

To head off blows, Kurt loudly asked Freya. "Actually I'd like to know who's winning the Trifecta at Aqueduct this Saturday?"

Freya frostily answered. "Those who have passed on don't do horses."

Kurt smiled evilly at that but as he opened his mouth Grace cut him off. "Freya, do you feel the spirit of Jersillda? This was her house. Did she curse her unfaithful husband? Did she cause the *Siren's* wreck?"

Closing her eyes again, Freya concentrated. "There is a woman scorned. Great, great anger here. She doesn't understand, she loves him so much..."

The medium was continuing, but Katherine overrode Freya. "I want to contact Charles! I want him to say who he really loves. Say he loves me! His wife!"

Diandra looked up defiantly, but held her tongue.

Freya continued. "¿Por qué no he hecho nada?"

Spanish again. Grace translated to herself. *'why, you'*–no I–*'why, I have done nothing?'*

Katherine hammered her hand on the table. "Charles doesn't speak Spanish!"

Suddenly, Diandra stood up yelling at Katherine. "Maybe he would have loved you, if you weren't such a bitch!" Crying, she ran to the doors and pulling one side open, Diandra slipped out.

Katherine screamed after to her. "You're not leaving! My husband is going to cry out who his murderess is!"

"Aw, hell." Disengaging his hand from Grace, Kurt had to follow after Diandra.

There was silence. Freya had stopping talking and her head was bend forward, her eyes closed. Sara nervously looked toward Bobby. He looked to Grace.

Standing up in a stately fashion, Katherine dramatically announced. "I think I've had enough of this nonsense for tonight."

Grace watched helplessly as Katherine left the seance room. She started to get up, but Freya, still with eyes closed and head bent, spoke. "No. Grace. Stay. There is an unquiet spirit. She is distressed. She's just floating–she can't understand. She wants to talk to you, Grace. Warn you."

"Who?"

"You were closest to her when she passed over." Freya said with frowning concentration.

"My grandmother, Helen?" Grace hesitantly asked. There was no one's hand she could reach, so Grace just set her palms down on the soft, black velvet, as eyes closed Freya's was breathing heavily. Bobby's concerned attention was on Sara, who really looked upset, but was still holding Freya's other hand. "Who is this spirit?" Grace asked again.

As if she was talking to herself, Freya said, "She..." Her voice stopped. Then, "She doesn't understand."

Grace asked, "What is her name?"

As if Grace hadn't spoken, Freya continued, "*¡Malditos! ¡No tienes derecho! ¡Ningún derecho a hacerme daño! ¡Que se pudran al infierno!*"

Freya was speaking in Spanish again. Grace tried to picture the translation in her mind, as if it were written out on a blackboard. '*¡Malditas!* ? *Curse them! ¡No tienes derecho! No*–something?--*hurt me. ¡Que se pudran al infierno!* "*Will rot in hell!* But if Grace remembered her Spanish correctly, there was an implied 'they'. '*They will rot in hell!*' Did the Spanish spirit woman mean '*he*' would rot in hell or was it a '*she*' who would rot?

Eyes closed tightly, Freya fell silent as the candle flames still danced in the old room's drafts and white wax dripped down on the black velvet. Freya pushed her self back in the seat, open mouthed and breathing heavily. She looked exhausted, but Freya was jubilant. "The recognition is coming, Grace! Soon!"

"The Spanish woman said that?"

Shaking her head, Freya said, "No. I just know. A feeling, an award. Grace, it's coming! It's in the mail now, not as much as you wished, but you will be recognized!"

Grace tried to smile. Why had Freya put that in? Diandra was gone and everyone at the table knew Grace had lost the Nobel. There would be no notice in the mail, at least not this year.

But Freya's mood swiftly changed from jubilant to almost one of grim regret. "We are finished for tonight." Bobby got up and turned on the lights, then Sara drew close to him, as Freya rose, spit on her fingers and used them to snuff out the candle's guttering flames.

As Bobby and Sara left, Grace started packing the incense and the first candelabra into Freya's suitcase. She kept turning over in her mind what the 'Spanish woman' had said, yes, it was only Freya's subconscious, but what were the words? *¡Que se pudran en el infierno!* That was wrong. 'She would rot in hell', would be *¡ella se pudrirán en el infierno!* That would be singular. But if it was a male, it would be *¡élse se pudrirán en el infierno!* Freya used *Que* se, the plural 'They'. "Freya, when you were speaking in Spanish, why did you use *que se* instead of *élse or ella se*? Was there a reason?"

Freya looked curiously at her. "Grace, you know I don't speak Spanish."

Chapter 43

"You must–you just did. Didn't you have it in college?"

"Two semesters, when I ruined my 'A' average by pulling two "Cs". If I couldn't remember enough to pass a freshmen test, you think I'm going to remember any of it twenty years later?"

Grace was trying to analyze the data. "Your subconscious mind..."

Freya almost pulled her suitcase away from Grace. "Don't lecture me on things you know nothing about! Scientists get results they don't believe in, so they make up a 'scientific pseudo-rationalization' that neatly explains away the inconvenient results. Your preconceptions are not allowing you explore the facts! If I hadn't been a departmental student aide, if I hadn't marked all the teacher's papers, I would have flunked Spanish because I couldn't understand it, much less speak it. And I couldn't have cared less."

"You can read ancient Norse."

"Norse is not Spanish."

Grace desperately wanted to repair their friendship. "Look, after tonight, I owe you a dinner..."

Freya closed her suitcase, not looking at Grace. "After tonight, I'd rather eat alone. I think you'd better find someplace else to go on Mondays."

Saddened Grace just watched her friend walk away.

That Friday afternoon the police had returned her laptop and all her computers to her lab, so Saturday she was in the lab, recreating her Murder Suspect spread sheet, filling in columns for Marshall, Miakos and Gigi. Miakos rows were easy. Suspects: Himself; Tina, his ex-wife; Kurt and some unknown scuba diver. Percentages for Means and Opportunity still held 95% for Miakos killing Miakos. The -5 % outstanding, was Motive: Why?

Suspect rows for Marshall's murder were more

complicated: Bobby, Kurt, Adam, Rachel, Katherine, Diandra and random killer. By the rather subjective percentages she had awarded, Adam, Rachel, Katherine and Diandra dropped out as serious contenders. That left Bobby, Kurt and some as yet unknown killer. This wasn't going too well.

She looked more carefully at the rows. Numbers were up for Diandra. Motive: Jealousy. Means: She was Athletic. Could use a boat. Had access to the ORR craft, but he percentages dropped off when it came to Opportunity: time. Grace could not see Diandra stupid enough to run off and commit a murder trusting that a drunk wouldn't wake up and report her missing.

Grace inserted a suspect row for Faith Brewster: 0% on Miakos. 0% on Gigi Ramirez , but for Marshall, a possible motive: self defense from rape. Means: Faith could have driven down from Boston and have been in the area. Did Faith have an alibi? Grace could start by checking with the Brewsters. When had they last seen their granddaughter?

Maybe she could call Faith. Start talking with her? Maybe drive up to Boston and talk with her, so Grace could watch the minute facial reactions that gave you the 'feeling' someone was lying. But with this investigation she had lost Bobby's trust and Freya friendship? After her transparent questioning would Grace still have a friend left?

She went back to the spreadsheet. Means: Faith was athletic, she rode a rowboat before she walked and she was familiar with the ORR campus. She had access to ORR's boats, but to kill Marshall? If he isolating her on the Octagon and started to paw her? Grace knew the Brewsters--Faith would more likely have kneed him in the balls. No. Faith as Marshall's killer came up with a weak total of 23%.

God, she was wasting so much time on this? Grace left a phone message for Mark asking, "Since I'm not arrested, can we assume they found nothing incriminating in the search of my apartment?" Then she walked over to the east wall and checked the bubbling tanks. Both blue tailed and the newly delivered normal lobsters, with rubber banded claws, were climbing about slowly in the cold water tanks, all set at the right temperature. Everybody was alive, a good sign. She e-mailed Brian Kancir, to tell him know what progress was being made and asked when he wanted *Affiliated's* photographer to get pictures of Kurt and her in the lab? Probably shouldn't show the lobsters, just stress 'marine creature pharmaceutical study'.

Going back to her desk, she had just started reading her new Niagara of e-mails, when her lab extension rang. "Grace?"

At first she didn't recognize the woman's voice. Why don't people have the simple courtesy to give you their name when they called? "Yes?"

"I went your lab earlier." Now Grace recognized the slight whine of Diandra's voice. "You weren't there."

"Yes." She wanted to snap '*I'm busy, whatever do you want?*', but didn't.

"But you're back now?" Diandra continued.

"Yes." That's brilliant, since she was calling Grace on the laboratory phone. "Is there something I can do for you?"

"Yes." Diandra hesitated. "I'd like to attend another one of your seances."

That surprised Grace. "But you don't believe in spirits?"

"When that Freya woman started I thought it was all pointless, but as she continued...I mean, I felt Charles was in the room."

Was there a scientific explanation for that feeling? Grace considered it. "Maybe it was because of Katherine? A random smell of Charles' residue in her hair or clothes? The olfactory nerve is strongly tied with memory."

"No. I felt Charles was standing beside me, needing to talk to me. I must try again to contact him, can't you and your medium friend help me? Can we please get her to try again without Katherine interfering? Without the others? Just the three of us? Please."

"When?"

"Now? Tonight."

The last seance had achieved nothing, but if she could keep her suspect talking. "I think the Library at the Roost is in use for the monthly Board of Directors' meeting."

A hesitation, then Diandra said, "That's okay. Your friend has the new age shop in town, I think Bobby's wife said that? Maybe I could meet you there? After it's closed we could sit there. She has a table doesn't she?"

It was Saturday. "She closes early. Freya and her son rent the Boatwright's barn from the Whaler Museum Conservatory where they're building the equivalent of a two person Viking fishing boat with period tools."

That seemed to stop Diandra. "How interesting." She seemingly thought a moment. "Maybe we could hold our seance there? Where is it?"

Grace gave her the directions, but then changed her mind. She wanted a safer situation. "No. We'll have the seance here in my lab." There will be people about and security near by, that sounded better to Grace. "I'll go get Freya."

"Should I come with you?" Diandra offered.

"No need." Grace was going to have to do a lot of persuading before Freya agreed to this. "I should be back in an hour. Meet me at my laboratory."

"Thank you. I don't think Charles is at rest and I'm sure he wants to communicate with me."

"Good." Grace hung up. Perhaps they could still get something out of Diandra. Maybe prove she was guilty? Or maybe even clear her? Grace logged off her computers, made her standard fast check on the specimen tank monitors, and grabbed her jacket, headed to her car parked back at the condo. The afternoon sun was just beginning to slant through the trees when she pulled on to the Main Road.

As she drove into Oyster River Harbor, she could see the lights were off in Freya's basement store. Grace kept trying to phrase what she wanted 'the spirits' to say to Diandra, knowing the hardest part would be talking Freya into this further sacrilege. She drove to Freya's house and parked. No answer at the door and when she walked around back the rowboat was gone. Freya loved to row and had probably taken it over to the boat building Barn.

Grace drove past the thicket of trees that formed the bird preserve and she turned off on a dirt road that ran through the woods, coming out to a clearing by the harbor, before a three story, dark-wood barn. Today there were no other cars there, but one of the barn's two, twenty-foot high rolling doors was open for light. Grace got out and walked towards the building, wondering just what she could say?

At its front the Boatwright barn had two, two-story high rolling doors and a third, human sized entrance. Its three other long sides were lined with banks of small paned windows for light. With one of the high, rolling doors open, Grace could see the cadaverous opening was darkening as the early afternoon shadows lengthened.

Inside the barn was totally open to allow building area and Grace could see Freya. She was wearing a leather apron, with her golden hair in braids wrapped above her head, as she wielded her trimming axe to plane a thick tree limb. As Grace entered, the limb slipped out of Freya's makeshift clamp.

"Damn." Freya said.

"To be in period, shouldn't that be a Norse curse?"

Freya looked at the offending wood stave and sonorously pronounced. "Hon varr Draconian, gamla vis Hruga uskit'r!"

"That translates to?"

"I am a Draconian and thou are less than a heap of

shit!"

Grace looked around. "Isn't Mac here helping you?"

Freya was wiping her sweating hands, one still bandaged. "Ben's sick, so Mac's off patrolling. More importantly, why are you here?"

This wasn't going well. "You still angry with me? About the seance?"

"Faking it? Yes." Freya was looking back at her stave.

"Well, I want you to do it again."

Now Freya's bright blue eyes were glaring directly at her, radiating anger, and Grace suddenly realized the formidable strength of this six foot tall woman who split huge logs with a trimming axe just for fun.

"Grace,..."

"Just think about it! Please–I haven't heard if the police found anything in my apartment, but I'm still their chief suspect."

Freya's anger instantly mutated into concern. "I keep asked Mac about you. He won't talk, but he's worried about you–I sense it!"

"Diandra called me, she wants a seance with just the three of us in my lab. She says she believes that with you she can contact Charles and that he wants to tell her something important, maybe who murdered him?"

Freya shook her head. "She doesn't believe anything!" The Viking maiden walked closer to the open door way. To usher Grace out? "I felt nothing from her at the seance. That woman hasn't a psychic bone in her body."

"But she knows something! Freya, I'm sure of it. If we can just keep her talking, she might let something slip!"

Freya was looking outside. "If she's the murderess, why would she want to contact her victim?"

That had Grace confused to. "Maybe to put us off the track?"

Freya shook her head. "I shouldn't have done that first

seance."

"I know you think faking things are wrong. It is wrong! But I'm not getting anywhere else. They're going to be putting me in jail!" Grace finished, her voice bordering on the hysteria she felt.

"It should be that Kurt MacKay!"

"Why?"

"He's sneaky and he's hiding something. I felt it the night of the first seance. Why were you with him when you found Marshall's body? Guilt was radiating from him!"

"Freya, will you run a seance for me tonight. Please?"

"Another phoney one?"

"No–not phoney–maybe we could just try..."

Freya wouldn't meet her eyes. She was looking out the open door at the long shadows across the clearing. "It's later than I thought and the tide's coming in. I came over here by row boat and left it pulled up on the sand, behind those trees."

"Freya?"

"Whether I go with you or stay here, the rowboat's got to be pulled up higher on the beach."

As she started to stride pass, Grace offered. "I'll help you."

"No!" Freya had a hard, unyielding look on her face. "You stay here. The walk will give me time to think." By herself, Freya pulled on the massive boat barn door, rolling it closed, and darkening the building, with just the banks of small paned windows letting in a fading, dusty light. Without turning to look at Grace, Freya exiting by the third, smaller door to the left of the big boat doors.

Feeling helpless, Grace watched her stride away. Freya was walking as fast as she could to get away from her and maybe when she reached her rowboat, Freya would decide to not even come back. Had Grace damaged their long relationship beyond repair? Was Freya still thinking her green healing auras around Grace? Or had Grace's abuse of something Freya believed was sacred, turned her to thinking of a punishing red light?

Balancing her cons with a pro Grace remembered that when ever she had a problem, Freya would always go alone to meditate with her spirit guides. Also that she hadn't totally refused. That her friend was still thinking about it was a positive sign.

From outside the barn, Grace heard scraping of gravel as a car pulled alongside hers. She went to the small door and looked out a square of dusty window panes. A bright red Miata was parking alongside Grace's car–Diandra's? Had she followed Grace?

If she followed Grace from Oyster River, she should have been just behind her? Why had she taken so long to pull in? Could Diandra be the killer? Grace looked fast to where Freya had disappeared into the pines and realized just how isolated they were.

Trying to calm herself Grace drew in a shallow breath, the boat shed was just lit by the windows and must look dark from outside. Had Diandra seen her? She would certainly see Grace's car parked there, but Grace wasn't prepared to talk with her now. Should she call the police? She fished into her pocket for her cell phone and remembered it was back home, charging, and what would she say if Grace had it to call? That she was being stalked by a woman who might be a killer, if she didn't have such a great alibi?

But then Grace remembered the Spanish words Freya spoke in the seance. Could it have been Gigi Ramirez , speaking in a language Freya couldn't speak? Gigi, a native born speaker, wouldn't make a mistake. ¡*Que se pudran al infierno!* Not '*she would rot in hell*'–'*but **they** would rot in hell.*' Suddenly, Diandra's alibi evaporated. Desperately, Grace looked about the boatwrights' shop, no phone, no back door and no hiding places. This barn was never even electrified, it only had kerosene and propane lamps.

Grace had fallen into a trap, Diandra hadn't wanted a seance, she had just wanted to get Grace and Freya off by themselves. Maybe she would have done the seance, and then stalked Grace as she returned home in that dark night. Grace moved back to a side window, trying to look out but still stay within the concealing shadows. Maybe she should just brazen it out, walk out past Diandra, and try to reach Freya? They could use the rowboat to escape or at least it would it be two of them against Diandra?

But a gray car was driving into the lot, parking close to the red Miata. That's why Diandra had taken so long to follow her, she must have been riding up and down the road, waiting for her confederate to arrive. Stepping out of the sedan was a familiar, stocky figure, Katherine Marshall. Now it was two against one!

Freya was back in the trees probably staring out at the water, thinking her 'healing light' of protection around Grace. With the harbor tide waves slapping on the sand and distant traffic on the road, Freya wouldn't hear Grace cry out.

Grace backed away from the door. All three front doors were closed, but building was only locked by padlocks outside. She frantically looked again for a place to hide, but the barn was entirely open for ship construction. There were some benches along the walls, the skeleton keel of the faering took up the center, with work tables in the back, so there wasn't anything really to conceal her.

She could hear their footsteps on the gravel outside, Diandra and Katherine couldn't know that she figured out what they had done. If she just kept her head, Grace could talk her way past them and get in to her car. What about Freya? Would they hurt her friend? Grace couldn't leave Freya alone with them!

The small door opened, and looking quite composed, Katherine entered followed by Diandra.

Maybe Grace could pretend ignorance. Still talk as if there was going to be a seance tonight and she would just appear friendly. The two other women looked calm, not threatening. Then, in the weak light from the small windows, Grace saw the gleam of steel in Diandra's hand.

Chapter 44

Like two sleek Doberman pinchers in attack mode Katherine and Diandra advanced. Diandra had a wide-bladed chopping knife and she seemed to be egging Katherine on, but Grace guessed that older woman would be the stronger. Grace backed slowly on the rough, wood planked floor. If she could get to one of the window walls, maybe she could break out and escape? But those windows looked awfully solid and the deadly pair were advancing.

Diandra smiled prettily. "Dr. Farrington. Yes, Charles was correct, you never do give up. You do keeping plugging away until you work things out, don't you?"

They were planning to kill her in broad daylight? With Freya over on the beach? Well, they wouldn't know about Freya. Grace grabbed up a heavy wooden mallet from a bench.

Diandra stopped, but Katherine didn't. Smiling still, she just continued to advance, with slow, steady steps, as she also held a knife, one with a long, narrow blade. "Grace, we just want to talk to you. There's money here, more than enough for all of us. I had Charles insured quite handsomely. The pompous fool believed that all the money would be used to fund the Dr. Charles Marshall Chair of Genetics at some suitably prestigious university."

Even as she moved forward, Katherine was slowly separating herself from Diandra, forcing Grace to deal with two moving targets instead of one. Grace found her head moving from side to side trying watch both of them. "Yes. I do need money for my research. Yes, I'd like to talk, but can't you put down those knives first?"

Not daring to take her eyes off of them, Grace still searched about desperately looking for a weapon better than the clunky mallet. In the muffled distance she could hear a siren. Maybe she should scream? Freya might hear her and call 911 but Freya didn't own a cell phone. Grace found herself slowly backing up again, afraid to look away from her killers, but needing to find a better weapon, any kind of a weapon.

She tried to remember Freya's self defense course. What had the Instructor said? Get the attacker off balance. Use his forward momentum to trip him up. But nothing in the course said anything about fighting two knife wielding murderesses at the same time.

Grace decided to try and talk to them. Bide for time. "Why Katherine?"

"He was divorcing me after all those years, all that I put up with. He was dumping me and Diandra, so he could marry that little bitch, Gigi."

Diandra let out a little sob.

Grace backed slightly more, then felt a hard wood bench cutting into her back legs. She was trapped, and could only try to keep them talking, even as they relentlessly drew nearer. "There were two boats out that night." She guessed, "Katherine, you took the first to the Octagon and tied up on the backside? How did you know how to pilot a boat?"

"Didn't you remember? Charles and I had that boat when we lived in Pasadena."

Why hadn't Grace had the brains to take her gun with her? "How could you get into the Octagon without keys?"

Katherine smiled as if enjoying a private joke. "Charles wanted extra copies made of all his new keys and he had Diandra do it."

And now Grace could figure out the rest. "And she was in the boat with him, luring him to the Octagon?"

"Oh, yes. He was cuddling little, dumb Gigi, but he still wanted to have sex with Diandra."

In anguish, Diandra cried out, "I loved him. He didn't even have to marry me!"

"That's enough!" Katherine turned back to her. "But you, Grace, you had to keep digging."

Could she turn them against each other? "It's daylight, your cars might be seen from the water and my car could be seen."

"So?" Katherine shrugged. "We parked here, if asked we'll admit that. That's if anybody even notices our cars, but I don't think they will. Diandra wanted a seance and I, the wronged, bitter wife, followed her to stop it. We even talked with you, maybe you asked us here. You, like that idiot Adam, were trying to negotiate a peace between us for the good of Oyster River. Unfortunately your foolish peace summit failed, furious, we both left at the same time. Both us will testify that you were alive and well when we drove off in separate directions. Poor Grace, another victim of the Harbor Mad Man."

Diandra sounded doubtful. "She was supposed to meet her friend here?"

Katherine looked contemptuously around her. "A friend? I don't see anyone and there's only her car."

Grace must keep them talking. "After you killed Charles, which one of you killed Gigi? How did you get to her?"

Again, Katherine seemed to find it all rather amusing. "Diandra went to the house Charles rented for Gigi and told Gigi that he wanted to see her. That he needed her."

Diandra sounded almost apologetic. "I tried to lure her to the beach by the library, but she got suspicious. Ran back toward the house where Katherine was in the shadows."

While Grace tried to think, she realized Katherine's strategy was to keep Grace talking until both she and Diandra could get close enough to kill her.

"Katherine got Gigi and I helped." Diandra half sobbed again. "Charles and Gigi, they both took so long to die! The newspapers said Gigi crawled almost to the road, but we stabbed her by the house."

If Grace was going to fight, Katherine would be the

one she had to beat and Katherine was moving ever closer a look of total confidence in her eyes.

Katherine spoke so softly. "Put down that silly mallet and we can talk about this, Grace. You were betrayed by my husband too, you can understand us, you are one of us..."

With both hands, Grace raised the mallet with determination, she wasn't going down without fighting!

Light and a rolling thunder sound. Freya was sliding the big barn door to the side, looking every inch the six foot Viking fury she was. "**Thor!**" Freya thundered.

Thor and Freya. Grace never believed she could be so eager to see two avenging Norse gods. Even if it was god-hood was by proxy, Thor, a.k.a. Officer Mac, held a very visible gun in his hand, ordering, "Ladies! Drop the knives! Both of you!"

"No!" Diandra desperately turned to Katherine, "We can..."

"It's over," Katherine said, dropping her knife. It bounced on the boards with dull clanks as she moved closer to her confederate. "Diandra, put down your knife or he'll shoot you."

"It wasn't our fault, Charles..."

Katherine cut her off. "Don't say another thing, until we get our lawyer." Katherine Marshall's voice was cold, but she put an almost gentle, loving hand on Diandra's arm.

Still staying with her legs pressing into wood bench Grace yelled to Mac. "They killed Marshall and Gigi!"

Mac had only one pair of cuffs, but the women showed no inclination to run, and soon a yard full of flashing, assisting police cars lit up the Boatwrights' barn. With the prisoners taken away, Freya and Grace soon stood nearly alone.

"How did Mac get here?" Grace asked.

"I called him on my cell phone," Freya said proudly.

"You don't have a cell phone."

"With dead bodies showing up all over the Harbor,

Mac kept nagging me. He bought one and insisted I learn how to use it."

Grace looked to her old friend. "You were so angry, I didn't even know if you were coming back."

Freya only smiled at that foolishness. "I was looking out at the harbor, thinking a white light of protection about you, and trying to think of some sort of reasoning to enlighten you. Then I heard–felt–knew something was wrong." Freya looked down at her. "I know you don't believe it, Grace, but somebody in the spirit world wanted to protect you. It may have been Gigi, you were nearby on the bridge when she died. She drew energy from you, but it wasn't enough. Gigi or someone told me to hurry back. That you were in danger!

"When I started to come out of the trees I saw both Diandra and Katherine going into the Boatwrights' barn and that didn't seem natural at all. The feuding wife and the girl friend, suddenly palling around? I called Mac. He was paroling up the road, and he did a full siren until he got near here. Why did they kill the husband?"

"Marshall was divorcing Katherine to marry the new girl friend, Gigi. Katherine and Diandra formed an unholy alliance, who could credibility alibi each other. Who would suspect the long suffering, jealous wife of covering up for the scorned girlfriend?"

"But getting together? Wifey and mistress?"

"Katherine had accepted her husband's infidelities for years, but I think she couldn't handle the loss of money and prestige a divorce would bring. Diandra really loved Marshall and couldn't stand to losing him to a younger woman. Katherine probably played on that. And once they killed Marshall, Gigi could have revealed their motive, so she had to die."

"But how did they ever force Miakos to jump in and drown himself?" Freya asked.

"They didn't. The *Siren's* curse fulfillment was just a

logical fallacy, at least the current day one. Just because three fish die in a tank, if fish one and fish two are proven to be temperature related deaths, it doesn't necessarily prove that the third died of the same problem. The deaths of Charles Marshall and Gigi Ramirez held no relation to Miakos' suicide."

"But Miakos was at the height of his career..."

"No, he wasn't," Grace replied.

Freya protested. "His show at the Harbor Gallery is sold out."

"Only after his spectacular publicity garnering drowning. When you first went to his one man show, you said there were only two red sales dots on the frames out of twenty-three works. Remember, his ex-wife had a newspaper route? He said she was delivering papers to keep herself fit, but she was keeping food on their table! Linda Hartz said the market for 'exploitive art' like Miakos' was running thinner and the big sales were going to young upcoming stars. When he was young, Miakos had been featured in the important, museum happenings, but he'd never made the permanent collections."

"So he..."

"Without the public buying his life's work, he had money problems. His wife was divorcing him and even Gigi, whom he considered a little tart, called him a dirty old man."

"But drowning?"

"He couldn't swim, so jumping into the Harbor was certain death. He chose a spectacular, public suicide as his last artistic presentation."

Freya was silent. "And the *Siren's* come hither curse?"

"Had nothing do to with it."

Freya smiled slightly. "Maybe, maybe not. It's still going to be the cover story in my next book, *Current Hauntings of Oyster River Harbor*."

"Will you have Charles Marshall in it?"

"A love quadrangle on an Octagon house boat? Oh, yes. That'll be fleshed out more." Freya looked down at her. "You know, when I do my Haunted Harbor tours, if I could get Kurt's boat to take them out to the lovers' tryst houseboat, where Marshall's ghost has been sighted..."

"Who sighted him?"

"You?"

"No!" said Grace definitely.

"You owe me–for two seances! And I bet if I asked Kurt MacKay and there was money in it for him..."

The last Police cars were leaving and nobody seemed interested in doing any more questioning of Grace so she turned to Freya, trying to ask casually. "It's not Monday, but did you want to get a fish burger with me?"

"Don't you have that formal dinner tonight?"

Grace looked at her watch. "Oh, my God, it's Saturday. The formal dinner reception in New York. I've got to get dressed." She headed back to her car. "Do you need a ride?"

Freya shook her head, as she followed Grace to her car. "Remember, there will be royalty there. Did you get that book on protocol?"

"From way across the room, I'll be staring at a minor member of the Japanese royal house."

"You may be introduced to him on the receiving line."

"With the Swedish royals, she put out her hand and I shook it."

"Maybe you should genuflect, like you did for Queen Elizabeth?"

"It wasn't the Queen, it was Prince Philip. You curtsy. I don't know what you do for the Japanese Royal house. Kow tow? That'll be messy on a dirty ball room floor."

Freya shook her head in disapproval. "You should have bought that etiquette book!"

Grace drove back to her condo. Her mailman was in

the lobby, filling the mail boxes, seeing Grace he handed her a stack envelopes.

"Thank you." She did a fast glance at the return addresses, as she hurried upstairs. The usual bills, scientific Instrument's catalogue, some college return addresses-- probably speech requests she would have to decline, and one long, stiff, cream colored envelope from the 'MacAlpin Foundation'. MacAlpin Foundation? Did she have a grant request in with them? No. But the name rang a bell, the 'Guru Award' people? What had Freya said at the last seance. *'A financial award and public recognition that will take away some of your worries.'*

She started to open it, but stopped. No time! Tonight was the pay back she owed Kurt. He might not be on time, but she would ready for his 'fancy do' in New York City. She had just time for a fast shower, before slipping into that fabulous blue, bamboo-print gown. Fortunately, Kurt MacKay generally ran on his own time and could be counted on to be running late.

Only, this time, surprisingly he wasn't. Grace was just zipping up her dress, when the door bell sounded.

She let him and his tuxedo in. His eyes lit up as he said, "Classy dress for a beautiful lady."

The temperature was dropping tonight, she grabbed her longer winter coat. "We could take my car?"

"I've rented a car."

"A car?"

"Limo–can't park the old muck splattered truck in front of the Jap Embassy."

"Parking will be rough. Maybe we should take a train?"

"Parking is the chauffeur's problem. He's also rented." Kurt offered his arm, Grace slipped hers with in his. She should have studied up more on Japanese formal etiquette, but Kurt MacKay was the last person she expected to take this stuff seriously.

They walked past the unopened, cream colored envelope. God, she wanted to open it and Grace considered taking it with them in the limo. It could be a nice surprise or just a disappointing invitation for her to speak at another symposium? No. She left it. Tonight was Kurt's night. As they started downstairs Grace asked. "Your friend, who is researching minnows?"

"Skipper? He said we would have time to talk during dinner, so I figure that means we'll be seated at his table. He's very interested in your 'Popcorn Gene Switch Theory' in relation to the evolution of fish innate behavior."

"Good. We'll have something to talk about."

The chauffeur held the door open for them as Grace continued. "Does this Skipper know the member of the Japanese Royal family who will be attending?"

"He is the royal hubbub."

She stopped and stared at Kurt. "And we refer to him as?"

"I call him Skipper, but you can address him as Your Royal Highness."

Oh, God–she should have bought that etiquette book.

The End

If you enjoyed this book please put a comment on your favorite social media, so that I can keep writing more Grace Farrington's adventures! Lynn

**OTHER GRACE FARRINGTON'S
OYSTER RIVER RESEARCH MYSTERIES:**

ORR: FATAL DNA

ORR: MURDER GENETICALLY ENGINEERED

THE WITCH TRIPLETS' SEAPORT MYSTERIES:

THE PSYCHICS' SEAPORT MURDER

On the murder of their witch mother, the young triplets, Holly, Frost and Noel were separated for seventeen years. The day of their long awaited reunion in a New England seaport, a murdered man is found on their mansion grounds, making brother Frost the police's chief suspect. Knowing nothing of her Old Craft heritage, Holly starts to learn the skills of her ancestors as she struggles to open Witch House as a viable Bed and Breakfast. To save Frosty she must also find the murderer haunting her family, while she is being so thoroughly distracted by the tall, muscular police sergeant, Paul Travinski.

MURDER AT THE WITCHES' ALTAR

MURDER AT THE WITCHES' MILL

ANTHOLOGY OF ADAM MARTIN'S LAW PRACTICE REPRESENTING WEREWOLVES, DYADS, GORGONS, THE REINCARNATIONS SISTERS, ETC.:

ADAM'S UNORTHODOX, UNNATURAL LEGAL PRACTICE

Inheriting his Great Uncle Quentin's unusual law practice, Adam Martin finds himself defending the rights of waterwitches, a semi-senile seer, mermaids, zombies and gorgons. He also finds himself writing contracts for werewolves, consulting with ghosts, as he struggles to protect unfairly accused fire starters. Rough assignments, but Adam must do this while trying to stand up to his six foot '*Cherokee*' law secretary and dealing with his staid, disapproving family of conservative lawyers led by the formidable 'hang them high' Judge Jeremiah Martin!

CENTAUR WARRIOR ADVENTURES

CENTAURESSES OF THE SILVER DRAGON

The Regiment follows the hoof prints of Jace, a ruggedly handsome centaur of Clydesdale proportions. Winning on their last field, but betrayed by treacherous princes, these sword wielding mercenaries are outlawed. Now as he hunts a patron to keep his band together, he must hide a worsening leg wound, knowing a challenge to his leadership will end in death!

Stumbling on to a dying bazaar, this legendary fighter finds a patron in the stunningly beautiful Silver Star, a tall, gray centauress with sea foam white hair, luxurious tail and ominous cloven hoofs. Star promises a vast treasure if the Regiment frees her rich mines from a rampaging dragon. But there are problems: Jace does not believe in dragons and the lady has not told him of her real enemies, the deadly Scarlur.

With the free ranging life style of centaur society Jace has always had many lovers. But none truly have touched his heart, since he was forced to slay Ginger on the battlefield. Slashing his sword down to give his true love a merciful death, he killed his heart too. Yet now Silver Star, this skilled healer and intriguing fast running she, awakens old desires within him. Beyond just mounting Silver Star, he must possess her! Even if her kin forbid their love and his warriors fear this silver siren is leading them all to their deaths!

CENTAURESSES OF THE JEWELED SPEAR